I Am Lazarus

I Am Lazarus

James Davison

RESOURCE *Publications* · Eugene, Oregon

I AM LAZARUS

Resource Publications
An Imprint of Wipf and Stock Publishers
199 W. 8th Ave., Suite 3
Eugene, OR 97401

www.wipfandstock.com

PAPERBACK ISBN: 978-1-6667-3196-5
HARDCOVER ISBN: 978-1-6667-2510-0
EBOOK ISBN: 978-1-6667-2511-7

OCTOBER 22, 2021 12:03 PM

Please note that all biblical quotes are taken directly from the King James Bible. They have not been changed or modified to fit the manuscript.

Cover:
The Resurrection of Lazarus, circa 1426
Giovanni di Paolo
The Walters Art Museum, Baltimore Maryland

I am eternally grateful for the support of a loving spouse whose intelligence and smile light up the universe around me.

For it is written: Eye has not seen, nor Ear heard,
neither has it entered into the Heart of man, the things
which God has prepared for them who love him.

1 CORINTHIANS 2:9

Introduction

What is God's plan for my life? This question should be the single most important thing every human ever born asks of themselves. It is a question I have wrestled with for a very long time.

Here are a few other questions for you to consider: If you were immortal, what would you do? Would you set out to accumulate wealth? Would you search out and catalog all the wisdom in the world? Would you take up arms and fight for a cause in which you believed, knowing no weapon could harm you?

I ask because I have tried to do them all, and yet, sometimes I feel the answer to that first central question continues to elude me, regardless of how hard I try to justify the gift of life I was given about 2,000 years ago.

The popular phrase 'time marches on,' holds no real meaning for me because my time does not march on. I have come to view my life as if it were outside time itself. One of my traveling companions, a young man you will soon meet, believes this as well. Throughout the years of my life, I have remained the same age I once was. It is both a gift and at times, a curse.

I have made many attempts at capturing the memorable events of my life. Some of my earliest work at collecting and organizing material was abandoned during quick escapes as the authorities closed in without warning. Luckily, I got into the habit of making copies of every letter, sermon, or scroll (which took time, let me tell you!), but I'm glad I made the effort. I probably should have suffered from carpal tunnel long before it was a thing. Anyway, I started burying copies of the most-impressive materials, and I do know that several of my previous attempts at recording details of the past have been found. In fact, most of what I'd written down was used as the template for the current Bible. Other documents with different details about the apostles were also found. But for some reason, after they announced the find, they never revealed to the world exactly what it was they'd found and who the author was. I made it clear who I was and why I left it, but, still, crickets.

This time will be different.

What follows isn't a perfect chronological diary like that of a young schoolgirl. If I had written a page for every day or month of my life, you'd be facing tens-of-thousands of pages. I mean, who wants to read that!

But I'm getting ahead of myself. As English rock star Mick Jagger once sang, "Please allow me to introduce myself . . . " my name is Lazarus. You may have heard of me. I'm quite famous. There is even a medical syndrome named after me. The "Lazarus taxon" is a scientific term, which describes organisms that reappear in the fossil record after a period of apparent extinction. An accurate description of me, I suppose. Symphonies and horror movies have been created which invoke my name. In the mid-1400s, my friend, the Italian master painter Giovanni di Paolo, painted a beautiful altarpiece depicting my resurrection from the grave. I wish I still owned that piece. If you close this book, you'll see his work on the cover. Go ahead, look at all the detail. Beautiful isn't it?

So, to be clear; I am the man that the Son of God raised from the dead a very long time ago. And trust me, I was kaput. Toast. A corpse. If I was posting to social media I would say that I was #ReallyDead.

I realize that if you subscribe to alternate religious beliefs, in which resurrections are not part of the narrative, then perhaps you'll toss this book into the pile for donation to your local recycling center. Whatever. But you paid for it (hopefully), so you may not want to be so hard-hearted that you can't even entertain the possibility you are wrong about God. At least allow me to tell you a bit more of my story. Maybe you will change your mind, or at the least, you will have found another spiritual philosophy in which you don't believe. I know that if you are an atheist then what I have to say regarding my life, death and resurrection may not sit well with you. My life contradicts the central thesis of your life: That there is no God. Well, my friends, there is a God, and he has a Son. The I last time I saw him in person, he very plainly said he was "coming back soon." When I heard him say those words I took heart, though I now realize we have different definitions of the word "soon." This is not conjecture. It is fact. I was once told that heaven measures time differently than we do on earth, which makes a lot of sense. But right now it seems like as good a time as any for his return. If you truly look at the murders, wars, rumors of wars, the media, politics, and politicians (of all stripes), the world today has all the makings of John of Patmos' writings!

This is why now is the right time to tell my story.

I'm sure you are probably thinking, "Man, what kind of psychological damage must this guy have to believe he is Lazarus?" Believe me, I've been shrunk by the best of them. The multiple personalities I have had to create to keep my true identity secret are the very definition of schizophrenia, or so my German friend Emil Kraepelin told me once. You might say I was patient zero for his landmark works. Keeping all these identities straight does get confusing sometimes. Trust me on that one too.

Think about the word "miracle," for a moment. It takes on quite a different meaning for me than it might for you. I was dead and brought back to life. Nothing can compare to that kind of miracle. Trust me. Anyway, I've never been seriously injured or faced death, other than that first time. I have often wondered if I had been captured and beheaded (a pastime for dealing with your enemies long before the modern Islamic State came along), would it have been curtains for me, or would my head have just kept living while my body tried to find the severed part that controls everything. (Picture what Agnew's body does in the Matt Groening cartoon "Futurama" when it doesn't have Nixon's head in a jar on top of it . . . and, if you get that reference, perhaps you should turn off the television and get outside more). Thankfully, I have not faced that particular state of being.

The facts are the facts: I was born, lived thirty-five years, died and after four days, I was no longer dead.

Most memoirs such as this are written as the subject is dying or already dead, often by authors who never knew the person but would like everyone to believe they knew them intimately. The biographer would replace personal knowledge with research, interviews, hearsay, written archives, or peer-reviewed material.

Let me be clear: I Am Not Dead. Nor do I think I am dying. There are no written-word archives, or libraries that chronicle my story. However, the Wiki pages on me are somewhat interesting. To be honest, they have helped me stay hidden. I log in on occasion and insert snippets or complain that information they present as fact doesn't have the proper back-up documentation or certification. It's kind of a fun way to spend a few minutes.

I write today in my preferred language, American Standard English.

On this grand adventure, I have been accompanied by two companions whom you will soon meet and come to know well. If you continue reading, you will discover that together the three of us have shaped much of what is known about the history of Christendom.

Some chapters will flow seamlessly into each other, and then there will be others that jump forward in time by hundreds of years to when things got more, well, interesting.

For my story, well, our story, to be as accurate as possible, I offered my two fellow travelers the opportunity to contribute to this memoir. I provided a few guidelines, i.e., describe yourself, your home life, how we came to meet, what you have been doing since our resurrections, you know, details such as those. While, like me, they have had to change their names, appearances, and life stories many times to escape danger, we use our real names in this narrative for simplicity's sake.

As the instigator of this endeavor and the tacit leader of the troika, I claimed naming rights. Thus, the title: *I Am Lazarus*.

This is the first book in the story of our lives, and I hope you enjoy it. There will be more, I promise.

Thank you for reading.

Feel free to contact me at thelazarustrilogy@gmail.com

I will fulfill my vows to the LORD
in the presence of all his people.

PSALMS 116:14

1

Lazarus

I once was a woodworker. I enjoyed taking a raw piece of wood, and with nothing more than the creativity of my design, and my two hands, crafting something that was both useful and beautiful. Don't be confused about my profession. I was not a carpenter. I just couldn't see building an entire home, or something similar. I preferred working on small, intimate things. I always thought of my work as important, though, at the time, I was just moving wood and creating sawdust. Today, if you break a cup, plate, or bowl during the preparation of your daily meals, you go to the store or, more recently, go online and purchase another. Back then, if you were not handy with your hands, you'd find someone like me. We'd choose a piece of wood that suited the proposed use, and I would create a replacement by hand. There were no big box stores around the corner. The difference between my chosen profession and that of a carpenter, at least when I was practicing it, was that you engaged a woodworker if you wanted new tables, chairs, eating implements, stuff like that. If your roof leaked, or if you needed a home constructed, you'd call a carpenter. You'd also call a carpenter if you wanted to build a place to house your animals, like a manger. Kind of ironic, right?

My specialty was furniture, specifically tables and chairs. I was good at what I did, building tables for local temples and religious institutions for use during holidays and special celebrations. This took a measure of skill, and I was fortunate to be known for the quality of my products.

On the day that changed me forever I was in my shop, which was located in what today we'd call a strip mall. I was focused on a large table for a wealthy Roman customer who always paid on time. I liked him, because his money was good, and he frequently commissioned pieces for friends and powerful families. Using a new, two-handed drawing knife I had just purchased from a local blacksmith, I was bent over, beginning to shave the wood I'd selected for the table legs when the door to my shop creaked open.

"Brother?" I heard a familiar female voice ask. "Lazarus, are you busy?"

Of course I knew this particular voice. It was my older sister Martha. Though she was polite to ask if she was interrupting, it didn't stop her from doing so. Since the death of her husband a year prior, she had returned to live in the family home I shared with a younger sister, Mary. It was where the three of us had been born and raised. My workshop was not too far away, and they were frequent visitors. I loved them both very much, and I smiled when Martha announced herself. I knew that no matter what my answer about how busy I was might be, she was going to come in, find a seat, and continue speaking. Without looking up, I answered.

"Yes, Martha? You can see I am busy with a very sharp tool. Can't whatever you have to say wait until I am finished?"

She didn't answer. Instead she entered and took a seat nearby. I looked up and could see the unhappy reaction on her face as I used my new knife.

"Oh, Lazarus, you be careful. That looks so very dangerous! I hate it when you pull a large knife such as that one towards your body. You could cut yourself to the point where no wound would heal. Honestly, it makes my flesh crawl just to watch you!"

"Well, you don't have to watch," I muttered as I inhaled and redoubled my efforts with the drawknife. In the process, I created quite a bit of dust and debris, some of which traveled in the direction of my waiting sister. I swear it was not intentional. Seeing the bark and wood shavings flying in the air, she gathered her cloak and wrapped it so that her ankles and hands were covered. None of what I was doing deterred her from speaking.

"Mary and I are going to the river to hear a prophet speak. It has been decided. You must come with us."

It was pretty typical to have roaming, charismatic prophets, and preachers in those days, much like the televangelists of the late nineteenth, twentieth, and twenty-first centuries. They would arrive, announce that

God had sent them to save us horrible sinners, perform things that appeared to be minor miracles or sleight of hand magic, and move on once the authorities had grown tired of their antics or pleas for money. As a man who followed the dietary restrictions laid out in the law, kept the commandments, and always was serious regarding my observance of the Sabbath, I found it hard to believe most of them ever heard directly, or even indirectly from God, much less believed in him. Not that I was as skeptical as that may sound. But I had become a realist, considering I thought that nothing they had to offer could impact my life enough to make a significant difference.

"Why should I go with you to listen to yet another prophet extolling the virtues of his version of religious life? I have no money to give him so, I am sure he would lose interest in me."

She looked around my workplace and shook her head. I could tell she was getting ready to say what I had heard her say hundreds of times before. I was not disappointed.

"You need to get out of this shop, brother. You breathe woodchips and fire smoke all day. How can that be good for you?"

I used the drawknife as a pointer and motioned towards the small windows framed by wood and stone. "Martha, as you can see, I get plenty of outside air. So, I see no reason to stop what I am doing and follow you to another one of those prophets talking about a new messiah or the end of the world."

"Oh, you are coming with us even if I have to go get Mary, and together, we drag you down to the river. And put your usual skepticism aside brother, this prophet is different, I assure you."

"Didn't you say that the last time?" I regretted saying this as I saw the emotional response begin to build on her face. I needed to apologize. "I did not mean to hurt your feelings. It is just that I don't think the traveling prophets that have cropped up recently have much to offer to me. I am a devout follower of Moses and the law. I pay penance for every misdeed, and I believe God accepts the sacrifices I make in his honor."

Martha was silent for a second. "This prophet is very different. He speaks of things no one has ever spoken of before. He doesn't seek money, followers, or goods. He seeks to change lives."

I considered this for a moment. There had recently been another prophet who spoke of the Messiah's imminent arrival, John, the Baptist. He was known for standing knee-deep in rivers and baptizing anyone who would come forward. I shrugged, hung the drawknife on the wall and took down a smaller, sharper one to refine the legs and prepare the slots and peg holes. I admit, I was curious about this new prophet who didn't seek money or fame though I tried not to show it.

"Well first, how can this new prophet make a difference if he doesn't seek money or power? And you are sure this prophet isn't the one known as John the Baptist?"

She shook her head and seemed excited. "No. This prophet is from Nazareth. I think you would like him; he is a carpenter like you. He is the one the Baptist has spoken of as the Messiah.'"

I'm sure I sounded quite exasperated as I corrected her. "I am a woodworker, not a carpenter. We have had this discussion many times Martha."

She found a small piece of wood within arms-reach and tossed it lightly my direction, "You know what I mean; he works with wood, just like you do. I know you will like him. He is very special. He heals the sick, makes the lame to walk. He speaks in such a serious and spiritual manner but is easily understood."

I was silent, so my sister took that as permission to continue.

"This prophet actually went to the river and was submerged into the water by the Baptist. As the prophet came up out of the water, the clouds parted, and the heavens above opened. A dove descended from the sky and actually landed on his shoulder! Then, a very strong voice was heard from the sky. This voice called the prophet 'beloved Son' and then said that he was 'well pleased' with him! Can you explain that? No trickery or deception can bring a voice down from heaven!"

At that time in history, everyone was accustomed to very odd, un-explainable, and what they thought were spiritually significant events or actions occurring. Every child knew of Elijah and Enoch, being swept up into the heavens by huge wheels of fire, and the stories of how Moses led the Israelites out of bondage in Egypt and into the promised land. His use of the staff of God was a prominent part of every Passover sermon. So, the fact that others had witnessed what appeared to be a dove fall from the sky and heard a disembodied voice after the Baptist had baptized this man didn't quite sound like a fable. It got my attention. I worked silently, thinking as I shaved wood. Finally, I could tell Martha wasn't going to leave until I stopped what I was doing and agreed to go with her.

"Can you give me a little more time so that I can at least finish this piece? I just started a new project, and I'd like to feel like I accomplished something today. Can your new prophet wait that long?"

Apparently, my reply satisfied her because she jumped up and hugged me.

"You will never know how much that means to me! This prophet will change your life forever. I just know it! Finish what you are doing and come to the house. Mary and I will be waiting."

Martha was not typically prone to exaggeration, so I was somewhat intrigued to meet this man who had so captured her heart and mind. I worked to complete the table leg and had an apprentice agree to take it to my customer. I liked to do this with expensive projects to make sure it was the product I was being paid to produce.

I closed my shop and walked the short distance to our home, unsure what level of enthusiasm to expect. When I opened the door and called out that I was ready to leave, there was no hesitation on the part of my sisters. I was not surprised to see that they were prepared as Martha retrieved a small basket of food and drink, and Mary handed me three large animal skins on which we could sit. Now well-prepared, we set off to hear this so-called prophet.

Soon we were sitting in the grass, surrounded by a few hundred others, watching, and listening to a man who stood on a large, flat outcropping of rock. I looked over the crowd, which was full of men and women with children. Off to the side, an entire cadre of the sick and infirm waited patiently for their own personal miracle. There was even a clump of Sadducees off to themselves. *Well, maybe they'll learn something* I thought. I smirked. Many of us would joke that these sect members were appropriately named. Three of their mainline religious beliefs were based on total denial. They denied the existence of spirits, the obligations of our oral traditions and the resurrection of the dead. Therefore, as we described them, we always said they were Sad–U–See. Who'd want to believe in that kind of negativity? No spirits? Refuting our oral traditions and no resurrection for the faithful? Their beliefs always sounded so unpleasant to me, so, in my mind, they were not relevant to my life or what I believed.

I put the Sadducees out of my mind and refocused on the prophet's words. His keen intellect and ability to connect with his audience were immediately evident. His voice was, in a word, perfect. Regardless of where you were in the audience, he could be heard. I sat and watched the tax collectors, religious authorities, even prostitutes and heavy sinners draw near to listen to him. I also noted that the religious authorities and temple leaders didn't try to mask their anger. I excused myself from

Martha's side and moved so that I was closer to them to get a better read on what they were saying to each other. I saw the leader of a local temple, and he acknowledged me as well. I inserted myself into their conversation for a moment, and without exception, they grumbled about the fact that this prophet was receiving those who were clearly sinners and even sat down to take food with them.

I nodded as if to agree and made my way back to Martha's side. The prophet had stopped speaking for a time to minister to those in the crowd who were ill. This seemed to draw the ire of the temple leadership even more than sharing a meal with peasants and sinners had. I watched, keen to see just how he might be manipulating the crowd, but I saw nothing that I felt was out of place. Soon he motioned for all who were standing to sit. Once the crowd quieted, he began to preach with an earnest voice. But it wasn't quite preaching, as I had grown accustomed to hearing. It was more storytelling but with a clear message woven into the words. As he spoke, his voice gained strength, seeming to resonate within me.

"What man of you, having a hundred sheep, if he has lost one of them, does not leave the ninety-nine in the open country, and go after the one that is lost, until he finds it? And when he has found it, he lays it on his shoulders, rejoicing. And when he comes home, he calls together his friends and his neighbors, saying to them, 'Rejoice with me, for I have found my sheep that was lost.' Just so, I tell you, there will be more joy in heaven over one sinner who repents than over ninety-nine righteous persons who need no repentance."

He stopped for a moment as the crowd began to murmur. I speak the truth when I say that what he said had shaken me. I tried not to look stunned as I considered his words. Leaving ninety-nine to find the one lost sheep? *The world is indeed full of lost sheep seeking a shepherd.* I didn't ponder the question too long, as there were those in the crowd whose murmuring quieted as he began to speak again.

"There was a man who had two sons. The younger of them said to his father, 'Father, give me the share of property that is coming to me.' And he divided his property between them. Not many days later, the younger son gathered all he had and took a journey into a far country, and there he squandered his property in reckless living. And when he had spent everything, a severe famine arose in that country, and he began to be in need. So, he went and hired himself out to one of the citizens of that country, who sent him into his fields to feed pigs. And he was longing to be fed with the pods that the pigs ate, and no one gave him anything.

Soon he said, 'How many of my father's hired servants have more than enough bread, but I perish here with hunger! I will arise and go to my father, and I will say to him, "Father, I have sinned against heaven and before you. I am no longer worthy to be called your son. Treat me as one of your hired servants."'

This did not sit well with some in the crowd. Some talked loudly among themselves and a man near me yelled, "How does this relate to my life? I am not rich. Nor am I related to anyone rich! The authorities take more than their share! I might as well be dead!"

The prophet took note and continued as he locked eyes with the young man who had blurted out his comment. The intensity of his gaze was startling.

"The young man arose and came to his father. But while he was still a long way off, his father saw him and felt compassion, and ran and embraced him and kissed him. And the son said to him, 'Father, I have sinned against heaven and before you. I am no longer worthy to be called your son.' But the father said to his servants, 'bring the best robe, and put it on him, and put a ring on his hand, and shoes on his feet. And bring the fattened calf and kill it and let us eat and celebrate. For this my son was dead, and is alive again; he was lost, and is found.' And they began to celebrate."

"What do they celebrate? The young son is a failure. He should be chastised for his mistakes and receive none of his fathers' treasures!" someone in the crowd yelled.

The prophet paused a moment, shifted his eyes, and kept speaking. "Now his older son was in the field, and as he came and drew near to the house, he heard music and dancing. And he called one of the servants and asked what these things meant. He said, 'Your brother has come, and your father has killed the fattened calf because he has received him back safe and sound.' But he was angry and refused to go in. His father came out and entreated him to rejoice with the family, but he answered his father, 'Look, these many years I have served you, I never disobeyed your command, yet you never gave me a young goat, that I might celebrate with my friends. But when this son of yours came, who has devoured your property with prostitutes, you killed the fattened calf for him!' And he said to him, 'son, you are always with me, and all that is mine is yours. It was fitting to celebrate and be glad, for this your brother was dead, and is alive; he was lost and is found."

"What does it all mean?" a man next to me muttered as he shook his head.

Somehow the prophet knew of his question. "Behold, those who are whole need not a physician. But those who are not whole, those who may be sick, they need a physician. For I came not to call the righteous, but sinners."

With that, he stopped speaking and motioned that it was time to receive those in the crowd who wanted to be healed. I remained seated for a while, mesmerized. None of what I was seeing was a trick. The people he healed were actually ill. I watched as the lame walked, as the blind began to see. I couldn't take it much longer, I had to get closer to him to see if I could determine how he was faking these miracles. I stood and with each step, I became more and more convinced that there was nothing false nor deceptive about this man. It dawned on me that perhaps he had been sent by the God of Moses and the prophets. My emotions churned, his words resonating over and over in my mind. Suddenly, it all made sense. I was that lost sheep. My shepherd had come looking for me, and now, I felt found. I knew. Martha had been right; this man was a very different prophet. The simple story he'd used to illustrate both a moral and spiritual lesson had taken everyone on a journey. His voice was kind. His expressions as he spoke were pure and conveyed the truth of his words. In my heart, I knew I had to meet him and understand the inner strength and beauty that had now captured me as it had Martha.

When the crowd began to thin, I made my way towards him. I wanted nothing but to thank him for his honest portrayal of God's love that had so touched my soul.

Approaching his inner circle of followers, he made direct eye contact with me and smiled. My heart jumped. The way he looked at me caused several pilgrims to make way for me to get closer. I believe they sensed I must be an old friend or perhaps a family relation. He drew me in, enclosing me into his arms in a hug.

He did not raise his voice. Instead, he spoke to me and me alone. "Lazarus, my Father loves you, and I love you." He held the grip for another moment. "You are not here by accident, for you have been chosen. All will be revealed soon. Come, stay by my side. Listen, learn, and watch. One day you shall be required to undertake a lifetime of ministry unlike any ever found on the earth. You shall stay with us for a few days, then return to your home, finish the project you have started, deliver it to the one who has paid for its construction and then come back to us to finish your preparation."

And with that incredible pronouncement, he took me by the arm and introduced me to his disciples. I guess it was normal for him to take people from the crowd and thrust them into the inner circle of his followers because they welcomed me with open arms and expressions of affection. Except for one. He seemed to be worried about something else.

2

It was a cool day. Winter was beginning to wind down as the sun stayed aloft longer and the air began to get warmer. My sisters and I had been following the man I had come to think of as my Rabbi Master for almost two months, sleeping where we could and sharing meals when possible. His message of love, compassion and healing was one I had never experienced. It moved my soul in ways I thought impossible. One day stands out in my mind. Later, in early spring he was preaching in an open field, with fires placed all around to warm the crowds. The Rabbi Master was answering a question. Well, it wasn't really a question so much as a not-too-thinly-veiled threat against those of us in the crowd, posed by one of the Pharisees regarding the story of a shepherd protecting his flock. I wasn't the only one who perceived the question as a threat. Many in the crowd began to question the presence of the Pharisees, who were eager to infer that although the Rabbi Master's followers may think we were safe from retribution by the authorities, we were not, especially if something happened to the Rabbi Master. The inference was that once our shepherd was out of the picture, the sheep that followed him would be easy pickings for the wolves and crucified for heresy.

"Very truly I tell you Pharisees, anyone who does not enter the sheep pen by the gate, but climbs in by another way, is a thief and robber."

Hearing the Rabbi Master reply in such a forceful manner I noted that the Pharisees took exception to being included in what we now call a "teachable moment" with the words "thief and robber." I knew trouble was on the horizon. I was right, so I listened with keen interest.

The bravest of the Pharisees used his arms to part the crowd so that there was a direct line of sight between him and the Rabbi Master. Then he posed his question.

"But sir, is it not true that anyone can call the sheep and they come? In fact, there is no need for a shepherd at all times."

Heads turned away from him and back to the Rabbi Master. A few in the crowd who'd never tried to herd sheep began to agree with the Pharisee. One or two did not understand why all this talk included sheep. The Rabbi Master nodded towards the Pharisee as if to say, "thank you for being so predictable" and launched into his quiet explanation.

"No. The shepherd calls his sheep by their name, and they recognize his voice. If one calls out to them and that person is unknown to them, they will run. They will not follow a stranger."

The Pharisee was quiet a moment. It was clear to me that he had never worked with farm animals a day in his life because he was having a hard time understanding what the Rabbi Master had said. It was clear we all knew it too, so the Rabbi Master continued.

"Truly, I am the gate. Many have come telling the sheep that they are the gate and the sheep have not listened to them. I am the gate. The thief comes only to steal and kill and destroy. I have come that they may have life and have it to the fullest."

"But," the Pharisee tried to interrupt. Now there was a gate involved, and that "thief" word again, which seemed to further stymie his attempts to trip up the Rabbi Master and show him a fool.

The Rabbi Master smiled as he spoke. "I am the good shepherd who lays down his life for the sheep."

That hit me hard. *Lay down his life for his sheep? What is he talking about? Is there something happening here that I have missed?* I took a breath and tried to refocus so that I wouldn't miss anything and took a hard look around, wondering if there were soldiers present, hiding in peasant cloaks.

"I am the good shepherd; I know my sheep and my sheep know me."

This was too much for the Pharisee. He cried loudly enough for the entire crowd to hear, "How can you people stand here and listen to this? He talks in circles! This man is demon-possessed and raving mad! Why is anyone still interested in anything he says?"

Many in the crowd shouted the Pharisee down, citing all the miracles the Rabbi Master had been performing.

"How is it possible this man is a demon? Can a demon open the eyes of the blind or heal the sick?"

Feeling the crowd turning against him, the Pharisee swept his cloak around his shoulders, turned, and ran from the crowd. I had the feeling that this Pharisee was in the crowd to plant the seeds of disbelief and perhaps hatred towards the Rabbi Master. I hoped it was just him, but part of me knew that the Rabbi Master was hated by many who, though they could see, were still blind to the truth of his divinity. Sitting nearby, I watched as the crowds pressed in, many seeking miracles or forgiveness for breaking one or more of the commandments. It seemed that the Pharisee's outburst did nothing to discourage them from approaching the Rabbi Master. *Perhaps the mission of that Pharisee was a singular one, and not connected to a larger effort. I hope so.*

One day later, as we made our way to the temple courts, a group of Sadducees and Pharisees stopped us. I knew this had to be trouble because the two groups were almost never in agreement. So, if they were together now something had changed. I silently figured they had been sent by the senior religious authorities to try and trap the Rabbi Master into perceived heresy so that they could charge and prosecute him.

The Sadducee nearest called out, "Teacher! How long will you keep us in suspense?"

A Pharisee jumped in and yelled, "Yes, if you are the Messiah foretold in our ancient prophecies, tell us plainly and we will follow you!"

Though the Rabbi Master said nothing, the look on his face clearly said everything. *I have revealed myself to you as the Son of God and yet you still refuse to believe. Therefore, simply telling you has not been enough to convince you.* His silence ate away at the group opposing him, and they all began to shift their feet and show disturbed, angry mannerisms. Finally, he answered.

"I did tell you, but you do not believe. Everything I do in my Father's name testifies about me and who I am. As I said two days ago," and when he said this, he pointed to the Pharisee who had been in the crowd, the one who had questioned him, then left quickly as the crowd turned against him. "You sir, were there. I said that my sheep know my voice and I know them, and they follow me. I give them eternal life and they shall never perish. My Father, who has given them to me, is greater than all. No one can snatch them from the hands of the Father. And the Father and I are one."

His answer didn't sit well with them, as you can imagine. Muttering, several of them produced large stones from a bag. It was clear they intended to stone the Rabbi Master right there in the temple courts.

He was non-plussed and stood his ground, spreading his feet into a stance that said, "I'm not going anywhere," he answered, his voice strong and clear.

"I have shown you many good works from the Father. For which of these good works do you stone me?"

A Pharisee on the edge of the group held a rather large stone and tossed it back and forth between his left and right hands. He seemed to be judging its weight for when it was time to throw it.

"We stone you not for a good work. But for this hideous blasphemy because you, a mere man, claim to be God."

The look on the Rabbi Master's face morphed into one of pain, but when he spoke his tone was very measured and reassuring. "Why do you accuse me of blasphemy? Because I have said I am the Son of God? Do not believe me unless I do the works of my Father. But if I do them, even though you do not believe me, believe the works, that you may know and understand that the Father is in me, and I am in the Father."

This was too much for them. They couldn't understand what he was saying. Then the one that had been tossing the stone back and forth missed it and the stone dropped with a heavy thud onto his foot. He howled, his foot clearly broken. He rolled around while the others contemplated if this was the Rabbi Master's fault, or just pure bad luck. I cringed as the Pharisee rolled in the dirt, screaming his distress. Part of me wanted the Rabbi Master to reach out and heal his foot. But I expected such an act of kindness would still not move his, or his colleagues' hearts in the right direction. The exclamations and curses created a significant distraction, and the noise was disorienting. The ones who had still held stones started yelling and reached out to grab the Rabbi Master so they could bring him before a court to face their unique form of justice. Turning away from the growing melee, the Rabbi Master and his followers scrambled to get out of the temple court and escape the city.

Over the following week, the memory of this interaction with the Sadducees and Pharisees stayed with me. With each successive day, the Rabbi Master spoke more frequently of a looming, great sacrifice that he was to make. It was heartbreaking to know that, given what I had observed, something was about to happen.

On one sunny afternoon, I decided to take a break so I could contemplate all I had seen and heard. Woodworking is often a solitary endeavor, and though I was engaged with the Rabbi Master, I found I missed the quiet time alone that I'd once enjoyed working in my shop or in the forest as I hunted for the best wood to harvest for my next project. Away from the sights and sounds of our camp of disciples, I began to wonder about where things were headed. *Here, he is loved by many. But the religious leadership that once seemed prepared to accept him as a prophet now express open hostility towards him and anyone associated with his ministry.* To me, just a simple woodworker, a peaceful resolution to the schism between the Rabbi Master and those who wished him harm appeared nearly impossible.

Discouraged, I turned my face towards the sun and was thinking about what I should do next, when I felt a hand pat me on the shoulder. I looked up and straight into his eyes.

How long has he been there, waiting for me to stop feeling sorry for myself?

I smiled and tried to convey my sorrow for missing his approach. Every problem I had been considering melted away when he helped me up from the stump on which I sat.

"Lazarus, walk with me."

"Of course," I said, falling in step beside him. As we walked, the flowers around us seemed more alive than they once were, and the sky even more beautiful than usual. We came upon two large rock outcroppings, so we sat down, facing each other.

He wasted no time.

"When you first came to us, it was because your sister's prodded you into making the journey to see me. Now, you follow on your own accord because you have seen the truth and embraced it. Yet, you have several projects to complete waiting in your workshop. I know that in your spirit, you know that your time with me is almost at its end. Just now, you were mulling over your future, curious about what you could or should do next. I have your answer. Return home and finish the projects that await your skills. Stay there. The next time you and I meet will be after the Father's glory has been revealed."

I was stunned for a moment. "You want me to leave your side? But I was not thinking of leaving! I was just worrying that the anger and hatred towards you could soon take a more aggressive approach. They were going to stone you just two days ago. Who knows what they will try to do tonight, or tomorrow? I cannot leave your side!"

He smiled. I could feel his glory penetrating into my soul, but I felt it important to continue my defense.

"Lord, please don't send me away! The authorities fear the crowds who support you! Everyone here stays the hand of anger they wish to raise against you. We all know they are waiting, watching, and planning for the day when they can come and silence you. Someday their reluctance to act in the presence of those who follow you will be overwhelmed by their hatred of you. I feel I must be there to help you!"

He never wavered. "Lazarus, in the coming days your life shall immeasurably change. A great charge from the Father will soon rest on your shoulders. Many events, such as those you fear, are being planned. They must first occur before you are to take up the mantle of leadership. I love you, as does my Father. He has chosen you for a great purpose, one which will be seen through the ages as essential to the Kingdom. Thus, do as I ask. Return to your home, complete the things that need to be completed, and wait. When they are finished, we will meet again."

That comment left hope in me, so not wishing to question the Son of God, I took my leave and did as he had instructed. I gathered my belongings and made the journey home. I confess that even today, the memory of stepping over the threshold of my workshop, the smell of wood and well-oiled cutting implements, still washes over me.

Apparently, Martha was nearby and saw me enter my workshop. I'd been inside a few minutes when she came over.

"You are back?"

"Yes. The Rabbi Master told me to return home and finish these projects. He said he would see me again very soon."

"I am pleased you are back. I won't bother you. Come to dinner whenever you are hungry." With that, she kissed the back of my head and left.

Sitting behind a large chunk of wood, I saw that the Rabbi Master had been correct. There were two items waiting for me that my apprentice had been working on. I took a favorite tool for shaving wood and bent into the task immediately. It felt good to get sawdust under my fingernails once again and I rediscovered my love of carving wood to create things for people. It troubled me that I was away from his side though. What if something happened and I wasn't there to stop it?

3

The last coat of vinegar-based pigment was drying on the chest I had just finished when I knew something was wrong. The immense pain in my chest was like the weight of a thousand heavy timbers. It almost prevented me from moving. I was dizzy, and I could not breathe. My legs felt heavy, the kind of heavy you feel when trying to walk in flowing water up to your knees. I dropped the sheep-wool mop I was using and managed to make it to the door of my workshop where I fell, half in and half out of the doorway. There was a loud noise when I fell, and I could see that I had knocked over two large shelves that held wooden bowls. Everything made quite a racket, and for a fleeting second, I hoped the noise would attract attention. The pain in my chest was sharp and lasted for a brief second or two before everything went black. As my eyes closed, I was aware of my sister Martha screaming as she ran across the alley in my direction. Well, she was probably wailing, but that was kind of her thing. I guess humanity wailed a lot back then.

When I was born, no one lived a decent life past fifty years of age, even though our oral and written histories inform us that our ancestors had lives that extended well past 600 years. Ugh. Can you imagine living that long without hand soap, toilet paper, or flush toilets?

Why is that important? Well, you should consider it in the context of what happened next. Now, granted, I was dead, so this is where I shall revert to a third party for information. I will quote from ancient texts, interpreted by folks in the fifteenth century.

Here is how you may know my story. What follows is taken from the King James Bible regarding the events surrounding my death and resurrection.

John 11: 1–44

[11] *Now a man named Lazarus was sick. He was from Bethany, the village of Mary and her sister Martha.* [2] *(This Mary, whose brother Lazarus now lay sick, was the same one who poured perfume on the Lord and wiped his feet with her hair.)* [3] *So the sisters sent word to Jesus, "Lord, the one you love is sick."* [4] *When he heard this, Jesus said, "This sickness will not end in death. No, it is for God's glory so that God's Son may be glorified through it."* [5] *Now Jesus loved Martha and her sister and Lazarus.* [6] *So when he heard that Lazarus was sick, he stayed where he was two more days,* [7] *and then he said to his disciples, "Let us go back to Judea."* [8] *"But Rabbi," they said, "a short while ago the Jews there tried to stone you, and yet you are going back?"* [9] *Jesus answered, "Are there not twelve hours of daylight? Anyone who walks in the daytime will not stumble, for they see by this world's light.* [10] *It is when a person walks at night that they stumble, for they have no light."* [11] *After he had said this, he went on to tell them, "Our friend Lazarus has fallen asleep; but I am going there to wake him up."* [12] *his disciples replied, "Lord, if he sleeps, he will get better."* [13] *Jesus had been speaking of his death, but his disciples thought he meant natural sleep.* [14] *So then he told them plainly, "Lazarus is dead,* [15] *and for your sake I am glad I was not there, so that you may believe. But let us go to him."* [16] *Then Thomas (also known as Didymus) said to the rest of the disciples, "Let us also go, that we may die with him."* [17] *On his arrival, Jesus found that Lazarus had already been in the tomb for four days.* [18] *Now Bethany was less than two miles from Jerusalem,* [19] *and many Jews had come to Martha and Mary to comfort them in the loss of their brother.* [20] *When Martha heard that Jesus was coming, she went out to meet him, but Mary stayed at home.* [21] *"Lord," Martha said to Jesus, "if you had been here, my brother would not have died.* [22] *But I know that even now God will give you whatever you ask."* [23] *Jesus said to her, "Your brother will rise again."* [24] *Martha answered, "I know he will rise again in the resurrection at the last day."* [25] *Jesus said to her, "I am the resurrection and the life. The one who believes in me will live, even though they die;* [26] *and whoever lives by believing in me will never die. Do you believe this?"* [27] *"Yes, Lord," she replied, "I believe that you are the Messiah, the Son of God, who is to come into the world."* [28] *After she had said this, she went back and called her sister Mary aside. "The Teacher is here," she said, "and is asking for you."* [29] *When Mary heard this, she got up quickly and went to him.* [30] *Now Jesus had not yet entered the village but was still at the*

place where Martha had met him. ³¹ *When the Jews who had been with Mary in the house, comforting her, noticed how quickly she got up and went out, they followed her, supposing she was going to the tomb to mourn there.* ³² *When Mary reached the place where Jesus was and saw him, she fell at his feet and said, "Lord, if you had been here, my brother would not have died."* ³³ *When Jesus saw her weeping, and the Jews who had come along with her also weeping, he was deeply moved in spirit and troubled.* ³⁴ *"Where have you laid him?" he asked. "Come and see, Lord," they replied.* ³⁵ *Jesus wept.* ³⁶ *Then the Jews said, "See how he loved him!"* ³⁷ *But some of them said, "Could not he who opened the eyes of the blind man have kept this man from dying?"* ³⁸ *Jesus, once more deeply moved, came to the tomb. It was a cave with a stone laid across the entrance.* ³⁹ *"Take away the stone," he said. "But, Lord," said Martha, the sister of the dead man, "by this time there is a bad odor, for he has been there four days."*

⁴⁰ *Then Jesus said, "Did I not tell you that if you believe, you will see the glory of God?"* ⁴¹ *So they took away the stone. Then Jesus looked up and said, "Father, I thank you that you have heard me.* ⁴² *I knew that you always hear me, but I said this for the benefit of the people standing here, that they may believe that you sent me."* ⁴³ *When he had said this, Jesus called in a loud voice, "Lazarus, come out!"* ⁴⁴ *The dead man came out, his hands and feet wrapped with strips of linen, and a cloth around his face. Jesus said to them, "Take off the grave clothes and let him go."*

From my perspective, those verses, written by the apostle John, the author of the eleventh chapter of the Gospel of John, among other books of the bible, don't fully cover the event. I'll describe it right now, from my point of view. Without warning, I fell ill and died. I won't get into the details of my experiences in the afterlife just yet. On occasion, it has become a topic of conversation, and when I have spoken of it, I have tried to be as honest and forthright as possible. However, it usually doesn't end well. Even in this modern, twenty-first century, as advanced and intelligent as the world is, the human brain still does not possess the ability to fully grasp what I would describe. To be honest, I sometimes wonder if it was real. There is still a pain in my soul when I recall what I saw and experienced. Another individual was there beside me the entire time, but I couldn't quite see who it was. However, I came to understand who was there later in life. You will understand it too if you keep reading. I struggle at times to see it with the clarity with which the Rabbi Master so obviously did when he instructed me to return to my home and prepare for a great awakening. But I will say this, where I was, I had no concept of time. However, I did know everything I had ever done. At the time of my death we knew growing season, wet season, dry season, the sun, moon, stars. These were our clocks. There was no Cupertino Apple Watch, no atomic clock, nor Greenwich Mean Time. When I died, I departed this reality of existence and immediately found myself in another one. A very unpleasant one.

And then, I was back.

I recall taking the largest breaths of my life. My chest heaved once, twice, as air filled my lungs. Then, the musty smells of a tomb carved thirty feet into the ground hit me. Those smells were soon overcome by the scent of perfumed linen. I took a few more quick, deep breathes. My mouth was dry, and my face was covered in burial wrappings. My hands and feet were restrained in the same cloth. It was clear to me that I had been entombed. Through the wraps, I could perceive a shaft of sunlight that seemed to flow like a mountain stream down the cave's stairs hewn from the earth. I knew that my dead body had been placed underground. My eyelashes brushed against the linens that covered my head as I remained still and quiet. I could tell that someone was tending me by removing the burial wraps. My newly opened eyes perceived a figure, beckoning. Someone next to me lent me their strength and helped me stand. Exposing my face and shoulders, I turned and saw the smiling face of my sister, Mary, who, through the tears flowing down her face, held new garments for me to wear.

I blinked as my eyes adjusted to the light. Clearing my throat, I croaked, "What happened?"

She started for a moment as if the fact that I was alive, and speaking wasn't enough. She turned, and the man standing in the passageway leading up to the surface nodded. Turning back to me, she answered. "Four days, brother. This is the fourth day since your death."

Death? Is that where I was? Eternity?

I turned to the figure that was still backlit. The person moved, and for a moment, a profile was painted in sunlight. It was then that I knew who stood in front of me, arms outstretched. Relief, love, and concern washed over me like nothing else ever has. It was the Rabbi Master. As my sister continued to unbind me, I wanted to express my deep concern for what he had just done, but my throat was dry, and I found it difficult to speak.

Martha moved to my side and unslung a bladder of water from her shoulder. She opened the cap as I tilted my head back and took a drink. The water soothed my throat. I spat it out and took another, longer drink that I swallowed. I was coming to terms with being alive again. I felt it imperative that my first sentence to the Rabbi Master after my resurrection was to address what he has just done.

"Master, why have you done this? You must know it will be seen as insurrection and heresy. I am not worthy, Lord. Especially if this turns the authorities even further against you!"

As I struggled to understand what had just happened to me, Mary made sisterly noises from beside me and provided a cloak and undergarments. I struggled with them for a moment, not truly alive yet, I guess. Once dressed, I stood there, tears filling my eyes. I knew what he had done, and it shook me. Martha hugged me, as did Mary.

Looking back on that instant in time, I believe he knew I was having trouble mentally processing the fact that I had just been resurrected from the dead. I had not moved, so he approached me. Saying nothing, he put both hands on my shoulders and smiled, his face no more than a few inches from mine. His smile drew me in. Seeing the fire of life in my eyes, he threw his arms around me. I clasped my arms around him and wept. Soon he released me and nodded. I was speechless.

"We shall speak later. The time is soon when all shall be revealed."

He pulled away after a minute and started to leave. He turned, twisting at the waist, nodded, and motioned me to follow. I did not want to. I could tell a crowd had gathered outside the tomb by the sheer volume of noise. Most of the yelling appeared to be people clamoring for miracles. Many were saying I had been asleep or pretending to be dead. I wanted to address every accusation of sorcery or trickery but knew from the tone in their voices that the ones who did not believe would never change their hearts or minds. I also knew that the pious religious leadership would not look on this latest miracle as a good thing. Why? Well, it sliced through the boundaries of life and death as a hot blade did through fat or gristle. While I was grateful to once again be alive, I knew that regardless of his reasons, what he had done for me was going to cost him. I wish I had been wrong.

Adjusting to being alive again wasn't easy. Though my tools hung right where I had left them, it felt like the spirit to move the wood was no longer in my hands. People stared at me and spoke behind my back as I walked. It was attention I did not want. Since Passover was approaching,

Martha thought a Passover supper in my honor would be a good idea, so she arranged for a few close friends to come to celebrate. When he opened the door, I knew she had invited the Rabbi Master, and I wondered at her decision. But it was too late to try and dissuade her. After exchanging pleasantries, we shared the traditional cups of wine and ritual purification.

Everyone looked to the Rabbi Master, and he reached over, took the matzah, and broke it in half, giving the larger half to Mary to wrap and hide for the children to find later. He then offered us the best Exodus retelling I had ever experienced, because we all knew he had experienced it as the Son of God. When he finished speaking, I knew that what I had just heard was special and tried to commit every new detail to memory. He looked around the table and could see we were stunned. He smiled, clapped his hands, and said: "Shall we wash our hands before eating?" It was such a simple phrase from the mouth of the Son of God, that we all laughed, washed our hands, said a blessing, and started the meal.

Before we could get to the bitter herbs, though, it became clear that having the two of us together in the same room–the man whom his followers believed to be the Son of God, and a man he had recently raised from the dead–attracted far too much attention. We tried to eat and enjoy our feast but the noise from out in the street continued to grow.

The chief Hebrew priests could be heard outside, calling for me to be put to death because I was an aberration unworthy of life. Now, I considered this to be kind of ironic since, well, you know, I had actually *been* dead, and they were very anxious to *make* me dead once again. In the back of my mind was the news I'd heard earlier that day. After my resurrection, I'd heard that while he was traveling and preaching, the Rabbi Master had resurrected two others, a young woman, and a young man. Though I did not know the details, I did know that these actions had set the authorities against him with renewed vigor.

Listening to the yelling I was concerned, but I kept my peace.

Mary and Martha did not.

"What if they break the door down and take you both?"

The concern for our welfare and that of the other guests was evident in their tone and on their faces. I turned towards him with an idea.

"You raised me from the dead Rabbi Master. Perhaps you could blind them temporarily so that we could make our escape?" To be honest, I asked because although I was concerned about his welfare, I was more concerned for my own continued survival. I liked being alive again!

He smiled that sad, not-quite-a-smile of his and answered: "Fear not Lazarus. Though my time approaches, your time is in the far future. Remember what I say . . . you listened and committed to memory the Exodus story. Retain that knowledge, for in such a way you shall nurture the faith while I am gone. Though you will live in the shadows for a very long time, you will survive and live far beyond other men and shall build on the great works many will begin in my name. Yours is the greatest charge of all, given to you by the Son of God; be the keeper of the faith. Keep my words in your heart for you shall do and see many great things." With that, he paused and leaned towards my right ear. "You will forever change the world."

Change the world? How am I, a woodworker, supposed to change the world? I'm not even sure I belong back in the world. What does he mean by that?

He could see that I was trying to comprehend what he'd just said to me, so he stopped for a moment, took a deep breath, and moved even closer. Taking my right hand into both of his, a light began to shine through his eyes that was brighter than any I had ever seen. It was clear he knew of the turmoil his words had caused inside me, and he wanted to comfort me. The light subsided, but I was mesmerized.

"Lazarus, we will not see each other again in this life, but I shall be with you always." He motioned towards the door. "Go now, for I have blinded them as you suggested."

From the wailing and screams of terror, it was clear that the entire crowd outside had indeed been struck blind.

"Make your escape. Travel to Caesarea Maritima (today the ruins are part of an Israeli National Park), where you will meet two who will be your new companions in the great work the Father has placed before you. You will be given the means to secure passage to Cyprus. Once there, you will find a friend prepared for your arrival. Stay for a time, then when the time is right, leave. Upon your life and testimony, a great ministry shall be built."

This was all news to me, and I foolishly blurted out: "Cyprus? Traveling companions? What am I to do in Cyprus?"

"Share what you know. Learn what you can. Teach the people. Always be prepared for what will come. As keeper of the faith, you must live and learn. You will face many hazards in the years that follow. Many will seem insurmountable. Others you will not see until they are upon you. Gird yourself in righteousness, be patient, be vigilant, and pray for strength."

With that, he smiled, kissed me on the forehead, opened the door, and turned my direction as if to say, "You first."

Not wanting to miss the opportunity to leave and out of a desire to follow his instructions, I held my sisters for a few moments, kissing them on the cheeks. I took one last look at him as he held the door open and with hesitation, I walked through and waded into the crowd.

Now quite blind, the men and women gathered around Martha's home groped at the air as if they could grab their lost sight and shove it back into their eyes. Their hands ran over my body as I pushed my way through.

To make sure they did not keep me from making my escape, I added my voice to the crowds.

"I am blind! This is madness! What has happened to us?" They let go of me and continued their verbal assaults.

I looked over my shoulder and saw the Rabbi Master in the middle of the crowd. He smiled and nodded. Turning a corner, I heard their collective gasps of anger and relief as their sight was restored. Many voices called for whoever was responsible to die. The voices calling for his ascension to the throne of power seemed fewer and softer.

Skulking in the shadows, I was unsure of what to do next. Must I follow his guidance right now and make my way to the waterfront? Was it so important to buy passage to Cyprus today? I hesitated. My human nature took over, and I decided to wait and see if the authorities tried to punish him. I secured lodging on the other side of town in a place frequented by prostitutes and criminals. Alone in the room, I changed my look by cropping part of my beard and trimming my hair.

I waited and watched from a distance as he was arrested the next day. There was talk that one of the disciples had turned against him, enriched by the religious authorities for the measly sum of thirty pieces of silver. I prayed this was not true. But after hearing talk around the markets and courtyards, I knew who had done this awful deed. I just did not understand why he would have done it! However, I was not surprised. I never liked the man, and I remembered that the disciples had never trusted him.

Both secular and religious hierarchy had grown tired of the miracles attributed to the Rabbi Master and his ever-growing popularity. Many of those who witnessed first-hand the miracles he performed had initially professed belief in him. But after hearing of his arrest, many who once followed him went to our religious leaders and invented crazy lies that were so far from the truth they were impossible to disprove.

Concerned at their perceived loss of power over the people, the chief priests, and others brought their concerns to the Sanhedrin, our highest court of religious justice. The best description today is that it was like the American Supreme Court. (I've always thought that the framers of the U.S. Constitution had the Sanhedrin in mind when they authored Article III in 1789.)

Talk amongst the crowds outside the courts was that although he had been arrested, the authorities were at a loss regarding what to do with him. I overheard two men near the temple discussing their options.

"This man has performed many miracles. If we let him go and he continues, everyone will believe in him, and then the Romans will come and punish us. We could lose our power and our nation."

"Then we must kill him."

"I agree. I will suggest that we take him to the governor. We must say that the prophet wants to overthrow Roman rule! That should get his attention!"

It was not easy to sit in the shadows, anonymously, listening to their plans to kill the Rabbi Master. In the back of my mind was the constant push to go to the waterfront and secure passage, as he had instructed. But I felt I also needed to see what would become of him. Throughout his arrest, trial, and crucifixion, I kept out of sight, sometimes changing my appearance and outer garments two times a day. I put a pebble in my left sandal and developed a limp to further my disguise, knowing that if they were to discover me, I would be dead once again. I sensed they still wanted me dead for the sin of being resurrected. I became quite adept at disguising myself in those few, short days. I even stood near my sisters for a time, and they never knew I was there. This was just the first of many times I would put this skill to use.

After being forced to march through the streets carrying the very cross on which they would crucify him, the soldiers directed the Rabbi Master towards a hill called Golgotha just outside of town. When they reached the hill and began getting two other men ready for their crucifixions, I stayed away from the crowds but close enough to hear the grunts of the Roman soldiers wielding the hammers as they drove long spikes into his hands and feet.

Even today, when I hear construction sounds of a similar nature, I think of that day with tears in my eyes.

The crowd of onlookers was small, so I hid near a large tree and watched as life escaped the only man I had ever loved other than my own father. It was crushing. I heard him yell something that sounded like: "It is finished!" The sky darkened. At the same time, an earthquake shook everything and everyone. I felt nauseated and had a sudden urge to leave, and to shake the dust of the land from my feet. I turned to begin the journey to the docks as he had directed.

With my mind swirling, I had stumbled into the city, and I noticed a woman in front of me. She was in the shadows leaning against a pillar and perked up as if she had been waiting for me. Her face was partially covered, so I could not see if I knew her. She moved to intercept me, and soon we were face to face. Now in front of me, she stopped, lifted her face, and looked at me as if she knew me. As I returned her stare, her eyes told me that she did know me. But I did not know her.

"What do you want?" I barked, false bravado leaking into my words. I hoped she wouldn't recognize me and announce to the Roman guards nearby that another of the prophet's followers was right here for the taking.

She held out a hand as if to stop me from moving. Her voice startled me.

"You are Lazarus of Bethany. I am Junia. The man you know named John, the one who follows the Rabbi Master is my uncle."

I stood, thinking. I wiped a tear and refocused on the face. *Yes, John has a niece whose name is Junia. A Roman citizen. What is she doing here and what does she want with me?*

She could see that I was unsure. With a furtive movement, she withdrew a leather coin purse from her cloak. By the way she held it without lifting it I could tell it was heavy.

"I was instructed to meet you here and give you this coin purse. It is for your use on the journey ahead."

This took me by surprise. *How could anyone know I was here? I was told by the Rabbi Master to go to the waterfront and find passage to Cyprus. I disobeyed his orders so that I could watch his trial and crucifixion. How is it possible that she knows of my disobedience?*

"How did you know I would be here?"

"I was directed to find you here in a way even I do not understand. I know that I am to give you this change purse and then leave Judea, never to return." The way she looked down at the coin purse and held it so gingerly made me think it was burning a hole in her hands. Once again, with emotion in her voice, she implored me to take the bag from her hands.

"Please, you must take this so that I can fulfill my part in his plans and leave this place of death! You must leave, too, as you were instructed."

I was shocked into silence but took the change purse. *How can she know any part of what she just said?*

Then she leaned closer and whispered: "Do not return to the place where you have been hiding. They wait for you there." I was stunned as she continued. "God be with you, brother Lazarus. God be with all of us." She muttered that last sentence in tears as she turned and began walking in the opposite direction of the three men hanging on the crosses that still stood on the hill behind us.

I sought out a doorway with a dark overhang, my chest heaving and heart beating so hard I worried it might burst through my garments. I tried to gather my wits. *They wait for me. I should have left town.* The change purse was a mystery. I risked a glance inside; it was filled with a substantial amount of silver and gold coins.

More than enough to begin anew in Cyprus. Taking some to use in barter, I put the rest into the bag I had slung over my shoulder.

With new determination, I started the journey to the waterfront. Given where I was, it would take at least a couple of days or more. I just hoped the shadows were sufficient to hide my face.

In the time immediately following the Rabbi Master's crucifixion, a few followers associated with his ministry fled as I did, or renounced their belief, which saved them from imprisonment or crucifixion. On their deathbeds, I have always wondered if they recanted their denials and await us in paradise. I hope my sisters took time to grieve. To spare them the added pain of not knowing what happened to me, before going to the crucifixion, I had paid a man I trusted to liquidate the tools in my workshop and give the proceeds to Mary and Martha. He was to tell them that the Rabbi Master had arranged for me to leave the area for their safety. I prayed they would accept my departure and make new lives, blending in with society to avoid further attention. However, there was still a price on my once-dead head, and I had no desire to stick around and see these murderous intentions towards me fulfilled.

4

Taking what Junia had said to heart, I snuck westward, towards the sea. It wasn't long before I heard the shrill calls of seabirds and smelled the salt air blowing in from the Mediterranean Sea. Soon I came to a seawall. The water was such a beautiful bluish hue and waves lapped gently against the rocks and wooden beams. I would have stayed and enjoyed the view for a bit longer, but the place was crawling with people, animals, and cargo. Taking refuge near the dock, I stayed out of the way and out of sight, waiting for a sign that I was even in the right place. I was reluctant to emerge from my hiding place because I had no idea which ship at the port was the one meant to spirit me away from Judea and to my destiny. The Rabbi Master had told me to go to Cyprus, and because of the distance to be covered before landing on Cyprus, I was hopeful I wasn't going to be traveling in a small boat. I had no real experience with sea travel and was reluctant to undertake a long journey of any length. I was relieved when a large, three-masted ship appeared, docked, and began to unload slaves and materials from the Egyptian port of Alexandria. Through the cacophony of noise, I overheard the master of the ship talking about his next port of call. Cyprus. This had to be my ship.

I approached the shipmaster once he was alone. He saw me coming his way and, busy with his preparations, tried to wave me off.

"What do you want? I don't like you people. You always have ways of making us all suffer. We don't take Jews," he gruffly spit my way, both hands shooing me away as if I were an errant child. I didn't move as he muttered a vile curse in my direction. I reached into my cloak and his expression changed as his ears heard the clinking of the coins. I held the change purse so that no one else could see what I was doing and shook it again. His attitude changed.

"Sir, if you have freight to ship, once we depart, there will be three stops. Cyprus, Sicily and then home. We can work out the fee depending on what it is we ship for you."

"I am a citizen of Rome, and I require passage. Does this help?" I asked as I slipped several pieces of silver out of the bag and into my hand.

He eyed the coins I was offering like a hungry child might eye their favorite snack food. With a furtive glance up and down the dock, he retrieved a large piece of cloth from his tunic. Wrapping it around my hand, he acted as if he was cleaning something off my hand, but instead he used it to slide the coins into the fabric, which then disappeared into a hidden pocket on his clothing. His movements were so swift and stealthy that it was as if nothing had happened at all. *Clearly, he has experience in the bribery game.*

"Welcome aboard. Go below or stay topside. Just don't get in our way. Do you have personal effects?"

I shook my head and opened my arms, indicating that I was bringing just what I had on. This seemed to satisfy him.

"Which port?" the man asked, as if I he suspected I was a criminal evading capture.

"Cyprus. There will be two others who shall approach you in a like manner. They are to be allowed to board as well." I saw a protest building in his posture and cut it off as quickly as possible. "They will have the means to pay just as I have." I'm not sure where that came from, but somehow, I knew it to be the truth. If the Rabbi Master had seen fit to provision me for this trip, then I was certain he had taken care of the other two individuals who were to be my traveling companions.

The shipmaster seemed to accept this news with a measure of glee, so he bowed and ended our conversation.

"This is agreeable my friend. Please board."

I was unprepared for what I saw once I looked up at the ship. Though not a sea-going man, I had heard enough about boats to know what lay before me. Tied to the dock was a recently decommissioned naval vessel. Everyone knew of the Roman Navy, and it's prowess against Rome's enemies, both external *and* internal. It had been a couple of years since Augustus and Marc Anthony had been at war with each other, but Anthony was finally defeated, and the score settled between the two men in an epic Ionian Ocean battle at Actium. After that, most of the Roman fleet was dismantled and burned. I guess instead of burning all of them, Rome must have sold a few, like the ship I was about to board. The five levels of oarsmen that once drove the mighty beast forward into battle had been replaced with masts and sails that soared above the decking. There was no great ram to disembowel enemy ships as most Roman warships had, but it was easy to imagine that one or more had existed. At least I wouldn't be pelted with the constant exhortations the whip master directed at the slaves, who no doubt once sweated, bled, and died at her oars.

Since the weather was good, I found a wooden bench near the front of the ship and took a seat. I was replaying what the Rabbi Master had said about the two who were to join me. I was intrigued, watching materials and goods leaving the ship and then others coming on board. The crew was proficient and knew what it was doing. As provisions were loaded, departure time grew ever closer, and yet, no traveling companions. Since I had never met them, I had no idea who to look for. I hoped that somehow, I would just know them.

Perhaps something happened to them? Maybe they are taking another way? Doubt began to creep in. *Did I wait too long? Did I miss something in the instructions? Was there another ship? Am I on the wrong vessel?*

I tried to remain calm and positioned myself to observe passengers as they stepped on board. Watching this process, none of them piqued my interest. I soon turned towards the ocean, wondering about the weather and if I would be able to ride out any storms across the water without becoming ill. Just the rocking of the ship while tied to the dock was unnerving. Each minute I was reminded that, after all, I was a mere woodworker, a man who moved and shaved wood into things, not a sailor. I had heard from the Rabbi Master's followers who were fishermen that if one were prone to seasickness on rough water, the bow or the stern were the worst places to be. But all the seating in the middle of this ship was below decks, and I wasn't about to be confined inside. I resolved to stay in the open and take my chances. With a sigh, I turned my attention back to scanning the docks and the deck.

I could tell we were leaving soon, as the crew began working with more purpose and stopped idle conversation. From the middle of the ship, a man who must have been the Captain started yelling, and dockworkers responded, assisting release of the lines that secured her to shore. Soon oars were in the water, and once clear of the other ships at anchor, our sails unfurled, and we headed into the open ocean.

As the shoreline shrank from view and disappeared, I realized that I'd been clenching my fists so tightly I had almost drawn blood. I laughed a bit at my own anxiety, took a deep breath of the salty air, and tried to relax. My escape had been successful. No soldiers or religious authorities appeared hot on my trail. But I was perplexed. I was also alone. I sat there, wondering if I'd made a mistake and somehow gotten on the wrong ship, or missed the other two entirely.

I will pause here to allow my two companions to introduce themselves.

Let no one deceive you with empty words, for because of such things God's wrath comes on those who are disobedient.

EPHESIANS 5:6

5

Elan

Let me begin with a simple statement: Every person reading this has heard of me, seen me on the news or read about me online. You've seen my interviews, my work products, and watched as I have made history. I foresaw many years ago that the coming technological advancements of the digital age would make hiding in plain sight difficult, if not entirely impossible, which is why I abandoned the ruse of making up fake names and identities every hundred years or so, and reverted to using my real one, albeit, with a minor change.

There is something to be said for a good plan, and since going "public" and beginning the run-up to my grand adventure, my positive press is almost unmatched. With more than 2,000 years' worth of intelligence and experience, is there anyone better suited than me for what I plan to do? The answer is, of course, no. And with what I have been given, how can I fail?

All my research and work has brought me to the point where I am almost ready to undertake the greatest journey in the history of mankind.

I'm going to find God.

I know he's up there somewhere, and I have one, singular question I would like to ask him.

I am grateful that Lazarus reached out to me and asked if I would be interested in participating in his book. I've thought about doing something similar many times. When he contacted me, I was reluctant at first, but after a bit of introspection, and a slight push from Sarah, I agreed to participate and write what you now read. Since that original communication, he has provided most of his material to refresh my memories about our journey through time.

I have tried to recall as much as I can of our adventures, both together and apart. I know that he has contacted Sarah separately, so I anticipate she will also provide a few details from her life, both before and after we three met.

But to begin, what I will share is just about me. Who I once was, who my family was, and how I came to be the man I am today.

I know that Lazarus was not happy when I decided to come out from under the blanket of anonymity. But even with my exposure, I have still not fully exposed myself. He has always been so guarded. I think because, from the beginning of our association, Lazarus was the adult in the room. Sarah and I were the out-of-control, young not-quite-adults of our threesome. But I believe he understands why I do what I do and what I have planned. At least he's never said I shouldn't try it. He's also rarely tried to stop me. I think he learned his lesson a very long time ago about trying to stop me from doing anything I set my mind to. He did try though. Once. It was a growth moment for us, and I have always appreciated him for that.

The Internet is littered with quotes attributed to me. One of my favorites goes something like this: "If you get up in the morning and believe the future is going to be better, then it will be better and brighter." I've always thought that the grass is greener everywhere, not just on the other side of the fence. You just need to change your optics or attitude if you don't see it.

Like all eighteen-year-olds, I went through my morose period. The difference is mine went on for more than 1,000 years. Then one day I realized I needed to grow up and be a better man. That is how I came to be a friend to Lazarus and Sarah, not just a guy with whom they were traveling. I was able to heal the wounds that my bad attitude had caused, which ultimately brought us closer together as a family.

If you've figured out who I am and are skeptical, know this: I have more than enough practice to appear to be anyone of any age.

Thank you for reading, and may God bless you all.

6

I once was a young man, full of life and optimism. I was the only child of two people who loved each other. I had young friends my age and the prospect of a lucrative future following my father's footsteps. I grew up knowing that one day I would be running his shipbuilding business. Then, disaster struck. While working on a new double-masted fishing vessel for a local fishing group, one of his employees fell, bringing several of the ribs connected to the hull crashing down. The collapse buried my father under a jumble of timber, crushing him to death. It was sudden and catastrophic and left my mother and me fending for ourselves. My whole life to that point had been preparing for a future with my father, building fleets of fishing vessels, and starting my own family. His death changed all that. Mother mourned far longer than normal, and I was pushed out of the business by the man my father had been grooming to take over, just in case I wasn't interested. He was more than eager to assume control. He even tried to take my mother from me, like she was chattel or an asset. Luckily, she demurred and continued mourning.

With no other prospects for employment, I did what so many young men (and today, women) have done. I sought my purpose and fortune by enlisting in the military, the Roman Army, to be specific. Rome was a military empire; my parents were free, Roman citizens and because of my birth, so was I. Since I lived in a Roman province, service in the Roman military was not forced but strongly encouraged, thus my decision was lauded by friends and family. I knew it would either kill me or make me a better man. I wasn't going to be building fishing boats for a living, so why not go kill the enemies of Rome? Soon I was wearing the garb of a soldier, training to defend Rome, and channeling my anger towards becoming the best soldier I could be.

I did not know that the Roman military was also the Public Works Department, the Department of Transportation, and the Roman Department of Sanitation. What does that mean? When not fighting our enemies, it was expected that we would be building and maintaining roads, public sewer systems, latrines, and the massive aqueducts that brought fresh water from the highlands. As a newly minted soldier of no particular standing, I was tasked with a group of other recruits to the Aedile (that's the name of the office. It's the modern equivalent to being the director of a large government agency). Sadly, that meant instead of heroically defending our nation against our enemies on the battlefield, I would be inside the public and private latrines. I could make lots of crude jokes about it, but I bet someone would just edit them out, so let me just say it was genuinely awful duty.

One afternoon, laying on my belly clearing a smelly blockage in one of the sewer systems that drained into a nearby river, I shifted my position in the square piping system slightly and felt a searing pain across my back. I finished my job quickly and left the covered ditch system where waste was to flow into a holding pond to dissipate. I asked a colleague to look at my back, and his reaction wasn't exactly encouraging. Though the actual date of the creation of iron nails isn't known, I can attest that they were used excessively. It soon became evident that I had dragged my back across several exposed nails used to secure sections of the covered sewer drainage ditch to each other. I was bleeding from two deep cuts across my upper back and I was in considerable pain. While a group of Greek-trained medical assistants debated amongst themselves about whether it was best to attach leeches to my wounds or a poultice made of horse dung and poppy juice, I waited in growing pain. I confess I wasn't real keen on their options.

Not long after they decided the poultice was the best idea, I was also given an amulet made of jasper. It seems silly today in this modern age to even type that sentence, but we did lots of stupid things back then and called it medicine. (In fact, I somewhat retract that statement; we still do today.) I was sent to a recovery facility that was not unlike a modern-day private hospital, but I yearned for home. With the permission of the poultice-makers, I traveled to my mother's residence to heal. It wasn't very long before things went from bad to really bad. The cuts became infected, and nothing the medical people did seemed to help. I was soon very ill, and when I consulted the healers all they did was hold up their hands and prescribe more leeches, dung, and poppy seeds.

I recall my death very clearly. My fever spiked. I was delirious and unable to understand what was happening. We'd never been a religious family. On occasion (mostly, when we needed something), my mother and father would offer burnt sacrifices, vows, and oaths to the various Greek gods the Romans had adopted as their own. Let's be honest here, we were straight-up old-world pagans. Mother abandoned the practices after Father's death and soon became a sullen mess, seeking no refuge in any religion. I believe she saw futility in asking a deity to intervene in the life of a "nobody" like me.

What I type now constitutes my recollection, many years later, of my death from what today we call 'sepsis.'

First came the wailing as my mother sat at my bedside. Though my eyes were closed, and my breathing labored, I heard every sob and every breath she took, preparing for the next sob. I understand why she was this emotional. My father wasn't even two years' dead, and here I was, at death's door. My breathing was difficult. I could feel my heart racing as I shook from chills. Through the chills and shaking, sweat ran from my body due to the high fever. It felt good for my mother to wipe my forehead with a cool rag, but the relief was momentary. I hallucinated that I was sliding or falling on a curved structure, which I guess were the ribs of a ship, not unlike those that had killed my father. I smelled horrible, as the infection had spread from my injuries to the rest of my body. I could not lie on my back because of excruciating pain. I felt my heart skip a beat, then another. I opened my eyes as wide as I could and tried to tell my mother I loved her. One second later, I closed them as I stopped breathing and stopped living.

I'm sure you, reading this, are very curious about what happened next. In the years I spent with Lazarus, I did get him to open up regarding some of the details of his experience in the afterlife, which sounded horrific. Sarah and I have tried through the years to address our individual experiences. Still, the only time I have ever discussed my personal experience was long ago when a religious scholar discovered our true identities. His curiosity was more about the fact that we had known Jesus and not so much about the question of whether we went to heaven or hell upon our deaths, which I thought was curious, but I never got the opportunity to address it in any real depth with him.

I will say this, heaven, hell, angels, demons? Totally real. My death brought me into contact with all four.

As I wrote earlier, my family was simple pagans. When I died, the place I went to wasn't pretty and wasn't nice, and I will do almost anything to avoid going back.

Anyway, I was there. I knew I was dead. All around me were the dead. I could taste death, smell death. I don't know how, but I had complete recall of my life before my death. I had a body, but it was wracked with pain. With every molecule of my soul, I wanted to escape to tell my family and friends that the afterlife and eternity were real. Perhaps I could get them to change their ways somehow and avoid it. I desperately wanted to tell them. I knew there was another side–a better place–and I knew the great gulf between the two was impossible to breach. It was soul-crushing, and I knew I could do nothing about it. Though I had no heartbeat, I felt the heat, and, yes, I felt pain. Lots of pain. I had no concept of time. I could have been there minutes, years, or millennia. I had no way of knowing.

Everything around me seemed to withdraw, like mice do when they run from the owl, and the brightest light I could ever imagine shone around me. I was startled and closed my eyes tight, yet the light remained. *Perhaps a new kind of torture?* I recall wondering if this would be the thing that might erase me out of existence permanently. Then, I heard a man. His voice was strong. It was impossible to ignore.

"Young man, I say to thee, arise!"

I sat up and opened my eyes. I tore at the linen that covered my face. I could see that I was outside the city gates, at a funeral. Mine! Not too far away there was an open grave. Once again, mine. As the burial linen fell from my face, I turned and accepted the hand of a beautiful man, his smile radiating love and peace. I slid off the wooden board used to transport bodies and was surrounded by my mothers' arms. People praised the Hebrew God, proclaiming his glory and that of the prophet who had raised me from the dead. The man looked at me, smiled, turned away, and was swept up into the crowd that had gathered.

I blinked. *Is this true? Can it be that I am alive again?* I cleared my throat and tried to yell, "thank you!" to the man, but the large crowd had swallowed him. As my mother smothered me with kisses and affection, I took a deep breath, thankful to be alive. I was also relieved beyond my ability to express it.

I had my second chance. I wasn't going to waste it.

Someone handed me a clay jar of wine. I drank eagerly. It was surreal. Moments ago, I had been lost forever in a sea of agony, pain, and loss. Now, I was looking into the eyes of my mother. I reached around to feel my back. There was no pain.

"Mother, we must go home. I have so much I need to tell you."

"Son, not too long ago I was mourning your death and facing life alone. Whatever you have to say can surely wait until I have had time to understand that you live!"

I nodded. I knew my mother was in shock, but she should have been me! I'm pretty sure I won the "I'm-in-shock prize" that day.

We returned home, followed by a massive crowd that grew with every footstep. The murmuring was also growing. I heard several times how we had faked my death, how mother was in league with the prophet, and that she had been paid richly for her performance. Go figure. Humanity hasn't changed much in these 2,000 years. I can imagine crowds today doing the exact same thing. I also heard several remarking that this wasn't an act of God Almighty but some unknown brand of sorcery. I knew it wouldn't sit well with some and I was right. It wasn't too long before the religious authorities showed up to examine me and to announce that I had most likely never been dead.

After the local celebration died down (funny turn of a phrase if I do say so myself), I had some alone time with my mother. I decided not to sugarcoat my words.

"Mother, please listen to me with your heart and soul."

"Son? What troubles you? Is there something you need that you do not have? Tell me, and I will get it for you."

"I mean it. You must do nothing else as I speak."

Clasping my hand so hard that it hurt a bit, she continued. "Yes, of course, I will listen to you, but what could be so urgent that you must talk now?"

"The afterlife."

"What? You know the gods will take care of us. They must have looked after you, had pity on me, a poor widow, and now they have brought you back to me. I ignored them for so many years. Now I must atone and make sacrifices to them, may they be praised forever!"

I had to stop that train of thought.

"Mother, there are no gods coming to help us. There is just one, true God. It is he who brought me back from the dead."

She was silent for a full minute. I was aware that her breathing had increased. I could tell her heart was beating faster than normal.

"Elan, what are you saying? What is the meaning of this? Only one God? Explain yourself."

I spent the next few hours telling and retelling my experiences in the land of the dead. While my friends and family said I had been gone a mere two days, to me it had been an eternity of unending torture and pain. It was then that I realized that I no longer felt any pain from the injuries that had taken my life. I removed my tunic, turned my back to my mother and asked, "What of the scars from my injury?"

She gasped. I craned my neck to see her face. Her mouth hung open for just a brief moment in time.

"There are no scars. There is nothing to indicate you were injured at all. Your back is healed. I smelled the dead flesh, saw the hideous scars as we washed your body for burial." I heard her inhale and exhale, then she spoke, her words soft and full of wonder, "How is this possible?" she asked.

Turning, I gathered her into my arms. "Mother, who was that man who raised me from the dead? Because not only did he rescue me from eternal damnation, but in doing so, the wounds on my body have been healed. Who is he? I must know the man who raised me from the dead!"

She looked startled for a moment. "He is a simple carpenter from Nazareth. His name is Jesus. He has been ministering to the sick and needy throughout the land. Miracles happen around him all the time. Many say he is the Son of God!"

"Has he ever done this?"

"Raise someone from the dead?"

"Yes."

"How am I to know such a thing? Not that I have heard, and if such a miracle happened before yours, I am sure the authorities would have noticed and made something of such a feat."

I recall this statement troubling me for a moment. Yes, in my heart, I knew someone in the local temple was probably speaking about my resurrection from the dead at that very second. I had no idea just how right I was. I suppressed those feelings and responded, "Mother, he is the Son of God. You must give up this misplaced belief in other deities. There are none. Yes, there is good and evil. There is also a place in the afterlife for those who follow the commandments and love the one, true God." I paused for a moment. "Tell me again how you came to meet him? You did not seek him out?"

"No. He was traveling with followers, and as we left the city gate carrying your body, he saw me weeping. He stopped and asked why I was weeping. I pointed towards your body and answered that my son had just died, and by our custom, burial must follow with no delay. I could see tears welling up in his eyes as he said, 'do not weep.' That is when he approached your body and spoke the words that brought you back to me."

"It was that simple?"

"Yes," she began to weep, hugging me so tightly that I thought I would die again.

Separating myself from her grasp, I held her at arm's length. What I then said to her is still somewhat of a mystery to me. I am not sure how I even formed the words. They seemed to tumble out of me. "Mother, the man who brought me back from the dead is the savior foretold in ancient prophecies: the Messiah who has been sent to rescue mankind. He is the answer to this tired world of death. We must believe in him!"

I could see the skepticism building. Even though her once-dead son was talking to her, I still had to shock her. "I have told you about the place I was after I died. Let me be clear if I wasn't clear enough before. It was not a good place. I cannot describe everything I experienced to you because you would not grasp just how horrible it was. In the distance, I could see a place I knew to be heaven across a great and terrifying gulf. I knew it existed. I knew I was looking at the entrance to the Kingdom of God. I also knew I would never be there, that you would never be there, that no one we ever knew would be there. This man, this prophet, Jesus, he is our only hope. He has come so that we can all live."

"Live? Like you live now?"

"No. Well, yes, maybe. I draw a breath, I am alive, so I am living. While I was dead, I learned that when we die, we are no longer living. But, if we believe in him, we don't go to that place where I was. It is so clear to me now. Across the great gulf were flowering trees, honey flowing like a river. The city was bathed in a bright and golden hue as if the brightest morning sun were above, though I saw no sun and felt no rays soothing my discomfort. I could hear singing! Singing! I want us all to go to the place off in the distance that I could see but never attain. I don't want to be alone or in pain for all eternity. I don't want you to be either. We must sell our possessions and follow the man who brought me back from that awful place, and we must do it now!"

This was not what she had expected.

"Sell our possessions? My son, we have nothing. With your father's death and then yours, I had abandoned myself to the whims of fate."

"Whims?"

"Your deaths changed me. I felt like a reed in the sand, being pushed to and fro by the wind from the north, then pushed by a southern wind, never standing still, but bending to the whims of the fates, the ground underneath worn away by unseen forces."

"Mother, there is no fate. If you have nothing of value to bring, then, it will be easy to gather what you need. Hurry, we are going to find the messiah and follow him."

7

As my mother and I followed in the footsteps of the man we came to call the Rabbi Master, we came across many people who related to us the story they'd heard of a young man being raised from the dead outside the city gates of Nain. Many expressed their opinions regarding whether such a thing could happen or not. Some said it reminded them of the time more than eight hundred years prior when a great prophet, Elisha, raised a young child from the dead in the town of Shunem, just across the hill from Nain. This all reminded me of conversations I had heard before my father's death. Rumors that the towns of Nain and Shunem were built over holy ground, consecrated thousands of years ago by prophets. This fact apparently made it possible to raise the dead in the right circumstances. I had listened with skepticism, secure in the knowledge that such a thing was impossible. Now, I was still in shock after discovering just how little I knew.

Everyone wanted something from him. Many hoped he would bring about a new era or raise their relatives from the dead. I know my mother wanted to yell that I had been resurrected from the dead. Fortunately, I had counseled her to remain silent, which she did. Reluctantly.

Once we caught up to him, we tried to keep out of view lest he recognize us and bring us forward. We stayed on the fringes of the ever-growing and rowdy congregation, watching, listening, and learning. Mother was speechless as every illness or malady fell before his healing touch. Sometimes all he had to do was speak the name of a disease and the person who was suffering from it was healed. I could see my mother coming to believe, as I already did, in the messiah. It brought tears to my eyes, knowing that now she would avoid the awful place I had been.

Days turned into weeks, and we remained at the edge of the crowds, undiscovered. When I was dead, I was acutely aware of my surroundings and what was happening to what I would call my "afterlife body." I would describe it as being a state where every sense was heightened, especially pain. After returning to life, I discovered that I retained, or rather, gained, a greater sense of awareness. I soon came to realize that I could determine if someone we interacted with was honest, or deceitful. I sensed that many in the crowd were not who or what they purported to be. Innately I knew they must have been sent by the religious authorities to spy and report back. I also knew that they meant to harm him. I wanted to scream their intentions, but I remained silent.

One day, I was lurking on the edge of a large group, all clamoring for miracles, when I was almost overcome with a sense of impending doom. I felt betrayal and anger and it was coming from someone nearby, a close associate of the Rabbi Master. It made me sick. It was at that moment that the Rabbi Master did what I had been avoiding. He turned and looked my direction. He nodded and smiled.

That night, I was shaken awake. I recognized the man who had woken me as one of his disciples.

"Come," he spoke so as not to wake up my mother.

We walked towards a tree on the edge of the River Jordan. The Rabbi Master waited, sitting on a large boulder. Shadows cast by the moon gave everything an odd shade of black and white. However, he was clearly illuminated in a shaft of light. He pointed towards a flat rock, and I sat.

"Elan, you have come a long way since being raised from the dead. Your mother now believes, and the testimony of those who witnessed your return to life has brought many to my flock. Tomorrow, I shall break bread at the home of a noted Pharisee." He paused. "This will signify that the end of my time here has come."

I wanted to interrupt.

"I know you have questions. You will have many more. You shall face trials and tribulations. However, you have been raised for a reason. Tomorrow, when I leave, you must leave too. You have been recognized by the authorities and as they scheme to take my life, they also intend to take yours and your mothers to serve as examples of why the people should not follow me. Do not worry, your mother will be taken in and will be well cared for by my followers in other lands. I do not send you out into the world alone. I am sending you to meet a woman to undertake the journey with you. You are to travel to the western well of Capernaum where you will find her waiting. From there, you will make your way to the seaside town of Caesarea Maritima and meet a man whose name is Lazarus. His journey shall be your journey. Help him. Learn from and with him. Your female companion may seem frail at first, but there is great strength in her that you will need. Now, return to your mother's side and prepare to leave."

With that, he reached out and touched my face with both hands, stood, and left.

I was in shock. His departing touch was such a loving gesture, so soft and personal. I was overwhelmed. For that one, singular moment, I felt enraptured. I'm not sure how much time elapsed, but I realized I was alone, and dawn was approaching. I gathered myself together and made a quick path back to my mother, resolved to sneak out of the encampment before dawn broke.

She was not very pleased when I woke her. "But why must we leave? Are you disillusioned with the Rabbi Master or his teachings?"

I had expected reluctance, but there wasn't time to be subtle or manipulative. I decided the hard truth was best. "There are spies in the crowd who wish us harm because of who I am. They also mean harm to you and to the Rabbi Master."

She reacted with anger and fear but remained silent.

I put my hand on her shoulder. "We represent what he is capable of doing."

"Who is it? Romans? Because if so, we are Roman citizens. This fact alone must carry a certain amount of weight."

I shook my head as I replied. "No. Not just Romans. Jews also. Remember how I told you that after coming back, my senses had been heightened somehow? Well, for the last week I have sensed that the Rabbi Master has a traitor in his flock, one who pretends to be a follower but instead is in league with his enemies. The authorities are looking for a reason to arrest the Rabbi Master, and our presence, being known now, gives them pause to consider just what this man can do. If he can raise the dead, it would be easy for him to overthrow a government just by raising their sworn enemies. Think about that for a moment. The Rabbi Master told me I have been given a special charge, to accomplish a task yet unknown to me."

This got her attention. "You have spoken with the Rabbi Master? What task has he given you and why can't I be part of it?"

"I do not know. He asked that I meet two other people and we are to go somewhere, perhaps to start a ministry. He told me that you will be cared for by his disciples. But we must leave now."

While she pondered this statement, I continued to break camp and prepare our belongings.

With a curt nod of her head, she decided. "You are right. We must leave. If the Rabbi Master has said it must be so, then, it must be so."

I was relieved to hear that. She was always very smart.

"Good. Let's make our way towards the coast."

As we left the camp, another man, unknown to me, approached. He handed me a small, black sack. Accepting it, I could tell that there were coins inside. He removed another from his cloak and handed it to my mother. "From the Rabbi Master. Now, you both must go your separate ways." He turned to my mother and said, "You will be watched. Take this silver and go, make a new life under a new name three towns to the eastern side of the Sea of Galilee. You will be contacted and watched over by those loyal to the Rabbi Master. Now, you must say goodbye to your son forever."

She started to protest but he held up one hand. "You shall see him again in the kingdom of God." He saw protest beginning in my face too, so he held my shoulders and said, "son, convey to your mother the love you have for her now for it shall be the last time you speak to her on this side of eternity."

I clamped my arms around her neck, and we held onto each other for a while. And as the sun began to crest the hills to the east, the man spoke once more.

"Mother, you must depart now. I have instructions for your son that you must not hear. Now go."

Our parting was sorrowful. She cried, but her tears were tears of love, not pain.

"I love you, my son. Go and follow the path the Rabbi Master has set before you. Be the man he knows you can be." With that, she hugged and kissed me, releasing me slowly. With a sad smile, she turned and departed, never looking back.

We both watched her disappear into the mist of the coming dawn. The cool air settled onto my shoulders as I anticipated what might be happening next. The man took me by the hand and led me to the edge of the clearing. "You must first travel to the western-most water well just outside the town of Capernaum. There, you will meet your traveling companion. She will be waiting for you after the next moonless night. Her name is Sarah. Together, you are to make your way to the port of Caesarea Maritima on the Mediterranean and secure passage on a three-masted ship that will be going to the island of Cyprus. You will be in the company of a man known as Lazarus of Bethany. You are to watch from a location of safety as he purchases passage with coins that will have been given to him."

He pointed at the change purse I had hidden in my pack. "After you see that he has boarded the ship, take a measure of what has been provided in this purse and purchase passage on the same ship for you and Sarah."

The man held out a hand and passed me another small sack.

"Here is a parcel of food to sustain you and Sarah. Once you see Lazarus board the ship, you and Sarah will do as he did. Approach the same man and offer a small bribe to secure a berth on the ship. Once you are on board and the ship is underway, you will find Lazarus on a wooden bench at the bow of the ship. He is to be your guide and friend."

With that pronouncement, he shook both of my hands and turned me towards the tree line. "Now, go with God, Elan of Nain."

My head spun and I could still taste the salt from my mother's tears as I made my way into the trees. The morning dew wet my feet and the edges of my cloak while I was repeating in my mind what the Rabbi Master had said.

Journey? Of course, I had heard of Lazarus. He, like me, had been raised from the dead. Why was I to meet him? And who was this woman, Sarah? It seems the Rabbi Master knows her. Why is she important?

For as by the one man's disobedience the many were made sinners, so by the one man's obedience the many will be made righteous.

ROMANS 5:19

8

Sarah

Hello, I am Sarah. Or I once was. I guess I still am. To be honest, it is hard to know sometimes, given the years, and all that has transpired.

It was gracious of Lazarus to offer Elan and me an opportunity to introduce ourselves and contribute to this history of our lives. I often saw him scrunched over a roll of parchment, vellum, or a scroll, and later, over paper stock. When movable type came along, he was quite happy. With the invention of typewriters, word processors and computers he was an absolute madman. But I'm getting ahead of myself. I use to watch him making notes about things we had done or people with whom we had been involved. I tried to sneak a look a few times, but Lazarus always caught me. It was like he always knew I was trying to spy on him as he would bend over and write down the things he remembered. I confess, since I became aware of what he was up to, I have been quite curious regarding what he might say about us. About me. Sometimes, when I saw him hard at work, I guess I sort of hoped it was a poem or a song, maybe a verse of two that would tell me he loved me as a father would love a daughter. I once engaged him in a conversation regarding how he lived before his death and resurrection, and I came to understand that he just was not much of an emotional person, which meant no poetry. I gleaned from our conversations that he wasn't much of a family man either. He never became attached to a woman through marriage, though he loved his sisters Martha and Mary. I believe dying, going into the afterlife, and being resurrected had a significant effect on him, to the point that he remained a singularly morose man, but with a tinge of hopefulness, if that makes any sense at all, given that he knew the way to avoid an eternal life of misery and pain. The Lazarus of today is still a bit distant, but he is far less morose. And, even though he's never penned poetry for me, or a song of any kind, I suppose he does love me as a father might, but it would have nice to hear it from him once in a while.

I know that could make me sound like the modern-day version of a spoiled brat. But I am not spoiled. On the contrary, I know that I am blessed. Perhaps it's just the trauma of my early life that has left me wanting sustained personal contact based in love. Perhaps, I am human after all.

What I have to offer here will not be the ramblings of a teenager adrift in the ocean of time. Though my body may be "stuck" for lack of a better word in the formative years of early adulthood, I assure you my mind has more than 2,000 years' worth of experience and knowledge, bottled up ready to share.

I pray you will find strength in what I write and hope for the future. Like that of Elan and Lazarus, my story is complex at times, given how each of us has experienced and interpreted the events of our resurrections and what we believe God requires of us.

Were we to build churches? Or perhaps start schools? Should we try to be political leaders? What would happen if we started telling everyone who we are? Would they believe what we'd have to say about our experiences in the afterlife? Would we be branded as heretics? Witches? Burned at the stake? To be honest, during our lifetimes, we three have faced various versions of all of these, and much more, and experienced the hatred you might expect to accompany such 'outrageous' claims.

At times, it seemed that just surviving the numerous attempts on our lives might be enough.

Anyway, thank you for indulging me in a bit of nostalgic reflection. I hope you understand that though I may appear to be a young teen, I am very old. I write going forward from someone whose mind, body, and spirit were born, lived, and died more than 2,000 years ago. Then I was alive again.

By the way, I still have the doll you'll read about it a few pages. She has changed personalities as many times as I have, and she has always been my best friend.

9

I was born and raised in Capernaum, a fishing village on the north shore of the Sea of Galilee, a beautiful freshwater lake we used for many purposes. I was the only child of Jairus, leader of the local temple, and his wife, Tamar.

Our home, which was located very close to the temple, had four rooms built around a central courtyard with a protective wall. Our animals–some goats, two donkeys, and three lambs–were kept in an interior enclosure. A cistern was there as well, to capture rainwater. If the water level was low because it had not rained, several wells were located all around the countryside.

From a very young age, girls not already betrothed or married were consumed with preparing to become housewives one day. I spent many days cooking, cleaning, keeping the household fires burning, and even doing the family laundry. As an only child, yeah, I got the worst of the household duties. My aunts, grandmothers, nurses, and other female relatives all saw that I was given every opportunity to learn what it meant to be a woman of modest means. I recall that the sewing, grinding, baking, spinning, gardening, and cleaning never seemed to end. I was pretty good at it, though; so I always believed my parents would find a nice Hebrew man for me, and I'd be the perfect wife, maybe even marry someone inside the temple leadership. Someone like my father, Jairus.

So much for best-laid plans.

At the time of my birth, science was little more than unmitigated sorcery and wild guesses. In other words, it was much like medicine today. Okay, I typed that partly in jest, but honestly, you wouldn't believe what healers did back then to try and cure a fever. I should know, I had a nasty fever, and what they did to try and heal me would be child abuse today.

One morning while tending to a baby lamb, I sneezed. This led quickly to a sniffle, which wasn't all that abnormal. Everyone sneezed and sniffled. I wiped my nose and kept feeding my animals. Later that night, I felt warmer than usual. The women all slept in a single room on an elevated bed platform to keep our bodies from contact with the cold ground. Such closeness made hiding my labored breathing impossible.

The next night I drew the attention of my mother, who raised herself up from her position and asked in a concerned-yet-I-just-woke-up voice, "Child, what troubles you? Why do you make such noise?"

I probably fake-cried a bit, looking for sympathy and not interested in being scolded. Seeing that tactic gained no traction, I gathered up some resolve and answered, "I do not feel well."

Feeling my forehead with the back of her hand, my mother withdrew her arm quickly and exclaimed, "Sarah, you have a great fever!"

Apparently, my father was woken by the commotion in the next room and stuck his head beyond the entrance to the room. After a grumpy comment regarding his lack of sleep, he offered to begin forming a remedy poultice.

My mother coughed and spat out, "What in the name of Moses and the prophets do you know about making a poultice? Please, you'd more likely kill your daughter with some dung-centered stinking bandage. Leave this to me, return to our bed and trouble yourself no more."

I heard him mumble acceptance of the rebuke, and soon he was snoring again.

Mother gathered her cloak and ushered me towards the door leading to the inner courtyard as an aunt began working on some potion she believed would cure me.

"Come, child, outside into the cool night air." Wrapping a blanket around my shoulders, my mother led me outside into the courtyard. I shook briefly at the chilled air. The night sky was beautiful. The stars were laid out so perfectly. Looking upwards, I felt my throat closing.

"Stay here. I shall go boil water for a compress."

I made a movement with my hands, indicating that I needed a drink, too.

"Of course, dear. Your aunt is preparing a drink for you of honey and wine. Make no noise or movement."

I wasn't about to move. My head was spinning, and I felt like my tongue was too large for my mouth. Soon, my aunt and mother returned and gently shook me awake at some point just before sunrise. Taking the steaming clay cup thrust into my face, I drank the mixture, which made me sleepy. Falling asleep in her arms, I felt somewhat better.

Two days later, I awoke as I regurgitated her latest attempt at medical assistance and the meal I'd eaten a few hours earlier. The pounding in my head was like nothing I'd ever experienced. I had sweated through my inner and outer garments.

Clutching my abdomen, I called out in pain. "Mother, help me. What is happening? Why does my stomach hurt so? What was it you gave me? Help me!"

She rushed to my side. "Be still." Seeing the vomit, she was somewhat taken aback. "Oh dear, you have emptied your stomach again. We must get the medicine back into your body."

As she said this, my body convulsed in agony.

"Papa! Where is papa?" I cried.

"He left soon after daylight. He has gone to see a new prophet with a reputation as a healer. Stay strong, Sarah. When he returns, the prophet will know what to do to save you."

As I slipped into unconsciousness, I began praying to Moses to intervene on my behalf with the Almighty. My prayer was a simple plea only a child would make.

"Father Moses, please ask the God of Abraham to have mercy and heal me."

Delirious, I went back and forth between conscious and unconscious. Mother fussed about for a while, changing my clothing, and always applying a cool cloth to my forehead. As I slipped in and out of consciousness, I heard relatives remarking that she needed to be prepared for me to die. She would angrily shush them and shoo them out of room.

My breathing became labored, and just like that, I was dead.

The transition between life and death was immediate.

A soft but radiant light illuminated the room around me and seemed to pierce me. I opened my eyes, and a beautiful being smiled the most calming and wonderful smile. I knew immediately it was an angel. He reached out both hands and clasped mine in his. Attached to his body and moving as if he were about to fly away like a huge bird were two sets of wings that arched at the top over his head and swept down. I looked over the edge of the sleeping platform and saw that the wings came to a point and rested on the floor. I heard a swishing noise when they moved, though they did not disturb the floor or the dust. His feet did not touch the floor.

I felt no pain and knew immediately that I had died. I wondered if this visitor had been sent to heal me. With no effort, he helped me sit upright. A bright orange and white circle opened in the ceiling above my head. Like him, it seemed to just float there, with no real structure or substance. Other angels came down from the circle of light and surrounded me. I could tell they were singing. It was the most breathtakingly beautiful thing I could ever have imagined. As their wonderful melody permeated my being, I realized what was happening. The angel had not pulled me upright as I believed because I could see my body on the sleeping platform just below me. I floated above my dead body. My mother lay prostrate, crying. I could sense her pain. My heart hurt for her, and I wanted to cry, too.

As I struggled with these emotions, the angel spoke. "Sarah, you have passed from the realm of the living into ours. Fear not my child, for in death, you shall reveal the savior. The faith of your father brings the Son of God to your side." The angel gestured towards the ever-growing circle of light and other angels, "See, even now the heavenly Hosts gather to witness the miracle of your new life. You shall be reborn through the will of the Father and his Son."

As the angel held my hands, I felt the power of heaven while more angels began to swirl around us. He continued to speak, and the words embedded themselves in my soul. I don't know how long we floated there, but it was as if time itself had stopped. I closed my eyes and felt pure love permeating my entire being.

Then I heard someone speak with such force that it moved my soul. "Child! Arise!"

I felt a surge of strength like none I had ever experienced, and I opened my eyes. Gathered around me were my mother, father, and four men whom I did not know. I knew the man holding out his hand had to be he who had spoken to me and brought me back from death. It was he whom the angel had called "the Son of God."

I placed my hand in his, and he helped me stand. His gaze shifted from me to my mother. "Give her nourishment. She needs to begin rebuilding her strength."

Nobody moved. My parents stood, mute.

It was my mother who broke the silence first. "Prophet, she was dead yet minutes ago. She has been two days dead. We have begun the mourning process as laid out in the Law given to Moses and handed down through the generations! How is this possible?"

The prophet's face changed from peaceful to stern.

"Tell no one what has happened today." The force of his personality was evident in the tone of his voice.

"What shall we say?" my father asked.

"Say nothing. Your faith has returned your daughter to you. Give thanks in the appropriate manner."

He then turned to me and smiled, and speaking to my parents said, "Her life shall speak for itself in the years to come. Now, do as I commanded and bring her food and drink."

Without moving his lips, I heard him speak.

"We shall never meet again in this life. You will understand what has happened and why it has happened at a point far into the future. Remember what the angel of the Lord spoke unto you, for it shall give you comfort in the years to come."

It was a lot for a teenage girl to comprehend. I had just been dead, speaking with an angel, seeing hundreds of other angels, and then I was brought back to life. My heart was filled with emotion. I signaled to him that I understood with a lopsided smile and a nod.

He returned the smile, ran his hands over my shoulder, kissed me on the forehead, turned, and left.

My mother and father hugged me and cried. They brought me figs and oil, slices of bread and honey, wine mixed with water. I ate my fill and as I was drifting off to sleep, I heard father say he was going to the temple to kill a fatted calf and offer it as a sacrifice to God. I thought that was appropriate, and under my breath, I thanked God for sending his Son to heal me. I was alive! In the back of my mind was something the angels had said to me. They'd spoken of a great mystery to be revealed to me once I was reborn.

Mystery? What mystery?

10

The murmuring started soon after I returned to life.

"She is possessed"

"How can she be living? I saw her dead body!"

"This is sorcery of the highest order!"

My father's senior position in the temple was of no use to him as he tried to stave off the criticisms. Everyone was soon inquiring about how he had heard of the prophet from Galilee and why he had stepped outside of the recognized and common medical pathways to pursue an unknown cure by a prophet known for stirring up trouble for the temples and their leadership. Much was being made of how the prophet was healing the sick and the lame, turning religious society upside down with his sermons regarding direct accessibility to the Almighty God. Days after returning to life, I sought out my aunt to discuss the rumors. Finding her, we walked and talked until we sat in the shade of a large palm tree near a local spring. I asked her a direct question regarding my death.

"You heard what happened to me?"

"Yes," she replied. "Against the wishes of the temple, your father sought out the one called Jesus, a prophet who is gaining a following for working miracles and wonders. Once your father found him, he asked him to come back and lay hands on you, which the prophet agreed to do. They began the journey to your home, and a small crowd followed, interested to see what would happen. Many questioned why the leader of a local temple was asking this upstart prophet for help. As they approached our village, a servant was sent by your mother to tell them to stop."

"Because I had already died."

She looked at me with an odd expression and continued. "Yes. The servant told your father and the prophet that you had perished."

"So, my father knew that I had died before the prophet was able to get to our home."

"Yes. And that information did not deter the prophet at all. On the contrary, he merely stated loudly enough for everyone to hear that you were not dead, that you were merely sleeping. This made many angry, and some began to mock him."

"What were they saying?"

"That perhaps the prophet your father had found was of a simple mind, unable to comprehend the concept of death."

Hearing this, I cringed inside. The sweet, perfect man I had met had no such disabilities. And I could tell that he had complete command over both life and death.

"And?" I retorted. "They did not stop, did they?"

"No. They continued the journey towards your home. Your father and the prophet arrived, and without saying a word he expelled all the mourners who had been sitting with your mother, beginning to observe the mourning period as required in the Law."

"He sent everyone away?"

"Yes. He cleared the house completely, except for your parents. At that point, he brought three of his followers into the room." She hesitated for a moment, and I interrupted because I knew how the story ended.

"At that point, he spoke to me in a voice I could not possibly ever disregard! I heard him very clearly say, 'Child, arise,' and I did just as he commanded."

The look of astonishment on her face was one I'd never seen before.

"How can you even know such a thing?"

"I heard him." It was then that I told her of the angels, of the singing, and about all the beauty that surrounded me as he brought me back to life.

She was taken aback by the intense spirituality of it all. Stunned into silence, she played with a twig, removing the bark slowly with her fingernails. I don't know who was more shocked; me to recount my experiences or her, to hear such a story coming from a young relative.

Finally, she found her voice again. "Then you also know that he commanded your parents to never speak of what he had done, yes?"

I nodded my head. "Yes. He told them to feed me and to tell no one of my return to life."

She was quiet for a moment and then offered, "You must never tell this story. It is the kind of thing that could get you stoned or even crucified.

For now, your father is a man of means within the community. There is still talk about his decision to seek an outside prophet, but he should be able to weather this storm since he has followed the prophet's words. He has told no one, and everyone assumes that you were just sleeping, and the prophet simply woke you up from deep slumber. Even the women who had begun to sit the mourning period now do not believe that you were dead. No one who was outside your home knows the truth of what occurred. I know because your mother told me that I might add against the admonition of the prophet. I have told no one, and it would be wise of you to be very careful and keep this story close to your heart."

I sat for a while, wondering what the angel meant when he told me that in death, I would reveal the Son. *Even the prophet had told my parents to tell no one, so how am I supposed to reveal him if I wasn't supposed to tell anyone?* It was a bit much for my young mind.

My aunt saw my internal struggles.

"Sarah, I cannot begin to understand the immeasurable gift of being reborn. Your new life is just beginning, so it is possible that the prophet had other reasons for returning you to your parents. Pray about it, take heart too, for whatever happens, you have met the Son of God, and you have seen beyond this life! You have a message to deliver, and one day, I know you shall deliver it. Now, take your leave to return home, but first, hug your aunt, I love you, now go hug your parents, for each new day is a gift from God."

I stood, hugged her, and did just as she had suggested. I ran home and hugged my mother, and when my father came home from the temple, I hugged him.

11

I followed the advice of my aunt, returned to my regular household duties, and kept quiet. That wasn't enough to satisfy the suspicions of our neighbors. It would seem that too many of them had been in the room with my mother, mourning over my dead body. Soon, the rumors started. I was sucking the blood out of babies at night. Then I was sucking the blood out of livestock or out of every other animal that recently died. Most of the rumors involved the sucking of blood. What can I say? We were kind of a ridiculous and superstitious people.

At the end of a tough day of enduring exclamations behind my back and watching the women make superstitious signs to ward off the evil they believed I carried, my father came across me sitting outside in the courtyard with one of my goats. The look on my face must have been one that said, 'talk to me. I'm feeling sorry for myself.'

He sat and started feeding the goat, pulling me close with his free hand. "Sarah, what is wrong?"

"Father, I can tell, the women in town believe me evil because I was once dead and now am alive. I know the prophet you brought to heal me instructed you not to reveal the miracle of my resurrection, but it would seem that everyone knows. I see them making faces and signs to ward off evil spirits when I walk to the well or market. Why don't they know that the man who raised me from the dead is the Son of God?"

"Yes, I know. Anyone who has not experienced what you have has no understanding of what has happened to you. And the prophet forbade us from speaking about it, so I cannot tell them how wrong they are to accuse us of falsely claiming your death."

"He has a good reason," and I related to him everything that had happened to me while I was dead.

The look on his face was one I'd seen before when he was interpreting an inscrutable portion of Mosaic law for someone. What I said had significant weight for him.

"Angels in our house. It is almost too much to comprehend. And the one who held your hands said that your death would reveal the savior?"

"Yes. And then I heard him tell me to rise up, and I did. That is when I saw you, mother, the Son of God and those other men."

My father considered what I had said for a few minutes. Then asked, "Do you know why the Son of God, as you put it, removed the mourners before he conducted the miracle of your resurrection?" He didn't wait for my reply and continued, "because there must be a greater purpose in your resurrection beyond a few townspeople witnessing your return. Greater than even your family and this town. I shall pray on it and offer sacrifice to the Lord of Hosts that he will reveal to you the true purpose. Open your heart, daughter, and he shall guide you."

I thought telling him something he didn't know might help.

"He spoke to me before he left and said that one day, far into the future, the reason for my resurrection would be revealed to me. How far do you think it might be? In a day? A month? Soon? Before someone does something evil to me because they don't like the fact that I have returned from the dead?"

"What do you mean he spoke to you? I did not hear it."

"Yes, I know."

"Your mother and I did not hear him speaking to you. This is curious." My father went quiet again, thinking.

"It was meant for me to hear and me alone."

The goat finished the carrot father had been feeding him and wanted more. My father smiled, patted me on the head, kissed my forehead and stood.

"I shall go and pray for guidance. What you have told me is emotional, and strange. Perhaps you should do the same."

I did what my father asked and prayed. Today, all these years later, it is clear when we pray for guidance, sometimes what we get in return isn't what we were expecting, and it isn't immediate.

Though I was praying, it was plain to see that keeping to myself and not speaking publicly about my experience was never going to be enough.

As I made my way home from the market one evening, perhaps seven days after my resurrection, an unknown woman joined me step for step. She was so close that it made me uncomfortable.

"They plan to take you tomorrow when you return from the spring you visit to the east of town. You will be killed. It will appear that a wild animal took you," she muttered under her breath.

I kept walking but hesitated for a moment, unsure if I had heard her correctly.

Then she repeated what she had just said. "There are zealots who plan to kill you tomorrow. The Rabbi Master is aware of the plot and is sending someone to meet you tonight. Your parents will be told you have left to begin a new life, one away from the threats against you. You must not return for many years. Your traveling companion is one such as yourself, raised from the dead by the Rabbi Master and now reviled in his hometown for the miracle that brought him back to life."

I kept walking but stumbled somewhat. "The Rabbi Master?"

"The one who raised you from the dead. The prophet your father sought out to heal you. He is sending a young man your own age. His name is Elan. He is from the town of Nain."

This was hard to understand, so I asked, "Who? A man whose name is Elan? Must I go?"

"Yes, there is no time. When I take leave from your side, make no further stops, and go to your home, gather a few things, garments, something important to you, that will remind you of your home if you must."

"Will my mother and father be told I am alive?" This was very important to me, given the threats made regarding my life.

"They will be told you are alive, but that is all they will know. Now, wait until full darkness. There will be no moon tonight. Go to the well near the western edge of the city. That is where you will meet your traveling companion. Do not wait for your parents to return. Now, go child. Go with God."

With that, she veered into a long, dark alley and disappeared. I ran home, my emotions running wild, not quite sure what to do. Bursting into the house, I inquired about my parents. The servants said my parents had been called away on temple business. It was clear to me. They had been distracted so that I could prepare what I needed to leave and not be tempted to stay.

Dismissing the servant, I gathered three favorite cloaks and undergarments, a doll made for me once by the mother of my father and waited in the darkness by a window. There was a tinge of orange glow from the sun on the horizon when I set off. Behind me, stars were just beginning to wink in the eastern sky. Intent on making my way to the well just as my unknown protector had instructed, a moonless night soon settled across the land. Snugging the hood of my cloak over my head, I stayed in the shadows and slowly made my way westward. The only sounds were those of crickets as they called to each other in the dark. I soon stood alone in a grove of trees near the well and put my pack of clothing on the ground. Selecting a large rock, I sat and waited for my traveling companion.

Without warning, a shadow appeared nearby.

"Sarah?"

It was a voice I did not recognize. Wary that this could possibly be someone from the temple seeking to entrap me, I paused before responding.

"Sarah! I know you are there. I see your breath in the cool night air. I am your traveling companion. The one you were told to meet. Come, we cannot tarry. We must put some distance between us and those who wish to do you, well, us harm."

This took me by surprise. *Us harm? Oh, that is right. He is like me . . . once dead, now resurrected.*

I cleared my throat. "Wait. How do I know it is truly you?"

His reply was instantaneous. "Silly girl, who else would be here on a dark night such as this? I know you were told to expect me. Come, no more games. We must leave immediately."

I stood. As he drew nearer, I could see that he was good looking, perhaps two-hands taller than me and approximately my age. He was sporting the growth that I was sure he hoped would one day become a fierce beard.

"I am Elan," is all he said as he took my small bag, slung it over his broad shoulders, and turned away. "Follow me. Stay beside me, as if you are my sister, and I am looking out for your welfare as we travel. Say nothing if we encounter others who may also be traveling."

I was preparing to interrupt when he beat me to it.

"To answer your question, we travel to the seaside docks, where ships come to off load passengers or freight, to meet a man who is like us. Since your father is highly placed in your temple, you may have heard of him, but perhaps you have not. According to what I have been told, we are to join him. He is much older and will protect us."

I shrugged, falling slightly behind. "Don't get too far ahead of me. My legs are not as long as yours, so please don't walk so fast," was all I could muster.

Elan snickered enough for me to overhear.

"I walk with purpose. I will slow when it is appropriate. Now, keep quiet and stay up. We have much ground to cover in the next few days."

I gathered my cloak, sinking into myself, and reassessing my original thoughts regarding Elan. I hoped he would not always be so authoritative on our journey.

I wanted to stop, to mourn what was lost to me, but the insistence in Elan's voice and the warning I had received from the woman resonated inside my head. Thus, I made every effort to keep pace with my new companion.

Already, I missed my mother and father. I hoped they would not be shunned or abused.

12

The journey to the waterfront had been uneventful, though I protested Elan's habit of walking too fast for my taste. We squabbled a
few times about it, but he finally began to slow, seeing that I wasn't lying
regarding his pace. I came to realize that he wasn't trying to be difficult;
instead, it was soon clear to me that he had never had a younger sibling,
much less one of the opposite sex. And it wasn't that I was weaker or
slower than he was, for I had grown up around animals my whole life, I
had brought back jugs of water from the well thousands of times, I was
as strong as I needed to be in those days. He'd been in the military, and I
was a girl from the country. Luckily, he recognized the need to adjust his
mindset because neither of us was what who we'd once been.

During the two days we traveled, we would hide whenever we felt
scrutiny from others that was outside of normal curiosity. Two days
later, we arrived at the docks. To be brutally honest, it smelled awful,
and the utter chaos was quite unpleasant. I'd never been to, or even near
the ocean, and to my mind, it was as if every human on earth was trying
to arrive or depart at the same time. Add to that the huge crates of food-
stuffs, animals, and the slaves in chains, and it was almost overwhelming
for a recently resurrected country girl.

Elan suggested we sit in the shadows and wait. So looking like a
couple of refugees seeking charity handouts, we kept our heads covered and sat for hours on a stack of wooden crates he found. The odor
of spoiled fish surrounded us and permeated virtually every pore and
stitch of clothing. It made me want to vomit. I never knew any fishermen, and I was happy for that fact. Elan seemed delighted, and after he'd
divulged his family history of shipbuilding I understood why he wasn't
as uncomfortable as I was. I mused that being married to a fisherman

required a stronger stomach than mine now that I knew what the water-front smelled like.

"Why do we wait?" I muttered several hundred times. I know I was impatient, which must have been unpleasant for Elan. Several times, after asking that question again, he would jingle the small purse of coins he'd showed me earlier and without looking at me would answer, "The person who gave me this told me to wait and watch for an older man with a similar pouch of coins. We are to follow him as he pays for passage and boards a three-masted ship."

He pointed to a ship not far away.

"That retired Roman warship is the only three-masted ship in today, so this must be the right place and time. Now, stay quiet. See that man directing everyone? He is the shipmaster, second only to the Captain. The man we're to meet, Lazarus, will have to go through him to get onboard. So, we wait and watch."

I didn't like him very much at that moment, so I focused instead on the flies crawling on a crate two feet away. I hoped this mysterious man would arrive soon. Closing my eyes, I relaxed a bit, knowing that eventually we'd leave this awful place. A thought entered my mind that this wasn't the strangest thing I'd experienced, which seemed to calm me.

Minutes later, Elan nudged me back to full consciousness, "There! This must be him!" he said under his breath.

We watched a single man, dressed for travel with no baggage, approach a shipmaster, and after a conversation, the two men cleverly exchanged something that could only have been payment for services, and the man boarded the ship. The shipmaster pocketed the coins with such deftness that it was clear he was accustomed to payments of this sort.

"What do we do? Are we to also purchase passage from the same sailor?" I asked.

"This has all played out as I was instructed. So, yes, we do as we just saw Lazarus do."

"That was Lazarus?" I asked in a hushed tone.

"Yes."

"Do we follow him now?"

We both watched as the man we were to meet boarded the ship and made his way to the front. Elan shook his head and snorted. "Apparently, he has never been on a ship before, especially one built for an ocean voyage."

I did not know what he meant, so I asked him.

"What is it? Why do you shake your head? Is it not him?"

"Oh, it is Lazarus. But he went to, well, I'll tell you why I shook my head later. Now, come with me," he said. Standing, he reached for my hand and without hesitation I took it.

Leaving the security of the shadows, I had a churning in my stomach that told me we were leaving our homeland, perhaps forever.

We approached the shipmaster just as we had seen Lazarus do and he smiled. Looking around, he made as if to shake Elan's hand and muttered something about being the richest man in the fleet.

"Cyprus, my friends?" he inquired.

Elan answered, "yes," and in a very clever fashion, just as he had seen Lazarus do, paid the man. Once the transaction was complete, he pointed us towards the giant boat and said, "Your companion awaits. Please board."

"Watch me and do as I do," Elan said under his breath. "I intend to mingle with other passengers in case anyone has followed us here. We wait until the ship is underway, then we will approach Lazarus. Do you understand?"

I shrugged, "Of course, I am not a little child. I understand your caution. I will follow your lead Elan."

A group headed to Rome was boarding, and we inserted ourselves into their boisterous group. We took seats and waited. Elan leaned over and whispered, "When the ship is away from the dock, say you need fresh air. That is when we will go topside and speak with Lazarus."

I nodded and sat, hopeful about this new life.

So do not fear, for I am with you; do not be dismayed, for I am your God. I will strengthen you and help you; I will uphold you with my righteous right hand.

ISAIAH 41:10

13

"Excuse me, sir. You are Lazarus, aren't you? Lazarus of Bethany?"

The shock of someone speaking to me and calling me by name took me by surprise. Am I undone? Are they about to take me before the tribunal and crucify me like they did the Rabbi Master? I was facing the front of the ship, so I turned to find two young people standing, waiting for an answer. I had seen children traveling with parents or relatives boarding and prayed my traveling companions were older. The voice that had addressed me was small, childlike, and shattered my false sense of security. Twisting in my seat, I saw a young woman, perhaps seventeen or eighteen years old. A young man accompanied her, and they held hands as if brother and sister, or as young spouses.

I fingered the twelve-inch dagger I had secreted in the belt of my robe. I had purchased it earlier that day, preparing for the worse. Though they were young to my eyes, the authorities were known to use such tactics to entrap followers of the Rabbi Master. I looked around for anyone who might be observing us. If the situation required, I felt I could dispatch them and continue safely on the voyage. Seeing no one paying close attention to these two, I answered the young girl.

"Do I know you?"

The young man smiled, but the girl spoke first. "We know you! You are Lazarus of Bethany. The Rabbi Master gave us instructions to meet you, and here we are."

I made quick motions with one hand to stop them from further revealing what they knew. The other hand remained on the dagger. I had never taken a life, but I knew I could do it if pressed. I was worried someone had overheard them calling out to me using my real name. But the raucous noise caused by the crew performing its duties and the sails flapping in the wind afforded us some privacy in conversation. Still, to be safe, I addressed them in the sternest, yet softest, voice possible. I patted an empty space on the wooden bench with my empty hand. "Come. Please sit."

The young man looked at me quizzically. "But you sit on the bow. Look at the slats of wood directly to your left. I surmise that you have spent no time on ships. That is the latrine. Perhaps we can move before we speak?"

I noticed the girl hold her nose for a second. Her expression was one of distaste.

"If that is true . . . "

"It is. My father was a shipbuilder," he interrupted.

"Then, perhaps this is the best place to avoid being overheard."

I could tell he didn't like it, but what was he going to do? Seeing his acceptance, I continued with what I had been about to say. "And, if you are who I believe you are, I caution you to never speak my name in public again. Do you understand?"

Both nodded very slowly, as realization dawned that I was the right Lazarus and that by speaking my name in public, they could have just confirmed our identities for someone seeking us.

I looked around. Every member of the ship's crew remained busy with his duties. There was a bit of security to be found in the gruff exchanges between the crew. The clamoring of metal against metal, the creaks and grinding sounds from the wooden hull, and the sharp, snapping of the sailcloth straining in the wind also provided cover. Others like me who had purchased passage were below, unwilling to sit so close to the salt spray, except for these two.

I needed to be certain of who they were. Even if they said all the right things, I needed reassurance they weren't part of some plot to ensnare me.

"Tell me, you mentioned the Rabbi Master sent you. So, who are you and what do you want?"

She spoke first, again.

"We were given instructions and the means to travel. We were told to go to the waterfront and wait for you. We did not stop to see the Rabbi Master's death."

I cringed. The pain in my heart clamped hard. I stopped breathing for a moment.

Pointing at the young girl, the young man filled in the silence for the first time.

"This is Sarah, the youngest daughter of Jairus, a very senior leader in the temple at Capernaum. She was very ill, close to death when her father left home seeking the Rabbi Master. He had faith that she could be healed."

In what seemed like an afterthought, he added, "I am Elan."

Before he spoke again, I interrupted the story. "How is it that you know this? Are you her brother?"

"No. I will get to who I am in a moment. I learned about Sarah's story from her. May I continue?"

I nodded, noticing the look of respect Sarah gave him as he spoke.

"Her father sought the Rabbi Master and convinced him to return with him, to heal his sick child. Before they arrived, a member of her father's household approached with the sad news that the Rabbi Master was no longer needed. It would seem that Sarah's illness was more serious than her father believed and in his absence she died. The Rabbi Master, on hearing this news, turned to her father, and was overheard saying, 'Don't be afraid; just believe, and she will be healed.' To those following, he turned and proclaimed that the girl was just sleeping. When they arrived home, the Rabbi Master took the girl's parents, his disciples Peter, James, and John, and entered the room where her body lay. Once he had removed all other witnesses, he took her by the hand and, according to her, commanded her spirit to return."

Elan paused for a moment, trying to judge my reaction.

"Most people would be astounded by this story or believe it false, but I see with you that is not the case. Therefore, you must know that what I say is the truth. You must also know that being raised from the dead runs counter to everything the Sadducees, Pharisees, chief priests, and scribes teach and believe. She is sought for trial and execution as a heretic and abomination. As am I."

As, am I? As, am I? Does he mean what I think he means by that? I was getting closer to believing them. I let that thought rest for a moment and asked the next, logical question, given her age.

"Her parents know she has run away?"

The young man puffed his chest a bit, which was kind of funny to see.

"First, she has not run away. She has left because of her life circumstances, her death, and her return to life. Second, yes, they know, in a way, but they do not know the details. It is best this way. Sympathetic followers of the Rabbi Master warned her about a plot on her life, so they helped her leave in the dark of night. Her parents cannot be tortured to reveal her whereabouts."

She wept a bit as she mumbled, "I pray they are left alone in their grief at my departure and not abused by the authorities."

I was somewhat shocked to hear a story that sounded rather familiar to my own. The fear she expressed was undoubtedly well placed. It is possible that at that very moment her poor parents were being tortured by the best interrogators available to the priestly cadre.

I understood her story. Now, I needed to hear his, so I tested him.

"Tell me of your involvement in this. You have not kidnapped her, but what exactly have you done?"

He shook his head very slowly, "Oh, Sarah was not taken against her will."

I looked past him at Sarah, sensing that what Elan had just said was the truth. But still, I wanted to verify it directly from the source of our conversation.

Her beautiful green eyes seemed to bore the truth through my soul. She could have spoken, but it was clear to me that she did not need to talk. She took a deep breath and, with a lilting, young girl's voice, offered a very simple and clear stamp of approval.

"What Elan has spoken is the truth."

I checked again to be certain we were not being overheard. We were not. Leaning towards him, I touched his hand. "Alright, I understand Sarah's presence. Now, young man, what is your story?"

The young man took a deep breath. Sarah grabbed his right hand, the one closest to hers and I saw the strength it gave him. He smiled at her, then at me, and started.

"My name is Elan. I am the son of a shipbuilder, who is now deceased, and his widow. I am from the town of Nain."

With that, he paused. Then I knew exactly who he was. Nain was, and remains even today, a small town in the Valley of Jezreel, just to the southeast of Nazareth and Mount Tabor. It's a lovely, green plain stretching for miles from Esdraelon to Megiddo. He realized further explanation wasn't necessary. I know he understood the distant look in my eyes and smiled sadly.

"Yes, I see it on your face and in your eyes. You must know who I am."

I did. His was the first of the resurrections the Rabbi Master had performed. I was still living when the story started making the rounds at the temples and markets. A young man from the town of Nain had died from injuries suffered as a member of the Roman Legion. As his funeral procession was leaving the city, the Rabbi Master was traveling on the same road. The funeral procession stopped when they saw the crowd following behind him and the Rabbi Master's heart went out to the young man's mother, as she had recently also buried her husband, a well-known local shipbuilder. Consoling her, the Rabbi Master was overcome by her emotion and made the decision to intervene. Telling the woman to cease her lamentations, the Rabbi Master approached the boards holding the linen-wrapped corpse, leaned towards the body, and with a loud and very clear voice was heard to say, "Young man, I say to you: Get up!" The story was that the young man immediately opened his eyes and sat up, linen falling away from his previously dead body. Several people fainted and even more started yelling, "He lives! He lives!" Raising the young man from the dead turned the burial into a praise and worship service.

When added to my own resurrection, I am sure Elan's and Sarah's were not well-received. I know the authorities who hated his message couldn't have him raising the dead. What if he did it to their enemies?

All that went through my mind in the blink of an eye. But I had to be sure.

"Thank you for explaining who you are. Now, what do you need with me? Why did you follow me?"

"We were directed to find you. We watched the docks from a distance, and once we saw you, we purchased passage with silver provided to us by a benefactor among his disciples."

Before I could respond, she continued. "We were once dead. We will never be accepted. The authorities seek us to return us to the realm of the dead. Both of our families know we have left, never to return, and that we intend to remain living. They will never know where we go, just that we have left to avoid trial and possible crucifixion in the manner they did to the Rabbi Master."

Her young eyes leaked tears that slowly fell. She looked up at me as she wiped the tears, drying them in the sea breeze.

"Elan and I had assistance escaping our homes from members of his flock. We heard of the crucifixion and were going to go, but decided to continue our journey to the docks, which is where the spirit of the Lord revealed your presence to us. We followed you and watched as you purchased passage on this ship. We did likewise. The man at the dock acted as if he knew we were coming, so we figured you had told him to expect us. We know the three of us are supposed to be together. Where you go, we are to go as well. We seek safety. We three are testaments to the Rabbi Master and his power, and they will never let us live if they find us."

I pressed my lower back into the bench. I had told no one of my intent to travel to Cyprus. Even the woman I encountered on the road with the coin purse only knew I had been told to leave. My destination and the detail regarding the means to get there had been between the Rabbi Master and me. That they were able to identify me, someone they had never met, through my disguise, was enough to believe they had been guided to my side. I also knew Sarah was right. Her reason for fleeing was exactly why I was on board the ship. When the Rabbi Master embraced me at Martha's that night, I was unsure. Now I felt a quickening in my spirit. I was no longer uncertain. It seemed that the decision had already been made for me.

Indeed, our lives are and have been intertwined since the moment of our resurrections.

The Rabbi Master did all of this for a reason, even if it eluded me at the moment. Reflecting on the last words he spoke to me, I now understood what he meant by "traveling companions."

It took a few seconds to settle my mind with what I was about to do, but with as much strength I could muster, I replied.

"I believe it is the will of God that we be together, and if so, then so be it. Yes, we shall all travel to Cyprus and may the Lord look upon our journey and guide our feet."

They both nodded quietly and sat back. I did the same. Since they were now part of my world, they needed to know the scope of my plans and be prepared for what was to come once we landed in Cyprus. Plus, there was no time for niceties. They must be ready.

"Listen to me and do as I say. Speak to no one else unless I say it is all right to do so, no matter how harmless they may appear. Think of new names." Pointing to Elan I said, "You are now my young nephew, so rename yourself and practice saying it." He indicated his acceptance as I pointed towards Sarah. "And you are his sister, my niece. I have the same instructions for you. Choose names you may be familiar with so that it is easier for you to remember them. Elan, maybe a relative? Sarah, the same. For your information, I am your uncle Cornelius, a citizen of Rome. We are moving back to Cyprus to increase our inherited fortunes.

When we land in Cyprus, we will seek housing and establish ourselves using the money we have been given. We will also change our clothes and appearance when we arrive."

Elan interrupted, pointing towards a small bag. "Oh, we have new clothes into which we can change. We both were provided these by the same person who gave us the money to fund our travels."

I sat back, stunned. Clearly, this was pre-ordained.

"I hope no one in Cyprus will be able to identify us immediately. But to be certain, the three of us must have different appearances when we arrive. I counsel you to be watchful on our journey. I have no way to predict our futures, but we must nonetheless prepare ourselves for whatever our fate is to come. Now, seek a private space below where you can change, do it and come back to me. Throw the clothes you now wear overboard at the first opportunity. I shall be right here, near the latrine as Elan has pointed out, waiting for your return."

Elan smirked and nodded. It seemed that hearing me speak with authority and confidence relieved a burden of uncertainty from their minds. It was evident in their posture and how they seemed to melt into each other for comfort. Mentally, I sensed that we would need to address the apparent mutual attraction I witnessed at a future point.

They've just met, they've been together on a long and potentially dangerous journey, so there is nothing to worry about, is there?

If only I knew then what the years ahead of us had in store.

14

The voyage from Judea to Cyprus gave me time to discover more about Elan and Sarah. When they returned, we sat on that wooden bench and passed the time relating our life stories to one another. Elan was distracted by the great ship, which made sense, given that his father had been a shipbuilder. He noticed and commented on every detail of the former Roman warship. After a good bit of conversation, he asked if he could be excused to go and speak to the crew. It didn't take long for him to be engaged with the men involved in rigging the sails, helping as they seemed to be repairing a sort of mechanism that raises and lowers them. It was intriguing to witness, and as they came to believe in his professed knowledge of ship construction, it wasn't long before he had gained their trust and disappeared towards the stern of the ship. Watching him, I hoped that my exhortations regarding his true identity would be enough to prevent any boasting.

His absence gave me the opening I needed to get Sarah to speak.

"While you and young Elan have just met, it appears you have already formed a close bond. Is that so?"

"We met two nights ago, at the western well in Capernaum. But I do not think of him in any way other than he was my guide on two moonless nights to find you," Sarah said. With just the slightest hesitation, she added tearfully, "Lazarus, I miss my mother and father. I miss my goats, too."

With those pronouncements, she looked up into my eyes, seeking reassurance. I did what felt right, I opened my arms, and she snuggled up to me, wrapping her arms around my midsection and held tight. I had never been around children, as neither my sisters nor I had any, so I stayed silent for a while and tried to comfort her without making it worse by stating the obvious.

Finally, I felt I needed to speak.

"I know you miss your old life. I miss mine, too. I once had a thriving business, one where I could be creative and work alone. We three have left our families and our possessions behind for an uncertain future. But everyone must leave their birthplace at some point and follow their own path. Think of this as the beginning of a great journey, to be undertaken with two friends."

She lifted her head which had been buried in my side and replied, "But I just met you and Elan. We are still strangers to one another. Perhaps one day you will be my friends. Thank you for trying to comfort me. I will try to be strong, but I still miss my home and the life I had."

I was impressed by the inner strength I heard in her voice.

She continued, "The woman who instructed that I leave my home and meet Elan said the Rabbi Master has a plan for my life." She hesitated for a moment and then asked, "Do you know what it is?"

A plan for her life? Then, is there a plan for Elan as well? Is it the same as my plan? She kept eye contact with me and clearly expected an answer.

"I do not know. Perhaps we will know soon. The Rabbi Master spoke of a plan for my life as well, so since then you two have been directed to find me, and I was told by the Rabbi Master to expect you. To me, it is clear that our three lives are intertwined in such a way that God has ordained it. Maybe we will help establish his kingdom. After my resurrection, the Rabbi Master told me I was to be the keeper of the faith, whatever that means."

She leaned away and looked up again, a slight smile on her face.

"I like the way you speak to me. It is as if I am just another adult. Elan treats me like I am still a child."

She inhaled deeply and seemed to inflate her chest with indignation. "I am old enough to have a husband and children! When he returns, would you ask him to stop?"

Oh Lord, perhaps this is why I never married. The knots running through the raw wood in my shop were far easier to deal with than the emotions of two young people. Please give me strength, Lord. As an afterthought, I added, *and wisdom.* I tried to recall how my parents had spoken to me whenever I complained about Mary or Martha.

"Sarah, I will speak to him, but you should also consider your actions and find a way to obtain common ground with Elan. We three have been put together for a reason. We may be traveling partners for a very long time. Think of us as a family. So, if you have an issue with your new brother, you must try to remedy the issue quickly. Never let bad feelings sit for too long. They take root and begin to grow. However, I would also counsel that you should trust your inner judgment."

She considered that for a few minutes without speaking. I could see she was working it out in her head, which impressed me.

"Yes, I understand what you have said. I will think of you and Elan as my new family. I am not angry with him, just frustrated. And I know you are worried that we will tell everyone we meet who we really are, but I do not feel it is necessary to relate my journey back from the dead. One day, I suppose I may, but now is not the time."

I was thinking about what she'd just said when she added, "And, although I miss my real family, and will for a long time, I understand why I needed to flee."

Though I agreed with her, I stayed silent a bit too long.

"You disagree?" she asked, the hurt creeping into her tone of voice once again.

Lord, remember that strength I asked for just now? I need more of it please!

"No. I am sorry I waited too long to answer you. I agree with you. Elan must not talk about it either. We are here on this ship, leaving Judea because the authorities will stop at nothing to take us. You, Elan, and I are examples of the true power of the Rabbi Master. I will reinforce that fact to Elan once we land and have secured accommodations."

This seemed to help, and it was good timing since Elan bounded up the stairs and returned to his seat next to Sarah.

"You should see the pegged mortise-and-tenon joints that they used to edge-join the planks together on the hull! My father would disapprove of their iron nails, driven from the outside. From the outside! I am amazed they don't leak to the point of overrunning their ability to remove the water! Honestly, sinking is a serious possibility!"

That was the wrong thing to say around Sarah. She threw an angry look Elan's direction, which caused him to backtrack his comment regarding sinking.

"What I meant to say is that she has a fine bow and is built so well even the strongest storms would mean nothing. Roman ingenuity at its best. I bet she made a fine warship! The hull is constructed primarily of Lebanese cedar planks and oak framing, which is how all the best ships are built. I suppose the nails used are sealed with pitch or resin. We should be fine, even in a storm. But the sea is calm today, so we have nothing to worry about."

None of that seemed to help as Sarah once again dug deeper into my side.

Are they my companions for a day? A year? How long Lord?

15

"Brother! Brother! Over here!" a voice boomed over the cacophony of sounds at the markets situated close to the docks. I turned to see who was yelling and was engulfed by the arms of a rather huge man. His embrace was impossible to escape, and I attempted to return it with equal enthusiasm, even though I had no real idea who was holding me captive. I managed to pull away and was taken aback. Marcus? This man, a member of the Rabbi Master's inner circle of followers, should not be here! He should be hiding, as I was confident the authorities were looking for anyone associated with the Rabbi Master.

He smiled a knowing expression that held no humor. "Yes, I see it in your expression. I should not be here. In Cyprus." Leaning over to my left ear, he began to whisper, "Many days ago, the Master gave me a coin bag of donations, gifts from wealthy followers, and instructed me to travel here ahead of you. I was to purchase property and introduce you as my cousin, a well-to-do Roman citizen in the company of two young relatives. It is by doing this that you may start your path towards securing the faith, whatever that means." As he released me, he nodded and winked. "So, I have purchased a large villa in town for you to use. It is well prepared for you and the other two."

With a look that must have displayed my surprise, I looked around to make sure no one in the crowd was paying close attention. Reunions such as ours were taking place all around, so I felt much safer.

"I changed my looks and clothes. How is it that you recognized me?" I asked.

"Cutting your beard and changing into better clothing cannot hide the fire within your soul. But you have no need to worry, here you are just another Roman."

"Just another Roman. Yes! I am just another Roman. I am Roman Citizen Cornelius Celsus Germanus."

Marcus stood back for a moment; his hands remained on my shoulders. His expression remained unchanged. I had heard of threats against his life as well. "Yes, I see it, you are taller than average, and by trimming your beard, your look is now more northern Roman Province than Hebrew, so you should have no trouble with your new identity. It's good you used that name; it is a strong one! Especially since I used it to purchase both of your properties."

"And your traveling companions, I suppose this muscular young man with the wonderful hair and bright eyes is your nephew, and this breathtaking woman, whose visage could lead an army, is his sister?"

I stepped back so they could come forward. "Allow me to introduce my nephew, Elan, and his sister, my niece, Sarah." I counted on the force of my introduction to carry the weight of truth with anyone who might be eavesdropping. I was also secretly testing them and their resolve to continue.

"No new names for them?" Marcus whispered in a conspiratorial fashion.

I shrugged slightly as I answered and replied in a lowered voice.

"I asked them to create new names earlier yesterday, but they protested a bit too much for me, so I relented. Perhaps later. I feel it is alright to continue to use their given names for the moment."

Marcus scooped up both Elan and Sarah, embracing them. Then he turned and embraced me again, holding the hug for what I considered to be a bit too long. Finally, he released me, herding us away from the marketplace. I noticed that two men who were with Marcus. They fell in behind us step for step. With a backward shake of his head, he addressed my obvious concern regarding the men behind us, "Pay no attention to them. They are with me. For the time being, they are my protectors and, by default, yours as well. Welcome to Cyprus, my friends."

With the twinkle in his eyes of a fellow conspirator, he continued, directing his voice towards Elan and Sarah, "Your uncle is a great friend, a man I trust with my life. The Master loved him, and that is enough for me."

He stretched out an arm and indicated the direction towards our new home.

"Come, we go towards the center of a town whose name is Kition. This is where I have purchased the home. It is near the middle of town yet in a quiet neighborhood. The property is attached to several other residences, which, in the coming years, I expect you will acquire and use as you see fit."

Marcus must have understood my uneasiness, given he'd yet to answer the question regarding the word 'properties.' Finally, he shrugged and offered: "I have also purchased an olive tree farm in a beautiful valley not too far north of the city. It produces some of the best Cyprian olive oil. Now, I know you are not a farmer, but I also facilitated this purchase on the strength of the direction of the Master. He seemed to know that you would need their use in the years to come."

With gusto he slapped me on the back and tried to bolster my emotional turmoil.

"Do not worry! Things here will work out just fine! I know you will love your new home in the city. It is large, with a central courtyard and windows that open to the street below. And the farm is so beautiful as to make me think of becoming an olive tree farm owner! Funds are remaining from the purchase, so I thought of using some to build a church focused on our Lord's teachings. I hope we are far enough away from the scribes and priests to escape their scrutiny. Perhaps when he returns, he'll approve!"

When Marcus said that he pointed towards the sky. It was if the Rabbi Master was about to arrive any minute with the heavenly Hosts to punish those most in need of punishment. His enthusiasm was evident, and I smiled. But inside, I was not smiling. At that time, I was unable to muster the emotions necessary to even pretend to share in his enthusiastic comments.

I grimaced. Instinctively, I sensed that whatever the Rabbi Master had in mind when he resurrected us required that we wait. I just didn't know how long the wait would be.

16

Sarah, Elan, and I settled into the home Marcus had acquired and established ourselves as the Roman citizens we purported to be. It was easier than I expected, as if we'd known each other forever, which was surprising given the commonality between us was that we three had recently been resurrected from the dead. Given the ease with which we settled into our new lives, I had hope for our future.

My plan was to spend as much time away from the city as possible, hoping to avoid anyone who might recognize me. As Marcus had said, I was not a farmer by trade. However, I was looking forward to learning about the olive trees and harvesting to produce the oil. And judging from Sarah's reactions to the animals on Cyprus, I expected her to hug every animal she could get her arms around at the farm. From the very start, Elan took to the olive oil farm quickly, intrigued by the science of the trees and the production aspects of the entire operation. A few days after we'd taken possession, he came to me with an ingenious idea for procuring water from a cavern located in the hills above the property. I could tell he had an inventive mind, which seemed to always be working on ways to solve the next problem that presented itself to him.

Taking a break from learning about the farm, I was enjoying a late spring morning, and thinking of the feeling a good drawknife in my hands might produce when my quiet introspections were pierced by the shrill tones of a young boy's voice. He was yelling: "The Tomb is Empty! The Hebrew Messiah's Tomb is Empty!" Over and over he yelled. I stood so quickly that my chair toppled to the floor. I leaned out of the window, curious about the boy and his message. *Ah, a newsboy*. Marcus had been right; the windows did look out onto the most heavily traveled street in the city. A small crowd surrounded him, each offering coins to purchase copies of the Acta Diurna. I'll digress for a moment; the Acta was the equivalent of the New York Times of ancient Rome. It was the official record of news blessed for citizen consumption by the powers-that-be. Every citizen of Rome read it with the same religious fervor with which the Times' Crossword puzzle is attacked today.

Hearing his words, my heart skipped a beat.

"The Tomb is Empty," I said to the air. "The Tomb. Is Empty?" *Does that mean I don't have to wait for his return with a heavenly army of angels? But wait, if his kingdom is to happen now, why tell me to leave Judea and travel to Cyprus? Why Elan and Sarah?* Something in my spirit told me this was not the moment he would establish a kingdom.

At that moment, Elan and Sarah burst into my room, breathless from running up a flight of stairs.

Both spoke as one. "Is it true?"

"Perhaps he is returning to establish his kingdom!" Sarah said with unfettered enthusiasm.

I held up my hands to stop them before they started packing and making plans.

"How am I to know? Like you, I am exiled here. Marcus is the only contact I have with the former members of the Rabbi Master's inner circle." Reaching into my money pouch, I handed two coins to Elan. "Go, purchase a copy. We must see what they say regarding this empty tomb." He snatched the coins from my hand, a huge smile plastered across his face, and turned to run down the stairs. Sensing his exuberance, I felt it necessary to tamp it down a bit. I reached out and grabbed his right arm, arresting his forward momentum.

"Wait. Be calm. Remember, you must blend in with the crowd. You are just another Roman citizen interested in the public affairs of the Empire."

Elan took a deep breath, and with a quick nod, I could tell that his heart rate was decreasing as the fire left his eyes. He stood straight, collected himself, and answered, "Yes, I understand. It shall be as you say." With that, he turned and exited.

"What if it is true?" Sarah asked, trying to contain herself.

What if it is true? That is the question. I took a second to gather my thoughts before I answered Sarah. I knew that whatever I had to say needed to be perfect, given the tenuous nature of her emotions.

I turned to answer but was unable to speak before she asked again, this time with even more enthusiasm.

"What if it is true? Can we return to Judea? What if the Rabbi Master is about to set up his kingdom? Are we to be royalty when he sits on the throne of the nations? I mean, he raised us three from the dead! We must be destined to sit at his right hand!"

She sputtered to an end, seeing my hands held upright in a feeble attempt to get her to stop talking.

"What?" she finally asked. "Please, you must have answers!"

Shaking my head, I spoke so that she would understand. "I have no way to answer you. No way. When Elan returns, we shall see what they report happened in the tomb where they lay his body."

"But . . . "

I stopped her from continuing. "No, I will not speculate. And how am I supposed to answer questions about a thing I have no knowledge of? I cannot give you an answer right now. I may never be able to give you an answer. Think about what you were taught in temple. In human history, there has been nothing like this. There have been no saviors, no Sons of God. Our experience with the Rabbi Master and his followers is unique. I do not know what happened in the tomb. You know this. Even if it is true that the tomb is empty, perhaps his body was stolen to enrage his followers into acting against the Roman government. Perhaps the Romans took it to prevent someone from stealing it and claiming he rose from the dead. Of course, it is also possible that he has risen as he said he would."

"But if he has indeed risen, then, he must be the Son of the most powerful Lord God Jehovah!" I could see there was almost no stopping her. Next, she started dancing, twirling, all the while singing softly, "He will smite the Romans and give us paradise!"

I sat down, feeling tired and uncertain of how to respond so I let her twirl. She *was* a young woman, after all. Her twirling seemed to be harmless and had the potential to dispense her pent-up energy. I was prevented from any other response as Elan burst into the room moments later waving the parchment paper.

"It is true, the tomb is empty. While the guards were asleep, the stone was rolled away, and the Rabbi Master is gone!" In an excited voice, Elan began reading. The news was now several days old.

"If this is true, then the Rabbi Master has been resurrected! This must mean we can return and take our places in his kingdom?"

Hearing this question, Sarah sat down hard on the floor and began to weep softly.

"Elan, read to us what they have written," I said as I laid a comforting hand on Sarah's shoulder. But before he could begin, a knock sounded at the entrance below. We exchanged worried glances. I cautioned Elan and Sarah to remain quiet and went to the railing, looking out and down into the courtyard. It was Marcus. Motioning him inside, I sent Sarah to greet him, telling Elan to sit and prepare to read the story aloud to the four of us.

"Have you heard?" Marcus said, seeing Elan with the Acta in hand. He smiled and asked, "What do you think of the news?"

"I know nothing of the news, just the rumor that Elan seems willing to accept as fact because it is printed in the Acta," I replied.

"No rumor my friend, the Rabbi Master has risen! We shall all be leaders at his side!"

I was skeptical when Marcus expressed his opinion that we would all be leaders at his side. I knew what he had told me. I guess he hadn't shared that message with Marcus.

"And how do you know this? Did he tell you? I think we are getting ahead of ourselves and the reality of our circumstances here."

Turning to Elan, I asked, "Has he appeared in the temple and asserted his authority as the Son of God? Does the Acta say he is forming a government? Has he deposed Herod? Or smitten Caesar with locusts and boils? He must have a special plague for those men who crucified him, right? Raising an army of angels to fight injustice? Does it mention where he has gone after leaving the tomb?" These many years later, I realize that my initial response could have been construed to border on blasphemy. But the wounds of his arrest, trial, and crucifixion were still fresh on my soul.

I asked Elan to scan the paper for more detail. He was silent as he read. Looking up, he shook his head. "None of what you ask is here. They report that the tomb was discovered to be empty, early on the third day after his death. The guards have no idea what happened, so they are being put to trial, charged with shirking their duties."

"They shall also be crucified. Ha! I bet they don't resurrect in three days," Marcus added, his insolent tone easy to discern.

Sarah interrupted. "But, if true, then we must return! If he lives, it is indeed a miracle! The Rabbi Master must need us, for we are special to his ministry! Isn't this, perhaps, why we were raised?"

I closed the distance between us and clamped my hand firmly onto her shoulder.

"You know we are never to discuss this," I whispered into her ear. I was glancing at Marcus as I spoke. I know he knew, but to hear it from the mouth of one who was resurrected from the dead might have genuinely been a shock for him. She struggled to remove my hand, but I kept it in place as I continued. "Calm yourself and stop. I shall release you, but you must not speak of what you believe to be our 'special reason for living.' Are you that eager to die again? Have you forgotten in the short period we have been here the true danger that forced us to leave our homes?" At the mention of home, she stopped the struggle and looked up. The tears started forming in those beautiful green eyes as she told me she understood. I released her, and she replied softly, still wringing her hands together: "I am sorry, Uncle. I shall be more careful."

Engrossed in the Acta, Marcus missed the nuances of what had just occurred. Elan did not. He understood perfectly and nodded in silence in my direction and spoke without moving his gaze. "If he is resurrected, it changes nothing. The authorities may simply find, arrest, and crucify him again, thinking he was not truly dead when they removed him from the cross and put him in the tomb. Like you, Uncle, I do not think it wise to believe we are safe to return."

Looking up from the news, Marcus replied: "Though when we met, I said I would establish a church here in Cyprus, this news is too exciting for me to ignore. I must return to Judea at once. I must go and see for myself. Perhaps I will be allowed to see the Rabbi Master again if he truly has risen from the dead and his body not stolen as you suggested!"

Sarah's small voice emerged from behind her clasped hands. "What if the reports of his resurrection are false? The authorities could be using falsified information and the hysteria generated by his trial and death as a means to discover supporters who have been in hiding?"

That question hit me very squarely between the eyes. I nodded, looking at her with newfound respect. Perhaps there was yet-untapped strength in the mind of this young woman.

"I would say, that is a very discerning comment. The authorities may be distributing falsified news just for the purpose you describe!"

Marcus folded the Acta and handed it back to Elan. "I don't think so. They would not use the official arm of the government to distribute fake news. Why would they do such a thing? If that were the case, no one would ever trust anything they read in the Acta ever again. However, perhaps what you say is true. I will book passage back under an assumed name and see for myself. If I never return, the grace of God be with you, my friends."

Embracing us, Marcus took his leave, exiting to the courtyard and onto the public street below. I looked out the window and followed his movement as he turned a corner and disappeared from view. I did not like his plans and hoped not to face similar suggestions to return to Judea by Elan and Sarah.

Turning away from the window, I noticed Elan and Sarah watching my reaction and waiting, perched on the edge of the wooden bench I had jammed against the inside wall. In the short time we'd been together, they had developed a shorthand body language. I am sure our circumstances required this, and a new, non-verbal means to express emotion was born out of necessity. Together, they nodded at each other and shrugged. Her left hand reached out and clasped his right hand. Thus joined, they asked in unison, "Tell us, what shall we do?"

Uncertain, I resolved to be smart, given this interesting news. It was then I recalled his last words to me.

"We wait and see. There is more to this than the eye sees, and the three of us would be a significant capture if the authorities did this to try and get the remaining members of his followers under arrest. We wait."

Saying that, I reached for the Acta, folded it, and shoved it into the fire.

"No more on this. Now return to your chores."

With reluctance, they acknowledged their acceptance, stood, and left the room.

17

Several weeks later, I was enjoying a hot cup of tea when Elan burst into my room somewhat breathless. Without preamble, he blurted out: "You are here in Cyprus and are causing quite a spectacle!"

Hearing these words shocked me. Turning to face the doorway, I noticed that Sarah was close behind. The looks on their faces told me something was up, and they were eager to share.

"What are you talking about? Of course, I am here! So are you!"

Elan laughed. "No, what I meant to say is there is a man in the square, a man from Judea. He is saying that he is Lazarus of Bethany, the man the Rabbi Master raised from the dead!"

"You cannot be serious?" was all I could squeeze out from my throat.

"Yes. He says that he is here to convert people to this new religion based on the teachings of the Rabbi Master and establish a church."

I could tell they were enjoying telling me of this imposter by the smirks on their faces.

"Have you seen this other Lazarus in action?"

"Yes. After seeing and hearing him, we ran back to tell you what we had seen. He is preaching right now. Come with us!"

I wasn't sure I wanted to go, so I thought about it for a moment, considering. We had succeeded in establishing ourselves as well-to-do olive farmers, keeping a very low profile, and I wished to continue our incognito lifestyle, which the imposter's presence could potentially threaten.

How does this man, who claims to be me, fit into the Rabbi Master's plans?

"Yes, take me to see, this other Lazarus. I am curious to hear what he, uh, I have to say."

I followed Sarah and Elan as they made their way into the town square. Ours was like any town square in virtually every town in the world. Commerce, religion, government, and citizens were thrown together into a mixing bowl of insanity and controlled chaos. In this instance, the town square was full of people listening to a man on a pedestal. It reminded me of when my sister Martha convinced me to see the Rabbi Master for the first time. As we edged closer, I could hear him speaking in a voice that was clear and not at all what I was expecting.

"The Lord Jesus died for your sins! You must repent! You must accept him as your savior! Otherwise, when you die, you will end up where I was when I was dead! Hades! It is hot, it is miserable, it is where those who die in sin go. And it is forever. You can never leave. Forever!"

As he yelled the word "forever," he thrust his arms into the air, fists clenched. People stood, shocked at such an emotional outburst.

Someone in the back yelled: "He is a heretic. Burn him!" Others just stood numbly, considering what he had just said. I was one of the silent ones. This man, this imposter, was speaking out and it caused me to reevaluate myself. *Am I am supposed to be doing this instead of him?* My emotions swirled, and I recall being a bit dizzy. *Am I a complete failure? Have I taken the gift the Rabbi Master bestowed upon me and hidden it, like the parable of the talents?* I resolved to speak to this Lazarus, but I knew I had to be very careful. He had begun to draw an increased level of attention from men whose religious authority was evident in their bearing as well as their clothing. I could see a few in the crowd, also silent, measuring those listening and their response to the man.

I pulled Sarah and Elan close.

"I am going to return to our residence. I anticipate the religious leadership will want some quality time with him. Remain here and follow him should he be taken somewhere or wander away. Act interested. Appear to be mesmerized by him and his story. Ask questions. Find out as much as you can and then return to me when you are satisfied." With that, I hugged them, nodded, and departed for home.

Towards dusk, they returned.

"Well? What have you learned of this Lazarus?"

Elan spoke first. "He claims to be you. He also claims that the Rabbi Master frequently appears, like a spirit, giving him direction. It would seem that he plans to stay and to begin raising a church. He says the Rabbi Master has given him a mission to spread his teachings and bring believers into the fold."

I considered this information, and then Elan continued. "His teaching has an interesting flavor."

"How so?" My interest was indeed piqued now.

"He stated several times that he had no intention of turning believers against the Roman government, and in fact, he was clear that as a Roman citizen, he was always going to be loyal to Rome."

That was not what I had been expecting. "Loyal? To Rome? That is very interesting."

"Yes. And, as he began to wind down, we were shocked to hear a booming voice yelling, 'Lazarus, my brother!' A man, who from his style of dress appeared to be a Pharisee, emerged from the crowd and embraced him!"

"What!?" Now I was disturbed. Was all of this just a cruel afterlife experience? "What?" I uttered once more.

Sarah nodded. "Yes, the man announced he'd just arrived from Judea. He then recounted an experience in which the Rabbi Master appeared to him and directed that he come to Cyprus and establish a church with you!"

I saw the look of confusion on both their faces. I am sure there was more than confusion on my face also.

"You are Lazarus of Bethany; we both know this." As Elan spoke, they exchanged knowing glances. "We know in our hearts that the Rabbi Master raised you from the dead. He raised us too. He sent us to find you at the dock and join you. We are alive! We know all these things to be true. But what of this, imposter? Why is he here? And why is a Pharisee here to bolster his claims to be you?"

I sat, silent. Finally, a certain peace came to me.

"I don't know how to answer you regarding this other Lazarus, nor the Pharisee who claims to know him. What I do know is this: I am who I say I am. This I know. You are who you say you are. It is evident. I must trust the Rabbi Master. We must trust the Rabbi Master. If a 'new' Lazarus has appeared, then there must be a reason, and we must keep our wits and heads straight regarding it."

They both nodded, accepting what I'd just said, so I felt it necessary to push forward and continue. "We shall go about our normal routines. If you normally go to the well for water, go. If we need something from the market, we should go. We will wait and see what is to come of this circumstance."

As they left, there was a fleeting feeling of discontent. Then, a measure of peace returned. There must be a reason for this development. Part of the plan, whatever that plan might be. With that, I returned to my work, content that we would come to understand this new development.

18

"Good Morning in the name of our Lord and savior!"

It had been weeks since Marcus had taken his leave to return to our homeland, and hearing these words shook me from the doldrums of a windless day, though it wasn't Marcus's voice I heard. When not at the farm, Elan and Sarah had been spending several days each week shadowing the other Lazarus, so I wondered if this new voice was connected. I was right. Standing, I encountered a well-dressed man in my doorway, a small sack that must have held a change of clothing and provisions in one hand. His eyes burned bright with an internal fire. It was a fire I had witnessed before. I relaxed, hopeful that the authorities would be unable to use a believer to entrap me.

"Sir, my home is yours. Sit, we shall break bread and drink wine!"

He smiled as he leaned a well-hewn staff against the wall and pulled the wooden bench close.

"No need to be so formal, Brother Lazarus. The Rabbi Master has brought me to you so that I may reinforce the message he gave you just before his great sacrifice."

I had to stop for a moment and think about what he had just said.

"What?" I sputtered, incredulous.

Laughing, he leaned forward.

"Brother, to prove to you that I mean you no harm, here is what I know of you and your companions. You are Lazarus of Bethany. Your sister brought you to the Rabbi Master. You are here in Cyprus because you fled Judea to escape religious persecution and possible execution for your perceived slight to the religious authorities, by being raised from the dead. You have been in hiding under an assumed name. Marcus, another believer, purchased a large olive farm for you. The two with you, Elan and

Sarah, were also raised from the dead by the Rabbi Master and were directed by him to meet you and become part of your ultimate mission. You hope to make a home here, to hide from the authorities who seek to kill those left behind. While you wish to fulfill the Rabbi Master's charge to you, it has not been clear to you just how to accomplish his plan for your life. Thus, you have been patiently waiting. Well, my friend, the waiting is over."

He stopped and sat back, crossing his arms. His smile was authentic, and he chuckled.

"I want you to think for a moment. How could I know these details? How could I, on my own, a man who has never met you or Elan or Sarah, have found you? If you have been as careful as I believe you have been, then no one here should know your real identities."

There was a pause as my visitor stopped speaking to gauge my reaction. I chewed on my lower lip and tried to calm my racing heart.

At that point, Elan and Sarah burst into the room, breathless. Due to the orientation of the open doorway and the bench on which my visitor sat, they didn't see him sitting calmly by the door.

"Lazarus, there is talk that a famous Pharisee has come to Cyprus! He may even be nearby! What if he has found us and intends to persecute us or take us to the lions?" Even though we had drilled our new names many times, in the heat of the moment, they used my real name. I closed my eyes in disappointment, and my heart sank as I pointed.

I saw the raw fear in their eyes as they realized what they had done when they saw my visitor. They froze in place. Their faces lost all trace of life for a moment, and I thought one or both would faint or perhaps attack him.

Elan was first to speak and what he said showed his acceptance of the event.

"This man is the Pharisee we were coming to warn you about."

Sensing the distress in the room, my visitor opened his arms in a welcoming gesture and indicated that he wanted them to sit on the floor.

"Elan, Sarah, greetings in the name of the savior. Please, sit."

They made their way to my side, eyes on the visitor the whole time. Like tiny pets seeking shelter near an owner, they sat on the floor.

Once they were motionless, he spoke. "My Roman name is Saul. It is my given name. Well, it was my given name. It also is true that I was once a Pharisee, an expert on our traditions and a devoted student of the writings that have defined and informed what it means to be Hebrew."

I remained silent, absorbing what he was saying and trying to calculate in my mind if I could muster the strength to kill him to preserve our secrets.

Correctly interpreting our combined silence, he smiled a warm, natural smile. "As I said earlier, you do not need to fear me."

"So, who are you, and why exactly are you here?" I asked softly, meaning not to offend this Pharisee who claimed not to be a Pharisee anymore.

"I spent the first half of my life persecuting those considered to be practicing our religion outside the Mosaic law. I have spent the last three years persecuting anyone who called themselves followers of the one you perhaps call 'Rabbi Master.' I did not see them and their beliefs as true to the traditions of our forefathers and our faith in the God of Moses and the prophets."

I shifted in my chair. Now I was curious.

Seeing this, he offered, "I am trying to keep my story short enough to maintain your interest, yet robust enough for your complete understanding."

Smiling, I held up one hand. "Please continue. I was just shifting my weight." Point of fact, I was shifting my weight, but only to better reach the blade I had secured long ago under my daily wear cloak. I was still uncertain if this Pharisee was being truthful or if he saw us as the next target of his persecution.

I believe he understood my unspoken emotions. "I do not know if you have kept up with the details regarding what occurred after the tomb was found to be empty." He paused a moment, anticipating an answer.

"We read a few stories in the Acta, and have heard some, rumors mostly, like people seeing him on the road or that he appeared to ten disciples and shared a meal of boiled fish before vanishing into nothingness."

"Yes, I can tell you that all those things and more happened."

He stopped again, seeing the astonishment on my face.

"You speak the truth? Was he alive? And he did appear and interact with his disciples before vanishing into the heavens?"

"Not merely interaction. He spent hours teaching them the meaning of many scriptures from the Law of Moses, the Prophets, and the Psalms. By their accounts, they spent 40 days with him as he prepared them for their various missions."

"Which were?"

"To spread the news of salvation to the most distant parts of the earth."

I sat back, intrigued. *So, his disciples also have missions?*

"Then, on the fortieth day after his resurrection, he took them out to a deserted field and reiterated to them his charge: They were to begin witnessing his glory to the world. He then was caught up by a cloud and ascended skyward until he was completely out of sight!"

Elan, Sarah, and I sat stunned into silence.

"The Master was alive and walking around, and we missed it?" Elan asked. I could tell the question hurt him to the core.

Our visitor sought to alleviate Elan's clear mental anguish.

"Young man, it was his way. I am sure every move he made had been planned to move the Kingdom of God forward, so you should not be angry or upset that you missed something important. You will have more than enough time to contribute to the Lord's work."

We all fell silent once again, although the last sentence this Pharisee had spoken stirred me back into action. I needed to know exactly who he was and why he was in my house. The last sentence the Pharisee had spoken stirred me back into action.

"I believe my interrogations took your focus off the information you wanted to share. Please tell us your story."

He smiled. "Ah, yes. Let me begin again. Some days after the Rabbi Master disappeared into the heavens, several of my Pharisee colleagues and I traveled to Damascus. Until that day, I had been very involved in persecuting the followers we could identify. We were prepared to bring charges against a particularly determined group of missionaries when, traveling along the road, I was suddenly nearly blinded by the brightest light I could ever imagine."

I blinked several times, and my heart skipped a few beats. "Inside the light stood a man. Though I had never seen the man you call the Rabbi Master, I instinctively knew that it was he standing in the light. He was real, and he was there right in front of me."

Our guest now had my full attention. I sat upright.

"This happened after his crucifixion and ascension?"

The man nodded. "Yes. And though I had never even met him, without hesitation he smiled and spoke to me!"

Maybe we were not about to be arrested, tried, and executed.

"He spoke to you?" I managed to croak.

"Yes. His voice was beautiful and clear. He asked, 'Saul, Saul, why do you persecute me?' Then just as suddenly as the light had appeared, my world went completely dark. I had no idea what had just happened and responded, 'Who are you, Lord?'"

"He responded, 'I am Jesus, whom you are persecuting. Now arise, go into the city, and you will be told what you must do.' Needless to say, my traveling companions were dumbfounded as they witnessed me fall to the ground and heard me speaking to someone they did not see! Only as I tried to stand did they realize I had been struck blind. They guided me to my donkey and made sure I arrived in Damascus safely." He stopped talking for a moment, clearly seeing the expression on my face. Elan and Sarah were also silent. Then he smiled and continued. "I took refuge in Damascus at the home of a friend and began praying for deliverance. I prayed for three days. On the third day, Jesus spoke in a vision to one of his prophets, a man by the name of Ananias, and told him to go to the house of Judas for a Pharisee called Saul of Tarsus."

Seeing my inquisitive glance, he continued. "Ananias told me that when the Lord was finished instructing him, he objected quite strenuously to going anywhere near a Pharisee named Saul! Can you even imagine objecting to the Almighty God? Ananias knew both my name and reputation, and because I had been so effective at persecuting those who believed in Jesus, he did not wish to ever meet me. But the Lord pressed on, telling him that I was a chosen vessel, one that would bear his name before the gentiles, and kings, and his chosen children. Hearing this, he repented his disobedience and followed the word of the Lord. When Ananias found me he laid his hands on me and the scales of dead tissue fell off my eyes! The first face I saw was his. I was overcome with joy, but that was tempered by Ananias, who spent more than a month with me, instructing me in the ways of Jesus and what it meant to follow him. I was soon baptized in the fashion of John the Baptist and left to begin my ministry."

The visitor paused once again.

"I would note that from the time of the scales falling from my eyes, I rejected the name I used as a Pharisee to persecute the followers of the Christ. I am no longer Saul. I am Paul, a disciple of the Son of God."

So, he has a new name too? This thought gave me hope. *Maybe he hides as we do, though a former Pharisee of his stature will undoubtedly attract attention.*

Paul paused, giving me time to think. I was relieved that he had not sought us out simply to take us before a Roman court for punishment. And his story sounded like something the Rabbi Master would have done. His clothing and mannerisms were indeed those of a Pharisee, someone whose words had weight and who was in command of every aspect of life. He also had a dramatic flair. I would learn later that he never seemed to do things in a small way. So, after hearing his story, I was left with one question. Opening my arms to encompass my two charges, I asked, "Then, sir, what can we do for you?"

Before he could answer, Sarah spoke up quite clearly. "And why are you with that other man, the false Lazarus? You just acknowledged that he," she said pointing at me, "is the true Lazarus, so that means you must know the other man is not truly Lazarus!"

It was clear he had anticipated that one of us would ask such a question because he pointed at me and responded. "Yes, Sarah, of course, I know your friend here is the true Lazarus of Bethany. And you are Sarah, daughter of Jairus. Your father is the leader of your local temple." He shifted his attention towards Elan and continued. "And this young man is the son of the widow from Nain, restored to life by the Rabbi Master. His father was a master shipbuilder of some renown."

We all gasped. Clearly our secrets had been shared by someone who knew of us, or else this Pharisee had actually heard from the Lord.

I did wonder why he had not answered her question. So, I pressed him, trying to stress the emotional context of my words.

"Well, it is plain that you know the truth about us. However, to Sarah's question, if you know who we are, why are you seen with this man who pretends to be me?"

He sat back for a minute, inspecting the nail of his right thumb as if the answer was hidden in the nail bed or cuticle. He rubbed it a few times and began to explain.

"Before I get to that, let me tell you something of the men and women who are left behind to continue the work of the Rabbi Master. First, they have begun to refer to their movement as 'the Way,' which I understand comes from an exhortation given long ago by the prophet Isaiah, who wrote that God's people were to 'prepare the way of the Lord.' Others call themselves Nazarenes, which is tied to the place where our Lord resided. More believers are coming into the fold every day, and though you three are to play a significant part in the future of our faith, those days are not yet here. You must stay in the shadows, learn, heal, thrive. And then, when the time is right, you will be brought forward and seen. Until that time, the Lord has specific charges that I am to give to you. You are living on the margin here. You think you have escaped, but being here, living here, going out amongst the people, sooner than you know someone will notice that you do not age as most."

At the time, we had no idea what he meant by that remark. Needless to say, his words took us completely by surprise.

"What do you mean, we don't age as most?" Sarah, Elan, and I asked at the same time.

He looked very pleased. "I realize this is information you did not know. Your resurrections have changed you. This detail comes to me from the Lord himself. It is one of the reasons I was instructed to seek you out. The Rabbi Master bestowed upon you an amazing gift, as well as a charge that must be fulfilled."

I was trying to understand, but the difficulty of what he had just said remained on my tongue.

"Explain what you mean by our 'resurrections changed us.' What does that even mean, and why do we learn of it just now?"

"What has happened to you has been done so that you can be witness to the glories of the Lord. You are to record everything that has and is to transpire and become lights in the darkness for those who have lost their way. He did not tell you because you needed time to regain your humanity once again. Now that has happened, he has sent me to give you the last measure of your great charge."

The three of us sat, stunned.

"Do you mean we are immortal?" Elan whispered.

"Yes, in a way. Your earthly bodies have been reset to the measurement of time as defined by God himself. I also know that you shall never suffer illness or injury"

"And you are sure?"

He smiled and laughed a bit. "Yes, I am quite sure. The Lord does not make mistakes. Ever." He stopped speaking for a moment, then continued. "As to the 'other Lazarus,' the Rabbi Master sent him to me and told me to bring him here so that he could take your place to preserve your secret for a time. After my conversion, one of the disciples of the Rabbi Master as you call him, Barnabas, befriended me to assist with my instruction."

"Barnabas? The man I know? He traveled with you?"

"Yes, but he did not want to come with me today to meet with you given that he is known as an associate of the Rabbi Master. When he heard I was traveling to Cyprus, he said the Lord instructed him to join me. I believe we will be here in a short time and then will move on to establish many churches in God's name. First, though, we seek to establish a church here. That is one way we plan to use the other Lazarus."

I guess he saw concern in my eyes, so he made sure to reassure us regarding our safety.

"You have nothing to be concerned about regarding the other Lazarus, me, or Barnabas. We will make sure that your location and true identities remain secret. This also is the Lord's plan. I believe you are being prepared for a great work, but the stress of your resurrection and subsequent exile from Judea remains fresh in your souls. Soon, you shall be called upon, but now, you get to rest."

He looked at Elan and Sarah and added, "The three of you get to rest for a time."

I considered his remarks.

"The Lord requires that we rest?"

"Yes, he does."

"Then, so be it. Thank you. My next question relates to your Lazarus. Is he to be part of your efforts to establish, what, a church? A ministry?"

"Yes. And this other Lazarus has been instructed to be cooperative with the Roman authorities, to fit into Roman life here in Cyprus, the stigma of being 'raised from the dead' will wear off, and he will be accepted as if it had never happened. Once there is a physical structure and congregants, I will anoint him as their leader. That is when I shall move on to the next place God intends me to go."

"Is that even possible?" Elan posed. I could see him pinching his arm as if to draw blood from his body in search of proof of life.

"Which part, Elan? The immortality? Certainly. God can do anything, as you have already personally witnessed. As to the remaining followers of the Rabbi Master, they are spreading out amongst the nations. I have left Judea and do not plan to return. Those who call themselves the 'apostles of Christ' are spreading the good news of the Rabbi Master throughout that part of the world. I intend to begin a ministry here in Cyprus and then to all of Rome."

"But the Romans are the ones who killed the Rabbi Master. Aren't you afraid they may do the same to you?" Elan inquired.

"No. Pilate applied Jewish law at the behest of the Jewish authorities who hated the Rabbi Master. The Sadducees, Pharisees, and chief priests of the temple are the ones with his blood on their hands."

He turned to look at Elan and finished with, "And if I am to be sacrificed for my belief, if they kill me for telling the truth about our Rabbi Master and salvation, then so be it. I shall be in paradise with him from the moment I leave this life."

As he paused, my head spun in turmoil and hope. *Maybe my idea to be out of the way and out of sight from the religious authorities just got easier. If this fake Lazarus is here, and if Paul and Barnabas help him, then perhaps we will be allowed to live quietly. But this is a former Pharisee. The authorities are sure to follow, wondering why one of their own has turned against them. It can only be a short time before he is jailed and perhaps beheaded. Or worse, the Romans will start inquiries and find us. Would he give us up to save his head?*

Somehow, he understood. "You need not fear my presence. I am here long enough to establish a church. I know you and your two companions have traveled here to escape. Let me assure you that I do not mean to involve you in my plans. No one will ever know the true Lazarus lives and works here."

Then he looked reassuringly at Elan and Sarah.

"Your presence here will also remain a secret. However, I have been given a charge by the Rabbi Master and plan to take action to begin to fulfill his charge to me."

When he said that, I was startled. He did not miss the emotions that flew across my face.

"I understand that the Rabbi Master has given you a charge as well. Perhaps, your charge is not dissimilar to the one he gave me on the road to Damascus."

I shook my head. "It is difficult to understand. You do realize that even acknowledging your question could put us both in considerable danger. The Jewish authorities have a considerable reach, spies everywhere, and even longer memories."

"Perhaps. But I believe the Lord protects us and keeps us from harm." Looking at Sarah, he suggested she fetch drinks for us all. As she left to fulfill his request, he started to speak again, "Now Brother Lazarus, let me tell you of the Lord's plan for Cyprus and for the many long years you are about to experience. I believe you should invest in a large amount of parchment and writing materials, keeping them handy at all times, for that is one of your new charges."

"The Lord wants me to write?" I asked. "What am I to write?"

"Of course, he does. You have a very long life ahead, and to do the work of the Lord, you will need to tell the story of his life, of your lives. What I am to tell you now comes from the Lord himself. Are you ready?"

Quill in hand, I was prepared. "Yes. Please begin."

19

The other Lazarus became quite a public fixture in Cyprus. Using his reputation as a former influential Pharisee, Paul made sure that our false Lazarus was granted access to the halls of power. Upon the power of those contacts, he was soon appointed to be the first bishop of Kition, Provence, and Marseille. The new title and its subsequent responsibilities involved extensive travel and the establishment of many churches. New Lazarus took to the task and folded his work and his story into establishing the legend of the resurrected Lazarus.

True to his word, Paul departed Cyprus soon after Lazarus was established. He was a very intense man, focused on following the guidance of his spiritual advisor, whom I believe was an angel. I kept up with news regarding his travels through all the Roman-held territories, and when I heard of his untimely death at the hands of the authorities, I was quite sorrowful at the loss of such a fine man.

Many years later, our false Lazarus appeared at my door one day. I was alerted to his presence by the soft salutation that announced his presence.

"May I be granted entry, sir?"

I turned, startled to see my older doppelganger. He clearly had aged while I merely pretended to. I wondered why he was here and what he wanted. He'd never visited with me, the man he purported to be, so this was the first time he and I had been in such proximity since he arrived on Cyprus. His hair and beard were grey, and unlike me, he had aged since we'd first met. I gestured towards the bench across from me. He nodded and took a seat. Something told me this was an interesting conversation that might go better with wine, so I asked a servant to fetch some. She smartly returned with a carafe of my best wine. Fortified, I settled back, curious why he finally felt compelled to come to speak with me. I watched as he took a quick sip and noticed that his hands shook. Placing his cup of wine on the table next to where he sat, he began.

"If I may, I would like to open this discussion with an expression of my extreme gratitude."

That was not at all what I had expected.

"Gratitude?"

"You, of course, know who I am."

"Yes"

"It would have been easy for you to uncover my deception, but you did not. For that, I am grateful."

I leaned back and responded in the only way possible.

"But that would also have exposed the truth. I admit, though, I was quite surprised when Elan came to me so many years ago and said that I was in the town square, creating a stir with my message regarding the Rabbi Master. But when you arrived, the former Pharisee, Paul, appeared, much as you did today, and related to me the reason for your presence here in Cyprus. But tell me, my friend, why would I have called you out?"

"Well, I never met the Rabbi Master; I was never a part of his inner circle. I wasn't even a member of the outer circle of his supporters. Paul, who wasn't a member of his original inner circle of disciples either, was my only link. And when he left, I had to create a persona and a life from whole cloth that may not have been what you, the true Lazarus, would have done."

I started to speak, but he held up a hand to stop me.

"Permit me to continue. Once Herod Agrippa the First began to seriously persecute followers of the Rabbi Master, many of his followers scattered through the provinces. It puzzled me that, as they left Judea to bring the good news, they all bypassed Cyprus. As if some heavenly intervention kept them from coming here and exposing the truth of my falsehoods. Add to that my observation that you have never once inserted yourself into my world. Instead, I have watched as you observed from the periphery. It gave me great joy to see you, Elan, and Sarah at worship on occasion. I felt it important to give you the space you seemed to seek, so I never addressed you three directly. Instead, I would only do so through an intermediary."

He stopped for a moment to take another sip of wine. Doing so, he lifted his left hand up and ran it over the surface of the omophorion he wore.

"You have heard my story regarding the provenance of this item, yes?"

I nodded. Indeed, I did know. Virtually everyone in Cyprus had heard the story of the beautiful and intricate vestment Lazarus wore draped over his shoulders during worship. It was seen as the most significant symbol of his spiritual and ecclesiastical authority within the church.

"I am not surprised. I have never wavered from the story that it was presented to me during a visitation by the Virgin Mary, who told me she had woven it herself." He paused. "I see doubt creeping into your eyes. I would think that you, of all people, would understand and believe. It is a true story."

I felt a measure of chagrin at that moment. Given my history with the Rabbi Master and his mother, I nodded my acceptance of his rebuke and motioned for him to continue.

"This omophorion is central to the belief, fostered by me, that a bishop of my high position must report to no one except perhaps the Mother of the Son of God. I use it solely to enhance my status with the other bishops here on Cyprus and in the territories where the autonomous churches I have created are located."

"All this I already know. Why do you come wearing it today?"

"I have spent thirty-one years traveling, preaching, teaching, establishing churches and congregations. Not just because it was expected, but because I truly believe. The churches I have established are strong. However, unlike you, I have grown old. I do not have the advantage of immortality. Even if I tried the tricks you employ to appear to age, I would be ultimately exposed as a fraud, which I cannot have. But with his help, I have aged beyond what many consider a normal life span. I have heard that parishioners attribute my long life to my interaction with the Rabbi Master when he resurrected me."

What he said took me by surprise. I sat, quietly contemplating what he'd just said. *People think that this man who calls himself Lazarus may have spiritual powers that delay the normal aging process, which could have been useful and problematic at some point.*

"I see your interest regarding that statement rising. But hold your conversation, brother. I believe that my age is a gift from the Rabbi Master so that you could have more time to better prepare Elan and Sarah for what lies ahead. Before you inquire, I have no information from the Virgin Mary or the apostles regarding what that may be, or when the Rabbi Master returns. I just know that you three will be involved somehow. I believe you know this. I feel the hands of time reaching from beyond to finally bring me back to the dust from which all humanity was formed. Before I depart this existence for the one promised through salvation, I wanted to say thank you and to pray a short prayer with you."

Once again, he ran his hands over the omophorion. There was no wear on it; though it was evident the action was one he frequently made. He stopped and continued speaking.

"I thought about giving you this omophorion and announcing your ascension to the position of bishop. But after a particularly vivid dream in which I was visited by an angel of the Lord, I am convinced it would be counterproductive to both our missions and ultimately bring those who seek you to Cyprus."

He stopped speaking for a minute and then continued. "I see the surprise in your face. You were unaware of the group that has been lurking around me?"

"What do you mean, lurking around you?"

"Of course, once I arrived, the details regarding my resurrection, well, your resurrection, were made public. There sprung up a group in Judea, which has gained strength. Their belief is that only the savior of mankind should be resurrected and immortal. They have been here, in Cyprus, for a very long time, always watching me, judging if my age is appropriate. That I have aged naturally has made them relax their surveillance. This is why I have never tried to befriend you, Elan, and Sarah. I would have led them to your door."

"They want to kill us I assume?"

With a nod he agreed. "Yes. So even after I am gone, I would be vigilant in your efforts to look older. Change your appearance every thirty or forty years; change your names, things such as that. I am unsure if they will believe I was the true Lazarus. So, be forewarned."

I sat back, thinking. This was news to me and unsettling. I did not wish to share it with Elan or Sarah, though I knew I must. For some time, I had been experiencing a stirring in my spirit around our false Lazarus, and now I knew why. He saw me thinking and kept speaking.

"I have pretended to be you for more than thirty years now, never meddling in your affairs, allowing Elan and Sarah to become instrumental in the business of the church. I do not know how long you will stay in Cyprus but giving you power over the churches would be dangerous and potentially lethal. I feel this in my soul. Thus, I will convene a council of elders from the various churches I am associated with to find a new leader. That new leader will be granted this omophorion, which will signify his power and significance to the church. I thought it good to meet you today to explain the actions I plan on taking and to offer a prayer for your continued success."

"Success?" I had no idea what he was talking about now.

"Yes. My success is your success. For you see, if the Son of God delays his return to earth to set up his kingdom, one day, far into the future, history shall record that his friend, whose name was Lazarus, was greatly loved by the Rabbi Master Yeshua. He died and passed into the arms of Father Abraham . . . "

Well, the first time it was not exactly into the arms of Father Abraham, I thought without actually interrupting him. He had never heard what happened to me in the afterlife. I guessed that he didn't need to know. Perhaps that was a good thing. He'd not seen my distraction, so he continued speaking.

" . . . And four days later, the Rabbi Master raised his friend from the dead. Lazarus then fled Judea after the arrest, trial, and crucifixion of our Lord and Savior. People shall know that he arrived in Cyprus. With the assistance of the former Pharisee Paul, Lazarus immediately began building congregations and churches, spreading the message of salvation offered through the birth, ministry, death, resurrection, and ascension of the Son of God. So you see, while I have undertaken a ministry in your name, you were able to you shed the mantle of your previous persona. Instead, you have embraced the life of wealthy Roman. Indeed, you have stayed so far in the background that you are completely unknown. Given your special circumstances, perhaps that will serve you well in the coming years."

He sat back, taking more wine. I confess what he said made sense, and he looked happy to have finished his confession.

"I am concerned though about one aspect of your life."

I was intrigued.

"What concerns you?"

"Sarah and I have spoken of this on occasion. I don't believe you have ever smiled during the more than thirty years I have been here. Why?"

His question hit me hard. It was not at all what I would have expected. He knew it, too.

"I see you understand. Is there something regarding your experiences in the afterlife that you can share with me?"

I shook my head for a second, once again trying to remove the images that had never left my mind. He smiled, leaned closer, and persisted.

"Tell me."

I hesitated. He sat back in his seat, hands clasped in his lap, waiting. I cleared my throat and decided the time was right.

"I do not know of the life you led before taking the name Lazarus and pretending to be me. But the life you have led as me is one of purity and godliness. I am not at all worried about your soul when you enter the afterlife. I am sure the Rabbi Master waits for you with open arms and the exhortation you have done well. What you will not see are all the unredeemed souls I saw during my time in the afterlife."

He shifted his body slightly and choked somewhat on his own spittle. "Unredeemed souls?"

"Before the sacrifice that the Son made on the cross, where did those who died outside the laws of Moses and the prophets go after their deaths? Heaven? Paradise? No. They all went to an awful place where there is no hope. Literally, there is no hope, forever, from the eternal circumstances of pain and suffering. I have never told anyone of my experiences, and I hope to never tell anyone again."

He offered an opinion.

"If I may, brother Lazarus, it is my belief that your experiences, good or bad, have been presented to you so that your witness will be stronger than any others. In the future, perhaps you shall have a significant contribution, outside what you have already done, to bring our Savior to the world. If you died and went to the place of pain and suffering, and returned, then you understand why it is important that we trust in our Savior and can give testimony to the grace of our Lord for his sacrifice and love."

That was an interesting interpretation of what I'd just said.

"Well, I am never far away from the images, feelings, tastes, smells, and experiences I had as a dead man. I haven't even been entirely forthcoming with you regarding the place and the suffering I saw because even you could not understand the complete futility of eternal life without the Lord Almighty."

He was silent for a few minutes, then offered his opinion.

"That has been caged up inside you all these years, so it is good that you have told me something about your experience, even if it is not the entire story. One day you should unburden yourself completely. Until then, try to understand the place you have had in furthering the message regarding salvation. Perhaps many thousands of believers will avoid what you experienced as a result. You should take heart with that thought as you go through what is to be your very long life."

I thought about his comments for a minute or two. His perspectives were interesting. I found one flaw in his ideas, though, so I felt compelled to correct him.

"You are not entirely correct regarding the statement that I haven't smiled since my resurrection. I believe I have smiled once. Elan and I once watched as a thief carefully stole a pot sitting on the ledge of a window. I thought it funny that a man, who was formed from the clay of the earth, was stealing a pot made from the same clay by which he and his ancestors were formed. I believe I remarked that the 'clay was stealing the clay' and Elan caught me in a smile."

He chuckled. "I see. Well, I stand corrected. Brother, I know that you, Elan, and Sarah have many long and perhaps dangerous journeys ahead, and I pray for your continued success. I wish Paul had survived but I know that he sees everything from his seat in heaven beside the Father. I love you, and the Lord God Almighty loves you. I will take my leave now; I believe I have said and done what the Lord wanted when he prompted me to visit with you."

My twin Lazarus stood, hugged me firmly, and held me at arms' length. "Now, Lazarus of Bethany, go with God, my friend." With that, he turned and started to leave. He stopped at the door and appeared to be deep in thought.

"One more thing. I have purchased a tomb into which I have directed my remains be placed when I leave this world. It is on the southern shore of Kition, a place I know well."

"You know of it?"

"Like you, I have missed Judea. I frequent the southern shore and look to the east, wishing for a glimpse of my homeland. I know it is too far by water for me to see, but in my imagination, I see the hills, the olive trees, and even Sinai."

I could not believe what I was hearing. Tears formed in my eyes, and I wiped them with one hand as I replied.

"I miss it, too. I also go to the shore wishing for a glimpse of Judea! Is your tomb hewn into the rocks near the water?"

He smiled a rueful smile. "See, perhaps, somehow we *are* the same person, except I am the mortal one and you are not."

He held out three small gold coins, grasped my hand, and un-clenched my fingers. As I tried to remove my hand from his, he tightened his grip and dropped the coins into my open palm. He then closed my fingers around the coins, his fingers wrapped around mine like a piece of dry parchment.

"I have made no plans for an inscription on the tomb and ask that you affix a message you believe appropriate to it. Something that has meaning to both of us. Take these. They were a gift to the church from a benefactor who directed they be used to cover expenses for burial of the dead."

I tried to deter him.

"I don't need coin; I can easily cover the expenses."

He was adamant. "No, you must take them. I have tried to always be transparent with the use of collections and alms that are given to the church, and I do not wish to approach eternity with the knowledge that I misused a resource given for the glory of God."

I unclenched my fingers and looked the coins. They were so shiny it was clear to me they were newly minted. He nodded, blinked, smiled sadly, turned, and left. I can still see the expression on his face today.

It came as no surprise to me when he called the bishop elders of his churches to Council just days after leaving my home. Within a week, they had selected a new leader, and ten days later, our Lazarus passed quietly into eternity.

Three days after his death, I stood in front of his tomb, my back to the roaring surf not far away. I could taste and smell the salt spray in the air. The stonemason I had hired was finishing the inscription above the entrance to the tomb when he turned to me with an inquisitive look.

"You sure this is what you want it to say sir?"

"Yes, it is exactly what I want people to see when they come to pay their respects to this man of God."

"Then, it is finished," he said, stepping back to admire his workmanship.

I was startled at his use of that phrase since it is one the Rabbi Mas-ter uttered as he died on the cross. Still, I resisted showing my emotions, and instead, approached the freshly cut stone and rubbed the inscription with my right hand, feeling the sharp indentations left by the mason's tools. I nodded my satisfaction and held out the three gold coins Lazarus had given me.

The mason was surprised by the amount I was offering.

"The payment you offer is far too much sir. I knew of this man's life and service to our community. I would have done the work for free."

I shook my head and insisted he keep the coins.

"Lazarus came to me, personally provided these coins and directed they be used to satisfy any debts associated with his burial. Please accept this payment. You may contribute whatever you believe is in excess to the poor or suffering in your community."

Reluctantly, he accepted the coins and bowed. I did the same and said, "Thank you for your work. God be with you."

I stood back and once again admired the inscription over the tomb, which was sharp and clear. The letters were so precise I believed at the time that they would be legible for thousands of years, clearly marking the tomb of the man people came to know as Lazarus of Bethany.

The inscription read, "Lazarus, friend of Christ."

20

After the death of our false Lazarus, we settled in and began to support the ministry he'd started as much as possible. I felt the hand of the Lord in every business decision I made in that whatever I invested time and energy into turned a profit. I tithed to the church and watched in amazement as our accounts brought in even more riches. To plan for the future, Elan and I began to sneak out of town, under cover of darkness, to bury a measure of our gold and silver in metal and wooden boxes I'd constructed. A few of the places we selected required overnight travel due to the remoteness of the locations. Most were hard to reach to prevent their accidental discovery. If we ever needed to escape, at least we wouldn't need to be impoverished or beggars while doing it. These trips profoundly affected Elan, given that he'd once been exposed to wealth as the Son of a popular shipbuilder. He noted that as our fortunes grew, it was a practice he planned to continue, no matter how long we lived or where we settled in the future. I agreed and was glad to see him thinking about a future where we were all still together.

Then, something happened that changed the course of my life forever.

One night, just as I was just about to drift off to sleep, a great light filled my room. I sat up, but my eyes were overwhelmed by the brightness that had engulfed me, so I waited for my eyes to adjust. When they did, I saw that there was a figure in the center of the light. There is just one way to describe the being I saw. Perfection. As I wondered if I'd died and been brought to heaven, I had an immediate sense of peace. The being smiled and held out both hands. He had six beautiful wings; each feather seemed to sing as it moved through the air. They moved silently, yet they held him above the floor. When he spoke, it was as if my entire body heard his voice.

"Lazarus of Bethany, the Lord shines his countenance on you. I have come to give you a specific command from the Almighty God. You are to go to the city of Ephesus, where you shall find John, a disciple who followed the Son of God. John is the son of Zebedee and Salome, brother to James, who also followed the savior. Mary, the mother of the Son of God is also there."

When he said that, I was shocked. *Mary? The mother of the Rabbi Master? How is this possible?* I had last seen her at the cross, watching her Son's crucifixion. When I turned away in shame and horror at what was being done to him, I had seen her face illuminated by a flash of lightning. It had been seared into my mind. I had thought of her on occasion and had even written down some of my experience hiding in the shadows during the crucifixion. However, I was embarrassed at my disobedience of the instructions given to me by her Son, the Rabbi Master. I wondered more than once what had become of her and Joseph, her husband. *Surely that information cannot be true.* The angel seemed to know my thoughts, as without hesitation, and quite forcefully, he rebuked me.

"You have no reason or standing upon which to question what I am saying! It is true. Mary, the mother of the one you call the Rabbi Master, which is as the Son of God requested. John has been persecuted and vilified, but he has shown the light of salvation to many through his persecution. He has also been given insight and understanding. His visions of the future shall be included in the books and letters you have been compiling. His material will be prominent in the time to come when you begin to fulfill the reason for your resurrection."

The reason for my resurrection? What does that even mean? I wanted to ask but found that I was mute.

"I see the questions rising inside you, but a hold has been placed on your tongue until you hear the words of the Lord. You have been recording the details of your life, death, and resurrection, yet you do not know why. You are to undertake a similar effort for Sarah and Elan. You shall also write of your time with the savior, of the great works and ministry you witnessed. Write of the men and women who came to believe and followed him. What you write is not for your consumption, though, but for a later work, one you will be moved in your spirit to produce. Far in your future it will be important and relevant that you have captured the details of the life and ministry of the Son. Take what you have written, prepare it for storage, and put it away for the time when it shall be needed. You must prepare, for there will be challenges. But you have been given the ability to overcome. John is the lone survivor of those who followed the Son, and he has been prompted in his spirit to create significant material, though he does not know the purpose yet. I shall go to him next so that he will be prepared to receive you. Take only that which is necessary for a short trip. You leave tomorrow. Sarah and Elan shall be looked after and protected. Your footsteps will be guided. Once you meet John, receive what he has to give, then return here. Copy everything and continue your pattern of securing your parchments from the hands of those who would seek to destroy or usurp the details of the Son's ministry."

He paused, and I looked into his eyes, which seemed to swim with color and light. He smiled, then his face shifted, and his voice took a more serious tone, "These are the words of the Lord. Your tongue is now loosed. Speak."

It was at that moment that I recognized him. The flash of memory made me wince in pain. He saw me reaction and said nothing. I, on the other hand, knew I had to ask.

"It was you, wasn't it? You are the one who was with me when I died on the floor of my shop back in Judea! It was you who took my hand, told me to remember everything I was about to see and experience. It was you."

The angel didn't even nod. Instead, his answer was steady and delivered without inflection.

"Yes. I was there. Though you were a friend to the Son of God, you were sent to Sheol to understand what it means to die in sin. Your proximity to him, his teachings, and your belief in him had become the foundations for your life. Thus, you were in no danger. The Lord delivered you from sin, and after you had the experience of eternity without the light of God, he delivered you from death. You needed to carry that understanding as you prepare for the next chapter of your life. These are the words of the Lord God Almighty."

I understood. I nodded, knelt, and bowed my head, and then he did the most amazing thing. With one motion, he reached down and pulled me up by the arm, his grasp firm. He shook his head and, in a stern-yet-soothing voice told me: "Do not kneel to a servant of the Lord, kneel only to the Lord himself. I see in your heart and soul that the words of the Lord have taken root. Now sleep, for tomorrow you begin a great journey that shall resonate through the ages."

I recall seeing that beautiful smile as I fell into a deep and restful sleep. The next few days were quite interesting.

When Jesus therefore saw his mother, and the disciple whom he loved standing by, he said to his mother, 'Woman, behold your Son!' Then he said to the disciple, "Behold your mother!" And from that hour that disciple took her to his own home.

JOHN 19:26-27

21

Islung the pack containing my clothes over my right shoulder, stepped off the ship and onto dry land. My legs wobbled, and I tried to compensate for the sudden lack of movement without much success. I steadied myself against one of the dock's wood pilings, turned, and looked at the horizon for a moment. It's a trick I had learned after disclosing that I was prone to seasickness with a man whose life had been spent on the water. I also said a silent prayer of thanks for successfully arriving in Ephesus. When we'd stopped the previous day in Athens, I had purchased new clothes, taking the time to remove more of my hair and beard to change my appearance. There I happened to glance into a mirror in the public square and realize it was the first time I'd seen my reflection in a very long time. I looked quite young and virile, which was still quite surprising to me. Now, standing there, holding onto the wooden pier, trying not to heave, I didn't feel so young.

"Are you okay, my friend?" an old man asked as he grasped my shoulder firmly. "Returning to dry land after a long ocean voyage can be taxing on the system. I should know. I once knew many a fisherman who spent more of their time on the water than on dry land. It takes time to get used to walking on solid ground that isn't moving with the waves." He then smiled, leaned even closer, and finished with, "It is good to see you again, brother Lazarus."

I released my hold on the wood, turned sharply, and looked into the face of this old man; he must have been more than ninety years old. But what held my interest, beyond the deep wrinkles and impressive grey beard, was the fire in his eyes.

"John?" I managed to croak.

He nodded as he took the pack from my shoulder, "Come, my friend, we should make haste to my home. You will find respite there, and then tomorrow, you take the five manuscripts I have written, as the angel of the Lord has commanded, and return to your home."

"Five?"

He nodded as he replied, "Yes."

I had no idea he'd written down his experiences until the angel told me, and now, to hear that he has five manuscript was quite exciting. I guess I'd not thought about what others who'd known the Rabbi Master might have written concerning their experiences. Now, I was anxious to get it. John hooked his own right arm into mine and turned me towards the center of the city.

"Come. Walk with me, then we rest and dine. Your journey has been long, and I am to return you to the sea as quickly as possible, so we must not tarry."

Still somewhat unsteady, I nodded and allowed him to guide me through the crowds and deep into the city until we stood at the entrance to his home. Entering, he pointed towards a doorway that led to a room away from his main living space and said, "That is for you. Go put your things down and come back, for we shall break bread and drink wine to celebrate your arrival. We have much to talk about, so do what you must and return."

After placing my pack on the wooden floor and throwing a splash of freshwater across my face, I returned to the main room. John was seated at a small table, a loaf of bread, dates, and figs on a plate along with a large dram of wine. He smiled, pointed towards a chair, and poured the wine into two goblets. I sat and relaxed for a moment, taking a drink from the wine. Reaching for the bread, I broke off a small piece and was about to take a bite when he held up a hand.

"Dredge your bread in this," he said, pouring a golden liquid into a shallow bowl. "I believe you will recognize it. When Paul lived here for a time, he told me you'd grown into quite the olive farmer." As he spoke, he also sprinkled salt into the mixture and what looked like dried herbs.

Doing as he said, I contemplated what he'd just said about Paul as I chewed.

"Though it was a shock when he first identified himself to us, we came to love and respect Paul. Those were good days, but they were also days filled with a measure of fear at being discovered and remanded to the authorities." Since John had mentioned him I asked, "Paul lived here?"

"Yes. After Paul left you, his travels took him back to Judea, to Rome, and to Greece. He came here, where we grew his ministry for almost four years before he felt called to the church in Macedonia. It still saddens me that he was beheaded by Nero, but we shall see him again when we join the Son in eternity. As to your fears, we all have had those kinds of fears. Most of us have been imprisoned or killed because of the Rabbi Master. It is good to see that you have survived unchanged."

As he said those words, I realized that what I was looking at was not a disguise; he was indeed an old man. I motioned towards his beard and long, gray hair.

"That is not a ruse to fool everyone, is it? Truly, you have aged?"

John smiled and nodded, "Yes, this is my real face, my real beard, and real hair." He motioned towards his hands. "And these hands are the same ones that once held the hand of the Savior. Though they are much older, I can still feel his strength flowing through them."

I looked down and felt compelled to continue with another question.

"You were there, weren't you? At the cross?"

He shook his head, and the look on his face made me repent that I had asked such a direct and emotional question.

"Yes. I was with Jesus in the Garden when he was betrayed by Judas. When the soldiers took him, I followed to the palace of the high priest. I waited outside for his release. Instead, he came out, bound and in the company of soldiers, and then was taken to Pilate. It wasn't long before I was standing at the foot of the cross. To be so close to his death, a man I loved without exception. It was almost too much for me to take." He stopped and locked his eyes with mine. "You were there too, weren't you?"

How does he know? I felt the shame of disobeying the Rabbi Master wash over me.

"Yes. I had to be there, but I was in the shadows. He brought me back from the dead, and I felt compelled to watch. Just before he was arrested, we had shared a Passover meal at my sister's home. As a crowd gathered outside, he took me into his arms and told me to leave. I was to go to the docks and wait for two others who would be traveling with me. But I had to go. If only to see what the authorities did to him."

John sat back and crossed his arms. He was quiet for a few seconds, and I wondered if I'd said something wrong. He leaned forward with a smile and surprised me.

"Ah yes, one-third of your group of three, Sarah. Did you know I was there when she was raised from the dead?"

With that pronouncement, he leaned back again, a smug look on his face. What he'd just said was news to me. I was shocked and pursued his statement.

"What do you mean you were there when she was raised from the dead?"

I sat, stunned. I had no idea, and Sarah had never mentioned the witnesses to her resurrection. I could think of nothing to say in reply, so I was quiet. John filled the gap.

"I know you've been traveling with Sarah and the young man, Elan, since leaving Judea. It is good that you three are together. You are the most powerful indication of the Lord's power. I suppose our enemies must have thought of that as well." He stopped, scratched his chin, and continued, "Ever think about the fact that the three of you make up a trinity? Perhaps, done by design? You, Elan, and Sarah?"

I had no response, so I didn't even try. However, I was able to form an answer to the question regarding those who still pursued us.

"Whoever it is that still seeks us has not relented, even given the amount of time that has passed since the crucifixion. However, we have prevailed with God's protection." Since I had no other details about John or his connection to the Rabbi Master, I felt emboldened. "Can you tell me more of your time with the Master?"

John smiled in reaction. "When you read the five books I have written, you will have a better sense of what I did at the side of the savior. However, I am not opposed to sharing the details. You mentioned the dinner you had at your sisters' home. Well, two days later, he sent Peter and me into the city with instructions to prepare a great Passover feast for the twelve men who were his closest associates. He said it was to be a last great supper. I had no idea that he was literal in his use of the word 'last.' We suspected a traitor in our midst. I believed a man named Judas was the one, but I kept silent. I wish I had not. Perhaps if I had killed Judas the Lord would still be alive. But then I suppose I would be damned for murder."

He stopped talking and shook his head as if the memories were just too painful. I almost implored him to stop, but he started speaking again.

"Two days later, I stood, silent, at the foot of the cross, as the Savior of the world hung there, dying. In one of his last breaths, he looked directly at me and instructed that I look after his mother. This is why she is here, now, under my care as needed. Although she is revered among the faithful, there is little I do for her now, other than visit every day."

His voice trailed off, and I could see the years of his life passing in his eyes. I felt compelled to ask, "You have written much of this for believers to read?"

He smiled, "Yes. It is all there. Pentecost, the tongues of fire that settled onto every head in the upper room, getting thrown into prison with Peter, my ministry after the Romans tried to boil me in oil in the Colosseum, my imprisonment on the Isle of Patmos, everything. I have even included letters I have written to the local churches."

"Boiled you in oil?" I asked.

"Yes. It was like being dipped in tepid water. I was unharmed, which converted hundreds when they saw I did not die a horrible death." He stopped again, and I could tell he might be testing me. I took a breath and recalled what the angel had said to me. I asked one more question.

"Even the revelations you've been given of the Lord's return and the end of days?"

John chuckled. "I see the messenger who sent you to me was quite thorough. Yes. Even my revelations of the end times are included." He suddenly became serious "What I will give you does not exist anywhere else. There are some who would pervert the Savior's words; even remove his divine birth, death, resurrection, and ascension into Heaven. They do not believe God created the heavens and the earth. One in particular, Cerinthus, has been a constant thorn in my side with his ridiculous ideas, so I am quite pleased the Lord sent you to take away and properly document and preserve my writings. I know God will be with you. Thus, my soul is at rest."

A sly look crossed his face at that point, and he tugged at his beard.

"You inquired if this was my real face. I am guessing, but you three must have been disguising yourselves, using some kind of wily subterfuge to throw off your pursuers or those who would be curious about your youthful appearances?"

I laughed. "Yes. The pursuers come and go. Recently, they have left us alone, but I know they will not stop." Then, it hit me. "You recognized me at the dock. How did you do that?"

"An angel visited me last night and said that you would be there. He also told me, very clearly, what you would look like. You seemed quite surprised to see me. I know the angel had been to see you as well, though I guess he did not tell you I was an old man. From your expression, you were surprised, weren't you? Did you think I was immortal? Like you, Sarah, and Elan?"

That took me aback. "You know about that?"

"Of course I do. Paul told me once, many years ago, that the three of you had been given a great charge by the Lord. Today I believe that one of your charges is to organize and catalogue a book of our Lord and Savior's life." He chuckled as he spoke, "There have been rumors, that once, in conversation with the Savior regarding the one who was preparing to betray him, Peter asked if I was the betrayer. I heard that Jesus answered something like: 'If I want him to remain alive until I return, what is that to you? You must follow me.' It is because of this that a rumor spread around that I would not die. It has followed me all these years, and I have made every effort to look my age and not appear to be anything other than a normal man."

"So, you're not immortal? Just making sure I understand you."

He laughed this time. "No. The Savior did not say that I would not die; he only said, 'If I want him to remain alive.' If. People are too quick to believe in wild rumors and speculation when their minds should be focused on ministering to the sick, those in need, and getting ready for his return. I tell you this: my visions of the end of days are such that I am very pleased that I shall not be there to see them. You, however, shall see it. So shall Elan, and so shall Sarah. There is no way around this information. It is my reluctant gift to you. I know this is something you did not anticipate, so take my words and hide them, for you have a very long life in front of you and a significant journey ahead."

With that, he took a heavy sip of the wine and stood. "Now, come. I want you to meet my associate, Polycarp. He has some of what I have to give you and is anxious to meet a man who once was dead."

Not knowing how to react to that, I drained my wine as well, stood, and followed him out the door. Minutes later, we knocked and entered a humble-looking stone house. A man, approximately thirty years of age stood, smiled broadly, and embraced us. John simply introduced me with: "Polycarp, this is Lazarus of Bethany."

Polycarp immediately embraced me again with renewed vigor.

"To meet the one, true Lazarus, the man our Savior raised from the dead. I have so many questions, especially about what happens to us when we die."

Ugh, the same old question. Perhaps I should wear a sign that says, "No, I don't want to talk about it."

He must have seen a change in my body language or in my face because he immediately replied. "But I suspect you may not wish to speak of your time in the afterlife. I shall hold my tongue and my questions until such time as you permit me to inquire."

This was quite acceptable to me, given that I had no desire to speak of my experiences in the afterlife to anyone and certainly not with a man with whom I had no history.

John sensed my discomfort and jumped in.

"Polycarp has the unique advantage of knowing and working with several of us who were considered disciples of the savior. He's also been quite effective in rooting out and exposing those whose teachings are false or designed to misguide the faithful. I place a very high value on his witness."

Polycarp let out a small laugh as John finished. "Yes, I will most likely be burned at the stake one day for challenging the heretics and gnostics. But their blasphemy must be met directly and without compromise by the truth of our Lord. Like John, I must be a steadfast witness of truth." He actually winked at me. "My friend, I'm sure if you spoke to them of the everlasting punishment prepared for the enemies of the Almighty God, they'd not even believe you, a man who has actually been there and experienced it. One day, I hope to stand before my God and be judged worthy of his eternal love. That is all I want to do."

"Well, you also want Lazarus to take with him the material of mine that you've been working on," said John. "Have you finished yet?"

"Yes. That is true. Come. Sit while I gather the material. It is in a satchel in the other room."

22

It was not difficult to become the wealthy Roman citizen I purported to be, charming, intelligent, and mysteriously healthy. Mistakenly, I began to delve into the political and religious circles of Kition, the beautiful seaport on the southern edge of Cyprus where we had made our home. In modern times it is home to Larnaca, the third-largest city on the island. And like the other Lazarus, I liked Kition because I could look out at the Mediterranean Sea and imagine my homeland just over the horizon. I should have paid more attention to Paul's words of warning (a reminder–he was beheaded at the command of Roman Emperor Nero) regarding hiding the nature of our resurrected bodies because I wasn't as successful at remaining undetected as I had imagined.

One day, there was a frantic-but-quiet knock at my door and the hinges creaked, as whoever was on the other side had put pressure on it and pushed it open, not waiting for permission to enter.

"Lazarus?" asked a voice I recognized.

His interruption stopped my silent moment of reflection. Turning, I acknowledged Elan, thinking how nice it would be one day if he had finally stopped calling me by my given name.

"Yes? What is it?" I asked, motioning for him to sit.

He shifted a chair and did not sit, which was odd. Then he began speaking, growing ever more agitated and forceful with each word. "I hear rumors. Though it has been many years, there are Romans and Jews alike who continue to inquire about us. Some have noticed and ask how it is that we seem to be healthier than most. They wonder what happened to the three who purchased this home and the olive farm more than seventy years ago. A few have suggested we must be demons. I even heard that a call has gone out to bring us in for questioning."

Immediately my mind went to the group our false Lazarus had once warned me about. *Could it be they have never stopped looking for us?* I confess I had actually begun to lose interest in constantly looking over my shoulders and changing my appearance to age. I had grown tired of simulating aging by using dyes and changing my walk to appear older. To be completely honest, it was disconcerting to be so healthy amidst a sea of unhealthy people. Sitting back, I knew what Elan had just said must be true. When raised from the dead, I could have never anticipated what the Rabbi Master had done. After Paul showed up and told us our resurrections had gifted us immortality, I did not believe him. Even today, approximately 1,900 years later, I accept it, but I still do not understand it. At that moment in time though, no one lived as long as we had. The three of us were now involved with the second and third generations of the people we'd known once we escaped to Cyprus. I had to confess that I had grown slack in my efforts to remain undiscovered. Now, apparently, those efforts were not going to be enough to prevent our discovery.

"If they are really coming, I believe it is time to go," he said, his voice low and unemotional.

How did I miss this development? I contemplated his question. "Really? Is it that serious? And where is Sarah?"

"I am here," she said, sliding through the half-open door. She took great effort to close and latch it securely.

"Has Elan told you what is happening? I have heard the authorities have sent people to take us in for questioning."

Thinking forward in time, I began to imagine what might be happening outside our control. I started gathering things that, in my mind, were important to our continued good welfare.

Sarah stopped me. "We gather nothing. We left Judea with nothing and have thrived. If we go, we must go and take only what we have prepared in the secrecy of our hiding places."

I marveled at the maturity of her mind. Of course, that maturity had been gained through three lifetimes that had been well lived.

I turned and blew out the candle. Glancing towards the window, I sensed that the pounding of multiple feet on the ground and the murmuring of men had replaced the normal sounds of the street. Risking a glance, two men were pointing in the direction of our residence. They motioned to men of arms just rounding a nearby market corner.

Well, that settled it.

"Yes, we go now. It is time." Looking at Elan I asked, "Did you latch the doors behind you in such a way as to delay them?"

"Yes. I broke the latches and blocked the door just as I have practiced."

"Good." I made a mental note to ask how he'd come up with the device he'd used to block the doors. I gathered a leather change purse with silver and gold sewed into its compartment and pointed to the secret exit we'd cut into of the walls fifty years earlier. The moneybag was heavy, but necessary if we were to purchase our survival. However, there were still caches of material Elan and I had buried in and around Cyprus, so if I lost what I was carrying, it wouldn't be the end of the world for us. Elan and I shoved aside the large fireplace, which hid the entrance to our escape route. What appeared to be heavy river rock was, in fact, just wood I had carved and blackened to make it appear to be a well-used fireplace. It was one of my best carvings ever. The tunnel it hid was dark and not very inviting.

"Inside, hurry."

I could hear pounding and clamoring downstairs. As I cleared the opening, I grasped the handle attached to the back and pulled it. In planning for our eventual escape, I had built the fake fireplace on top of a quarter inch of reed, giving it a silent swing. I had made a habit of meticulously cleaning the floor in front of it and had laid down a heavy mat of woven reeds tacked to the floorboards, so that if we ever had to use our escape route, there would be no telltale arc in the dust as I closed the fake fireplace back against the wall. Utilizing the locking mechanisms manufactured by a local blacksmith, I secured the fireplace to the inside of the wall. Hopefully, no one would ever guess a series of hidden tunnels were just behind what appeared to be a real fireplace. I lit two candles and, with Elan's assistance, replaced the pre-made panel of stacked stone behind the fireplace so that if the deception were discovered at least, it would appear that the tunnel did not exist. Once that had been accomplished, I patted Elan on the shoulder. "Move if you want to live!"

In the years since our escape to Cyprus, through what is now known as "shell companies" and using false identities I had created, I had acquired the entire block of homes attached to ours. It had taken time and secrecy, as I wasn't interested in drawing attention to myself. Over the years, Elan and I had secretly built several long tunnels hidden inside the façade and false walls of the buildings attached to ours. Honestly, I believe we were the first "home renovation show" so popular today as we vacated the buildings and built new walls and structures to hide our

escape tunnels. Then when we were finished, families and businesses returned to the buildings. They never knew what was behind those new
walls. Over time, we prepared the tunnels with clothing and some dried
food. We even connected a hearth to one that already existed, using a
unique system that Elan thought up to vent any smoke above the roof,
where it wouldn't be noticed. The hearth provided heat and the ability
to boil water collected from the cisterns we built to catch rainwater. The
tunnel also had all the materials needed to assume new identities. Sitting in the tunnel with several dozen feet between our pursuers and us, I
thought it prudent to calm Elan and Sarah.

"We are safe. While we wait for the authorities, or soldiers, whoever
it is to grow tired and depart. We must begin our transformations."

Elan sighed a heavy sigh as he prepared to use a razor in the candle-
light. I knew he mourned shaving the pathetic attempt at a beard he had
been growing. As he did so in silence, I turned to Sarah, who had scissors
in hand and was already halfway through removing much of her hair and
offered my assistance. With my help, over the next hour, she completed
the task and dyed it darker than her reddish blonde. While she washed
her hands, she took a deep breath and made a simple statement.

"I understand now why you never smile."

I was taken aback. Her comment stung and reminded me that the
other Lazarus had said almost the exact thing. I was surprised. To hear
her say such a thing was very unusual. To pass the time inside our hide-
out, I seized upon the opportunity to learn more about the mind of this
extraordinary young woman I thought I knew well.

"What do you mean?"

"You never smile. Living with the burden of living beyond our years
and hiding in fear of discovery probably weighs heavily on you. I am sure
you were unprepared for the life you have been living, just as Elan and I
were unprepared. Now I understand why I have never seen you smile."

I had to acknowledge her perceptive comment.

"I used to smile, mostly in the presence of the Rabbi Master. With
my sisters and family. Yes, I smiled. But like you, I have seen the afterlife.
Though your experience differs from mine in that I experienced the great
gulf separating those who have faithfully followed the teaching of Moses,
the prophets, and the Rabbi Master, and those who did not. It was enough
to remove the smile from my face. Perhaps one day it will return."

She considered this for a moment. "Yes, but the teachings of the
Rabbi Master, his death and resurrection have changed all that, right? He

taught that belief in him is the new covenant established by his sacrifice. That and that alone has altered how we are accepted into the afterlife. So, what you and Elan saw, the great gulf separating those who loved God, kept his commandments and laws and those who did not. It no longer exists, right?"

"Perhaps. Something John told me long ago comes to mind. The Rabbi Master preached that no one comes to the Father except through him, so I suppose that belief in him may be enough to avoid that awful place. John reminded me that during his crucifixion, two criminals–a thief, and a murderer–were crucified on either side of him. At one point, John said he saw the Lord's head raise, and it was clear that he was speaking with the one on his right. Everyone had heard the one on the left mocking him. However, the one on his right said something like, 'Lord, remember me when you come into your kingdom.' Without hesitation the Rabbi Master told him that they'd be in paradise together that day. That has stuck with me all these years and is why that in some of my writings I have tried to find and examine what the prophets of old said regarding eternal life after death. Perhaps you are right."

"Perhaps? If the Rabbi Master said it, then it is true. And he did say exactly those words, so I believe he has vanquished sin and Satan, and we only need to believe in him, just as he directed."

I was curious and felt it necessary to inquire. "How is it that you know of such things?"

No longer wringing the dye from her hair, she tied it up in a piece of cloth and smiled. "I have been listening to the street preachers spreading the word of the Rabbi Master. I spent many days with the other Lazarus, listening to his words and watching his behavior. And before he left, your friend Paul spoke with me at great length about the Rabbi Master and his plan for salvation. So, I now understand that we are all saved through the Rabbi Master; we just need to accept him."

I should have known. Before I could stop myself, I blurted out, "You spoke with Paul?"

"Of course, I did. He was visited by the Rabbi Master on the road to Damascus after his crucifixion! And spoke with him directly! When we met Paul, he was fulfilling the Rabbi Master's plan for his life. So in my mind we had much in common. I spoke with him as many times as possible until he left us to pursue his ministry."

Absorbing this information, I was impressed with her inner strength and conviction, so I and sat, waiting.

She continued. "Paul was a great man, one day, he will be considered a Saint. When the news of his execution came to Cyprus, I cried."

"Why did you cry?"

"For a loss that should be felt in the entire world as we know it. The authorities killed a man of God without hesitation." When she said that, she paused. The realization hit her eyes as they widened a bit.

"This is why they seek to take us into custody, isn't it? If we are who they believe we are, then we are also testaments to his ultimate power and divinity."

"Yes. That is true. But you see, they seek us without the assistance of God, and we escape from them *with* the assistance of God. Therefore, we shall always overcome."

She nodded. "This is God's plan. I accept it."

With that, she slumped into a corner, withdrew from the world for a while, and pretended to nap until she actually began to sleep.

Several hours later, hearing nothing more from our former residence, I stood and roused Elan and Sarah. Rubbing the sleep from their eyes, they looked at me with anticipation.

"Gather your things. It is time to go."

Elan didn't move but whispered, "Surely, they left spies hidden nearby, whose sole duty is to keep watch on the house, thinking we have been hiding this whole time?"

Good point. I thought. *The boy's instincts are spot on.*

"Yes, that is a good observation. We take the furthest exit into the alley one at a time. We meet at the location we predetermined. Remember, it is a day's walk from here. Make no noise as we proceed through our hiding places to the alley."

Half a day later, as we worked our way silently through the passageways inside the connected structures, we emerged into an alleyway one by one, three simple pilgrims in clothing that said we were not worth bothering and instead perhaps were beggars on whom to show mercy. I had stowed my coin case inside a basket Sarah had woven thirty years prior and left inside the escape tunnels. It screamed "old and dusty" and helped sell my new image as a beggar. Knowing whoever was looking for us might be watching the waterfront, we spent three days in the foothills of the mountains first. Then, with our clothing and appearance changed again, we made slow progress back to town and mingled with the crowds. Satisfied that we'd fooled our pursuers, I began looking for my contact, a man with whom I had previously arranged to leave should the need arise. His vessel was large and ocean-worthy, fully capable of taking us far away from our pursuers. I remade our acquaintance every six months or so, knowing that someday we'd need his services. It was not a given that he would be in port, so I searched earnestly for his vessel. Finally, I was happy to see him in the distance, haggling with a street broker over some chickens. Making my presence known, he acknowledged and motioned me to join him at a stack of fishnets that needed mending. Pretending to discuss my expertise at purchasing nets, we addressed my current dilemma.

"So, the time has come?" That was his only question, as he pretended to show me the nets.

"Yes. And I am a man of my word." Holding out a small stack of coins I had promised would be his, his eyes lit up with the thought of riches he would not be sharing with his workmates.

"This should cover any additional expenses related to our journey."

He nodded, his head inclined slightly towards his ship. "Board. We can depart at any time." To further our diversion he finished with, "I shall make sure the nets are delivered on time to your place of business."

I chuckled. "Yes, please, do that," I said as I motioned to Elan and Sarah, who followed as I jumped from the wooden dock onto the deck of the ship and went below to the space we'd purchased. The voices of the dockworkers and sailors, the smells, and the motion of ocean as it rocked us back and forth were eerily familiar.

"I guess traveling on the ocean has remained unchanged since we first escaped from Judea," Elan said.

"I still don't like it," Sarah said.

As we left the harbor, headed to a new and unfamiliar place, doubt crept into my mind.

Lord, is this truly what you had in mind for your Keeper of the Faith?

23

After two days on the Mediterranean Sea, we disembarked into the wilds of coastal Gaul, what is now modern France. Moving slowly, we made our way towards one of our buried caches. The plan was to retrieve what we needed to start over somewhere else and begin again. I had a feeling that this part of our post-resurrection lives was going to be played out more than I'd like.

When I was a young boy growing up in Judea, superstitions regarding the stars in the sky, changes in the seasons, even heavy rains or storms ruled much of life. To the soothsayers, the stars foretold disasters, births, major life-changing events, and of course, deaths. As they looked to the heavens, the people of my birth time also saw pathways to spirituality and the afterlife. That thought drifted in and out of my mind as Elan, Sarah, and I sat around a smoldering campfire, eating a fresh rabbit Elan had skillfully hunted. Before taking a large bite, Elan looked over at me, then up at the sky and back to me.

"Is God up there? I wonder, given our collective experiences in the afterlife. Personally? I don't believe that the afterlife is in this level, or plane, of existence. Our world, perhaps even the stars in the sky, are like a piece of that parchment paper you are so fond of."

I could tell, even by firelight, that he looked pretty happy with himself for that statement, so I had to ask.

"What do you mean?"

"It's simple to explain. Hand me one of your smaller pieces of parchment."

I decided to indulge him, so I did what he asked and reached into a nearby bag, pulled out a rolled-up parchment I intended to use later, and handed it to him. Taking it, he unrolled it and placed it on the ground. Using four small rocks, he pinned the corners to the ground and began.

"We live on the top of this parchment, the part that faces up. Everyone and everything alive is also there, though the earth is not flat, this represents every part of the world, both earth, and water."

Sarah interrupted, beginning to see his logic but unable to resist poking him a little.

"Do we really know the earth is not flat? And, what of the other side? The side that faces the ground?"

He nodded and smiled, acknowledging her interruption by scuffing dirt her way.

"Yes, you little heathen unbeliever. The world is round. Now, let me finish. As I said, our world is the parchment facing up. Everything else is on the other side of the parchment. The places we three went after deaths are on the other side, literally on the other side. I believe our world; our entire lives are spent on the side of this parchment that faces up. When we die, we go to the side that faces down. The world on the other side of the parchment is divided into good and bad places. I believe the Almighty set up this system so that one side could never see or visit, even by accident, the side where they do not belong."

Sarah looked thoughtful for a moment and then demonstrated once again her incredible intellect and the ability to get right to the point.

"What about angels? Or demons? How do they get from the bottom of your parchment world and into ours?"

Elan smiled once again.

"Let me show you something. You don't know it, but, you have gotten to one of my central ideas." Taking his knife, he cut a small slit into the parchment. "Now, before I used my knife on this parchment, it was whole. There was no way to travel between the sides. Now, with just one touch, there is a way for, let's say angels or demons, to travel between the top and bottom of the parchment." Pointing his knife upwards towards the sky, he concluded: "There must be a mechanism, some portal perhaps, through which beings from the other side can travel back and forth. I believe this is something, and it is either here, on the earth, or is it up there among the stars. One day I'd like the opportunity to go up there, find the portal, travel in it, meet God, and ask a simple question."

I didn't like the tone of his voice nor what he was implying. "Careful, Elan. He restored your life. He can just as easily take it from you. And he has been helping us this entire time. How do you think we've escaped the authorities? It has not been through our own strength or knowledge; it is because of him we still live."

By the light of the crackling fire, I could discern the features of his face. He had spoken with no malice or ill intent, he was being truthful, and his pain was evident.

"While I understand those facts, I grow tired of escaping my comfortable life in the middle of the night, leaving behind the things I have grown attached to. I am tired of running from those who would hold us captive or kill us. What do they wish to accomplish? Why do they continue to pursue us? What have we done to them that keeps them so motivated in finding our location? And, after all these years, we remain unchanged from when we first met. I am stuck between my childhood and my manhood. I am not sure I know what I am or how this helps the Rabbi Master. What are you?" he asked, pointing towards me. Pointing towards Sarah, he continued. "I don't know what she is either."

"Well, I know who *and* what I am," Sarah replied with force. "Maybe you are just confused. And I don't live on the side of dirty parchment paper either." She turned towards me and switched topics. "Since we are on firm ground, I feel it is necessary to say that I am not looking forward to spending another day on the ocean. Next time, that is if there is a next time when we must flee, can we try to escape by horse?"

I'd been expecting that comment for a while, given that during our ocean journey, she'd spent a considerable amount of time with her head pointed overboard, throwing up. Elan had made the transition from land to sea without trouble, as had I, but Sarah couldn't take the motion of the ship very well.

"If I am to be immortal, why must I also be seasick," she muttered.

"Perhaps it's to show that a touch of humanity remains," Elan answered as he ducked the stick she threw his way.

Her pout was visible even in the firelight.

I sat back, disquieted. I should have been planning the next iteration of our lives, but what Elan said had upset me.

Elan took another bite and chewed. I could tell he was thinking, but what he said when he spoke surprised me.

"Sarah, let me help you next time we must do this. I know a couple tricks my father taught me once that sailors use to ward off seasickness."

She relaxed a bit and smiled.

"If we find ourselves taking the ocean path again, I will. You grew up around the water. I did not. Thank you, Elan."

Elan smiled and nodded. "Now, back to what I was saying. One day I am going to find a way to get to the portal between the two heavens, and then, I'm going to find a way to ask our Lord a question."

He lay back against his bedroll. "One day," he repeated several more times, staring up at the stars until he fell silent.

I fed the fire and looked up at the stars, wondering if he'd get that chance. Would God even allow it?

Give, and it will be given to you. They will pour into your lap a good measure—pressed down, shaken together, and running over. For by your standard of measure it will be measured to you in return.

LUKE 6:38

24

We walked until we could walk no more. After spending a few nights under the stars, a storm system set in, and we sought dry lodging at a stabula. (Think of it as the Motel 6 of the time period.) I was too tired to discuss the future any further and fell into a deep sleep.

This is when I had another visitation from my angel guardian. While in a deep sleep, I heard, "Lazarus. Awaken. The Lord of Hosts has a message of hope for you." I blinked awake with a sudden start. In front of me was a spectral being I can only describe as blindingly, perfectly beautiful. I knew it must be an angel. He held out a hand. "Touch my hand and feel the presence of the Lord for when you touch me, you touch him." A beam of light struck me that was so bright it lit my entire universe. I clenched my eyes closed as forcefully as possible and bowed my head.

The angel spoke again.

"Lazarus. Come forth."

I heard this phrase, but not with my ears, with my entire being. I reached for his hand, and he helped me stand. Not aware of whom to address I began blurting out in a stream of consciousness. "Father, I am your servant to command. I am trying to keep the faith alive as your Son commanded. Your apostles have all been killed long ago yet their ministry lives on. Should we return home and become part of what is left of their efforts? Though it has been many years since your Son raised me from the dead, I do not understand why we are still pursued by those who wish to kill us. My two companions are reluctant to continue and do not see the greater mission . . . " Then I went mute as the angel squinted and held up one hand. His countenance was so bright that I closed my eyes, and then, he began to speak.

"Lazarus, you are a good and faithful servant. The ministry of the apostles is not your concern. The church must exist and begin to transition. Your walk with the Spirit of God is just beginning. You are to make your way across the land, seeding churches, and believers. Move when you believe you have been successful. Your destination is the Bithynian city of Nicaea, where you will be asked to establish a great church and provide council to a gathering of Christian leaders. This shall be a great work to gain consensus among the church assembly. You shall not lead the proceedings, but you will be recognized as one who speaks for the Lord."

Her stopped speaking, then I felt his hand on my chin. He lifted it up slightly and continued, "Lazarus, beloved of the Lord, open your eyes and see."

I opened my eyes and timidly looked up. The light diminished enough for me to see into the eyes of the angel. He smiled and continued. "You, Elan, and Sarah are three testaments to the Son and the Father. Continue building the faithful. Tarry not in one place long enough to raise the suspicions of those who seek you for they have hatred in their hearts regarding the Son's message of love and forgiveness. The Lord and his angels watch over you and shall always be with you." He hit me with a blinding smile and then said, "Now, you may speak."

Looking back on this moment, I should have used my first question to an angelic being for something more, substantive. Instead, I am still embarrassed that I blurted out a question that had been on my mind for a time.

"Are *you* immortal?"

He smiled as if he'd been anticipating such a silly line of inquiry.

"Yes. All the heavenly hosts are immortal."

"Demons as well?"

His face changed slightly with this answer.

"Yes, for now. Judgment day comes for all though. Even the legions of Satan shall be judged and punished for their disobedience. Their ultimate and permanent fate is tied to that of Satan himself. As you can attest, the lake of fire is real, and the punishment for disobeying the Lord is eternal separation from him."

I considered his answer. I had not even asked about judgment, given the painful nature of my experience while I was dead. Since I'd been given the opportunity to speak, I pushed forward with a topic that was close to home.

"Do you ever get bored, given that you are immortal?"

He looked concerned for a moment, then asked, "Are you asking the Lord to remove the gift he has given you before you have fulfilled his purpose in doing so?"

I shivered slightly. *Have I overstepped?*

The angel shook his head. He'd heard my thought.

"You know that nothing is impossible to the Lord, whose reason and purpose in action need not be understood nor ever revealed to you. You should be more concerned about the tasks which remain to be done."

"But, it has been such a long time. There are moments when each of us; Sarah, Elan and I, wonders how much longer until the return of the savior."

"You are here for a purpose, and that purpose remains to be done. Until the time is right, and all the signs and wonders foretold have occurred, you should focus on the charge given to you and not on how much time has passed."

With a measure of sadness, I relented. I guess the angel saw that since I had been chastised, he decided it was okay to answer my initial question.

"For us, time is different. Days, years, even millennia for you are in fact mere moments for us. You shall see. Though you, Elan, and Sarah were returned to your earthly life, your bodies are no longer tied to the lifespan of humanity."

With that answer in mind, I surged forward with another question.

"What of the afterlife? Elan and I experienced eternal separation from God. Sarah saw the angels in her room before she was resurrected. What is the house of the Lord like? Can you tell me?"

He seemed to relax as he smiled.

"One day you shall see the Lord's house. In it he has built many mansions for those who love him. Elan saw the pit of fire and knew the loneliness of eternal damnation. Your four days was more than enough for you to see that a life lived well is not enough to enter the kingdom of God." With that, he stopped speaking, laid a hand on my head, and said, "Now, sleep once again. When you wake, recall every detail of our conversation. Enshrine it into your heart so that your path forward will be illuminated by the spirit of the Lord Almighty."

When he withdrew his hand, I fell deeply asleep. When I woke the next day, I was surprisingly refreshed and made sure to put every detail the angel had said onto parchment.

That was the first time I began to get serious about writing down the things I knew that the Lord expected from me, kind of my own list of commandments. It has changed many times throughout the years, but that discussion with my angel remains one of the most instructive and important to what I came to consider as my mission in life.

25

By the mid-third century, we had made our way across the northern territories of the Roman Empire. With Elan yearning to be closer to the ocean, we traveled to the beautiful port city of Athens and began to make yet another new life. As was our custom when relocating to a new place, we would arrive looking older and less wealthy than we were in reality. Once settled, we would purchase space in a different neighborhood, and begin to transform into our younger, wealthier selves. If questioned, we'd simply pass each other off as relatives of our older, more public selves.

We experienced no real setbacks, and it seemed that the authorities who had been so devoted in their desire to find us had either lost the will to continue or had all died off. Then came Emperor Decius. He was the governor of Germania Inferior (the modern capital of Cologne, Germany) and a much-beloved member of the Roman Senate when he led a rebellion against the emperor, Phillip the Arab. Decius killed Phillip, and supported by loyalists in the Legion, was recognized as emperor by the Senate. Though he initially was unwilling to ascend to the throne, fellow members of the Senate implored him to take command of Rome. During his reign, he enacted measures intended to restore stability to the Roman state and unify all her citizens under an official, government-sponsored religion. In addition to this awful idea that seems to never go out of style, his drive for a one-world-government and religion brought about what is now known as the "Decian persecution." Many prominent Christians were summarily put to death without a trial or even a time of incarceration. Think of it as a prequel to the Spanish Inquisition, but with more deaths.

When Decius took power, there was no longer the pervasive persecution of Christians that we had seen in the first few centuries after the
crucifixion of Jesus. However, there was still plenty of suspicion and dis-
trust. This all changed with his decision to establish an Imperial cult. He
saw to it that anyone who did not participate in his religious conformity
was subject to the death penalty. While today it might seem a radical turn
of events, back then, it was somewhat common for every new emperor
to decide an entire chunk of his populace needed to die. During this
one-year reign of terror, many Christians believed there was no choice
but to publicly reject their belief in Jesus and espouse their love for the
official religion of Rome. As a result, the church went underground and
continued to exist in secret for almost one hundred years before the Edict
of Milan in 313 AD, which officially established Roman toleration for the
nascent Christianity, thus ending the long persecution of Christians by
the Roman state. By this time, we had had moved to the city of Nicaea,
just as the angel had directed.

Soon, brother Cassius (my new identity) was a regular preacher. I
had been fortunate in that my ability to hold an audience's attention was
an extension of my true personality. It wasn't long before I was invited to
attend and then join a ministry of some size. This was sufficient to put me
in a position to represent the faith when the announcement came that
Emperor Constantine the Great was convening a learned council of more
than 300 elders in Nicaea. I had spent more than fifty years cultivating a
name for myself within the local church, trying to match my own aging
with that of my congregants as they aged, and I soon rose to the position
of bishop. As such, I was selected to be a senior representative to the
select group of council elders whose task was to create the first uniform
Christian prayer and doctrine that could be used by all worshipers. My
decision to participate had been made years earlier by a higher power.

At the emperor's direction, we were to create some statements of
belief for the Christian faith. How were Christians to demonstrate these
beliefs, and how could we bring a sense of true unity among the various sects calling themselves Christians? Then we were to test these new
sacraments of belief with our various constituent Christian groups. Once
tested and agreed upon, these statements–which would become prayers,
dedications, supplications, and songs–would form the structure of our
Christian religion.

The deliberations opened on May 20, 325 AD. Hosius of Córdoba, a
noted bishop from the Spanish church and a legate of the papacy, a man

I had known of and respected from afar for many years, was named the council chair, and he ruled with a velvet glove. He was considerate of opinions he did not share and frequently changed the order to fully discover the root causes of any disagreements the elder bishops expressed.

We'd been meeting for weeks and, despite some spirited debates, managed to form agreements on a book of common prayers. Satisfied, we turned our attention to creating a creed that would explicitly detail our beliefs–something that could be led by priests and repeated by the congregants for generations to come. Hosius thought it prudent to pray over our continued success.

"Let us pray for further guidance on our achievements . . . please bow your heads," he said to the group. Every man bowed his head. "Brothers, pray with me the very prayer as the Son of God himself instructed."

I bowed my head but kept my eyes open so I could see if these men were sincere or just going through the motions of the prayer every Christian had been taught. As he led the men in prayer, some clearly demonstrated their individual piety through their over-exaggerated vocalizations of the Lord's Prayer and their theatrical-like hand and head motions. I immediately thought that they were the ones I probably needed to keep at a distance. *No, in fact, I should continue to befriend all of them to determine where they stand.*

"Amen," Hosius said quietly. His "amen" was loudly overtaken by that of the most personally pious around the table.

I smirked.

Taking a sip of red wine, Hosius gathered some papers, looked over at a scribe who gave him a slight head nod indicating he was ready, and began. "Alright now, where were we?"

I sat back, waiting to see who would speak first. It was a bishop from my first place of refuge, Cyprus.

"We started with a declaration of belief in God the Father Almighty."

Hosius indicated his agreement. "Yes."

"But is 'Father' the right word? Is God truly a 'he?'" one of the others blurted out.

Sadly, for this group, what the bishop blurted out wasn't a novel thing. Several in the group had indicated their discomfort with the thought of a male God. They lobbied that instead of using "Father" or "he" or "him," we should choose a word not associated with a human male. They supported the use of a word or descriptor that lacked the associations to a human figure. I believe they were still associating humanity with the Eternal. The group momentarily devolved into chaos.

After the most boisterous had their say, things began to calm, and I saw my chance.

"In all the historical knowledge of mankind's interactions with our God, he has always been described as 'he,' and I see no reason to change. There are millennia of historical and religious documents to support God as our 'Father' and to deny our congregants the opportunity to worship God as their Father is to deny them a true representation of the relationship he has with us, his creation."

Hosius sat to my left, still. "Bishop Cassias, your argument is a forceful one with which I do not take issue."

Hosius turned to the scribe. "Please, refresh us on the contents of the prayer such as it currently is."

The scribe cleared his throat and began.

"Bishop, what I have written thus far is 'We believe in one God, the Father Almighty, Maker of all things visible and invisible' . . . "

"May I request that we pause, please?" interjected a bishop from Italy.

"Yes?" Hosius asked, somewhat perturbed though it showed only in the downturn of his jowls, not in his inflection.

The Italian Bishop cleared his throat, took a drink of wine, and offered, "We have all come into contact with and know of the pagans and the gods they worship or venerate. It would seem to me that they have a god for virtually every circumstance, season, and reason."

Everyone around the table shrugged their agreement and nodded.

"Then, I propose adding one little word that solidifies our belief in the only God. The one, true God," the Bishop said quietly.

"You suggest adding the word 'one' to what we are constructing? In other words, if we refer to 'one God,' just that word shall strengthen the prayer and wrap the entire Christian religion together? Just this one word?" I asked.

No one spoke for a few ticks of my nails on the table. I frankly was surprised at his ability to distill the argument for adding the word. "Yes. Directly forcing a declaration from worshipers that the God to whom we pray and the God we worship is the same. This is critical to Christianity. It is also important to our benefactor, the emperor. By saying it in the prayer we acknowledge the oneness of God the Father, God the Son, and God the Holy Spirit."

"Did not Christ teach his followers to speak the Lord's Prayer?" Hosius muttered, injecting the other contentious item the council was exploring into the conversation.

Italy immediately pounced. "There, see! Brother Hosius is correct. When asked by the apostles how to pray, Christ instructed them to begin the prayer with 'Our Father. . . ' so there can only be one Father. One! We must add that word!"

I leaned back, hoping every word wasn't destined to be as parsed out and dissected as the word "one" was. If so, it was going to be the next century before this council reported out any progress, and while I would be fine with that, every last one of these bishops would be dust in the ground by the time we got agreement on anything else.

Hosius stopped speaking for a moment as he took a note of some kind from an assistant. He smiled after reading it, leaned forward and in a low voice said, "Brother Cassias, why don't you take charge for a moment, lead them towards consensus on the next few sentences. I have a matter to which I must attend. I shall return shortly."

I bowed my head and accepted his charge.

He stood and rapped the knuckles of his right hand on the wooden table. "May I have your attention, please?" As they quieted down, he continued. "I must leave for a while. I am placing Cassias in my shoes while I am absent. Please work together and try to make more headway on this prayer. Our charge from the emperor is clear–create a simple prayer, a mechanism that can be repeated by believers, which will bring them closer to God and will unify the faith they share. I believe that through Christ, this august body is capable of successfully meeting the Emperor's charge. Perhaps you should pray regarding your individual participation in our endeavor and how you would introduce our prayer to your respective flocks."

With that, he nodded my direction, gathered his materials, and left.

I assumed his seat and looked around the table.

"It is settled then, the word 'one' shall be inserted into the prayer. Yes?"

Spain smiled at me and reached out to grasp my hand. "This is very good; you Cassias are a leader among men. Please, continue."

"Scribe, once more, read from the beginning."

The scribe began. "We believe in one God, the Father Almighty, maker of all things visible and invisible. And in one Lord Jesus Christ, the Son of God, begotten of the Father, the only begotten; that is, of the essence of the Father, God of God. Light of Light, very God of very God, begotten, not made, consubstantial with the Father; by whom all things were made [both in heaven and on earth]. Who for us men, and for our salvation, came down and was incarnate and was made man. He suffered, and the third day he rose again, ascended into heaven; From thence he shall come to judge the quick and the dead. And in the Holy Ghost . . . "

"Stop," the Bishop from France quickly said. "I accept that we acknowledge him as the maker of all things. But 'begotten?' Will the average hungry, dirty, peasant, intent on the absolution of their sins, in any of our churches or meeting houses understand what the word means?"

Italy stood and looked my way as if to require my approval before answering. I tipped my head slightly. He took a breath and began.

"First, I'd not describe members of your flock, be they rich or poor, as 'dirty.' It is demeaning and too easily would lead to their separation from the faith if they heard the way you describe them. Second, what would you rather say? Most know what the word 'begotten' means. And anyone who does not will repeat it anyway and inquire as to its meaning after the fact. By using this, long word, we imbed in our prayer a sense of reverence. It is a beautiful word. Would you rather insert some phrase such as a crass 'our God created everything?' By using this word, they acknowledge that God created his Son long before creating our universe. It infers that God, simply through his being, had already set in motion the means for our salvation from sin. By using this particular word, and placing it exactly where we have placed it, we honor our central belief: that God Himself created the one who came to free us from sin, his Son before he ever created any other part of our universe."

I was impressed. This bishop had a clear grasp of salvation and God.

There was silence as the Italian bishop sat down. The silence was usually a good indicator that there was general agreement among the elder council membership.

I motioned the scribe to continue.

"And I believe in the Holy Ghost, the Lord, the giver of life, who precedeth from the Father and Son, who with the Father and Son is worshiped and glorified, who spake by the prophets; and I believe in one catholic and apostolic church. I acknowledge one baptism for the remission of sins, and I look for the resurrection of the dead and the life of the world to come. Amen."

"What of the decision to leave out the words the emperor wished to be used in his prayer?"

I had hoped this issue had been forgotten. But I was mistaken, so I weighed in, hoping for the best.

"The words he wished to be used for his prayer. You mean, Unity, Holiness, and the universal nature of Christianity?"

"Yes. His direction is that we frame a prayer based on the supposition that all Christians form a single, united group. In other words, a body of Christ, if you will, founded by his disciples after his ascension into heaven and their baptism by the Holy Ghost on Pentecost. His order was very clear. Create a prayer to be used by every Christian in the entire world. Have we accomplished the task in such a way that we can claim success, seek the agreement among the 300 waiting to vote on the prayer, and forward it to the Emperor? I, for one, do not wish to test his supposed tolerance for the Christian faith with my neck."

General mayhem ensued, and it persisted around every syllable of every word well into the afternoon.

I let one argument swirl for a while, and then I clapped my hands three times, restoring a semblance of order. We were so close. I truly wanted to present Hosius with a finished product when he returned.

"The Bishop from Germania is making a good point. However, I believe that the inclusion of the word 'one' provides the unity and inclusiveness the Emperor sought from this council. As elders, it has been our responsibility, despite our differing opinions, to craft a prayer that the whole of Christendom can use. I believe we have accomplished the task set before us. Besides, our prayer, as it is currently, demonstrates that there is unity in the entire Body of Christ through our addition of the words 'catholic' and 'apostolic,' since both can be construed to cover the whole cloth of our faith."

Someone out of view spoke loudly enough that we all heard his words.

"But is our faith universal? Does this prayer force doctrine onto our respective flocks that perhaps is outside the bounds of what Christ and his apostles gave us?"

At that moment, Hosius strode in.

I quickly stood and resumed my previous seat.

"I have been lingering just outside the room for a while, listening to you, my esteemed colleagues. Your intelligence, your strong objections, your strong arguments for keeping or removing certain words and phrases has given us a robust, exceptionally powerful prayer that, mark my words, shall be spoken by the faithful and the believers in Christ and his resurrection for thousands of years."

Needless to say, the turn of that phrase caught my attention. *What did he mean by that? I haven't been worried about those who had been so intent on capturing the three of us for hundreds of years. Should I be concerned?* This and more flashed through my mind. Suddenly, I was just a bit more uncomfortable.

"Who believes the prayer as we have structured it meets the emperor's requirements?"

I made a mental note to check in with Elan and Sarah immediately following our vote and the delivery of the prayer to the other council membership, all waiting in a large anteroom downstairs for their consideration.

Around the table a show of hands was unanimous.

"Good. Then, tonight we take the prayer to the full council for a vote. I shall not entertain changes, as you, being their representatives, have created this prayer from the whole cloth of Christendom. What shall we call it, this new prayer for the masses?"

"The prayer of Nicene. We created it here. Thus, its name should reflect the time and emotion expended in its creation," the bishop from France offered.

I had a different idea and spoke up. "I appreciate my brother describing what we have written as a 'prayer.' However, I would like to present a differing viewpoint. Perhaps, we have bested even the emperor's requirements."

The room went silent. Hosius looked my way with an interesting expression and indicated I was to continue.

"Let me explain. I believe what we have created is much stronger than a simple prayer that a child recites from memory each night before turning in to bed. The true significance of these painstakingly chosen words, which we shall present to the emperor, is intended to endure the test of time. It must, and I restate that word, must, have a name that acts as a sign that we not only met the charge given us by the emperor, but exceeded it."

The table murmured a bit. "Interesting," a few remarked. "Exactly what are you suggesting?" the Italian bishop asked.

Hosius thought about this for a second and motioned for quiet. "Brother Cassias makes an excellent point. I support the need to use the name of this holy place where we have done the work of the Lord

Almighty. I shall get back to that point in a moment. I believe that, when it is presented for his approval, the emperor needs to know that what we send him, in name alone, is proof that we have met his reason for calling this esteemed council to order. He expects nothing less. I ask you, what is it that we have created? It is a prayer? Perhaps. But what exactly is prayer? Is it a simple construction of words, put together, and designed to ask for something from heaven? It must get tiring if all humanity does is ask for the Lord's intervention regarding a stubborn mule, perhaps a bad business deal, or a fight with a spouse."

That brought a few chuckles from the gathered bishops.

Once again, the Spanish bishop displayed his ability to state and restate what was obvious to everyone. "To me it would seem that a prayer can be anything. It can ask for help from God or offer praise to him for the works he has done on our behalf. Honestly, prayer can be literally anything that anyone calls a prayer. I could pray for rain, or for a full belly, or for someone who is ill."

Bishop Ambrose, a man with whom I had nothing in common regarding Christ and his followers, took the table by surprise when he interrupted our discussions. "Must we offer penance for free? Why cannot we require a stipend or tithe before we offer forgiveness or access to this prayer?"

I could not resist. "A ridiculous idea. As representatives of Christ, we do not offer penance. Christ does through his sacrifice on the cross. And, as I recall, Christ already answered your question when, according to the letters we ascribe to the apostle Mark, the Lord drove the vendors and money changers from the Holy Temple."

"Yes, perhaps, but did all of that actually occur?" Ambrose was quick to reply.

This line of thought I had to squash with a vengeance. "Bishop Ambrose, belief is the central tenant of our religion. An additional question would be how are the poor to 'purchase' absolution for their sins? They are poor. Is absolution only for those with the means to purchase it? Honestly, this idea runs contrary to the teachings of Christ and his apostles. The issue is one that I cannot support, and no one around this table or who believes in salvation offered to humanity through belief in the Son of God, should either."

Ambrose looked quite unhappy, and it made me wonder what his motivations were. However, he acquiesced when Hosius intervened.

"Bishops. These are issues we can thrash out later. For now, we have met one of the tasks put before us by the emperor."

I nodded, and bishop Ambrose did as well, though he couldn't resist trying to push another idea with which I thoroughly disagreed.

"I accept your leadership on the matter, Hosius. I have one more idea though: Can we begin to think about a prayer for the dead?"

I answered before I even knew I had formed the thought.

"No. The dead are beyond help and no longer require prayer on their behalf."

Hosius glanced my way, and I thought I perceived his eyes blink a few too many times as if he was trying not to say something. However, he regained his composure momentarily and nodded his agreement.

I felt it critical to bring the group back to our main reason for being here.

"I heard consensus on the exact nature of what we've written. Now, can we come to an agreement on is it a prayer, or something greater?"

Hosius spoke next. "Instead of a prayer, what we have constructed is a statement of facts regarding our Father in heaven. It is proof to our premise that God loves us and sent his Son as a living sacrifice for all humanity. It is a sincere statement of our Christian beliefs through which we can also guide the sinner to salvation. If they listen and take to their souls how we assembled the words, there is truth and healing. Therefore, I put to you that this is not just a prayer. Instead, it is our central statement of Christianity. It is our creed!"

A moment of stunned silence was shattered by thunderous shouting. "It is a creed, by God, a creed!"

Hosius looked very pleased with himself. "Is there a second?"

"Second!" said every bishop with one thunderous voice.

Hosius rapped his cup on the table. "The Nicene Creed it is. Scribe, please make note of our agreement and prepare copies for the 300 delegates. When finished, come find me. I shall be speaking with bishop Cassias in my chambers."

We all shook hands, hugged, and ended with a simple prayer thanking God for his spiritual direction that had led the council of elders to the creed and for the sacrifice by his Son which provided for the forgiveness of our sins.

While I watched as the chief scribe began instructing his apprentices on which quills to use to show the weight of each word, Hosius gathered me by the arm. "Come, bishop, walk with me."

26

While Hosius and I walked the stone-encrusted halls adjacent to the great cathedral, I was reminded of Solomon's Temple. Before and after my resurrection, I had occasion to visit the second temple when it was in use. It's always fascinated me that modern humanity, in my opinion, builds many of their places of worship patterned on the historical descriptions of the Second Temple. The only person who truly knows if they got it right or wrong is me, and I'm not going to offer a critique.

Hosius broke the silence of our walk. "I asked you to accompany me so that we could discuss an important matter."

It was not lost on me that two of his assistants fell in behind us, though I thought nothing of it at the time.

I interrupted him a bit too eagerly. "The emperor's next challenge? I know he wants to compile the stories written by the apostles and disciples who knew the Lord into one manuscript. I also look forward with great anticipation to a spirited discussion amongst the bishops and the eventual agreement on when and how to celebrate our Lord's crucifixion and his resurrection three days later. It should be the second-most important feast of our ecclesiastical calendar, second only to the day of his holy birth!"

Of course, in the back of my mind were my experiences with the Rabbi Master; witnessing his crucifixion, fleeing Judea, my time in Cyprus, and then three days later, the news of his resurrection. I had always encouraged the false Lazarus to preach that believers should celebrate his resurrection.

My own resurrection wasn't even a part of that thought process. I guess it should have been.

"Yes, I agree with you. It shall be a very spirited debate. I would love to have you lead our discussions on the life, death, and resurrection of our Lord. However, you will not be a part of it."

Mentally, I quickly began to prepare a vigorous defense of my position when he opened the door to his chamber and ushered me inside.

"What is all of this?" were the only words I could manage. Before me, seated, bound, and under guard, were Elan and Sarah. Today, I know that my heart rate and blood pressure must have been spiking out of control. Back then, I didn't know of such things. I only knew something had gone terribly wrong.

"Have a seat," Hosius said very slowly, "Brother Cassias. Or should I call you, Lazarus?"

I started to muster my best defense, but the look in Sarah's eyes and the slight shake of her head was enough to stop me. I knew then we had been discovered. It crushed me.

Hosius motioned towards an empty chair. He addressed the two guards directly: "Leave us. Dispatch two more to the waterfront to stand by while the captain continues to prepare the Sanctus for a voyage." Pointing to three pieces of travel bags constructed of leather and brass, he continued: "Take these with you and make sure you arrive safely. I authorize the use of deadly force, in the name of God, to anyone who seeks to waylay you."

The Sanctus? Isn't that an ocean-going vessel owned by the church? As this thought swirled through my mind, I was relieved to see one piece of our luggage that I always thought of as essential to our future well-being. My attention to it did not go unnoticed by Hosius.

"Yes, you need not be concerned. We brought the means for the three of you to begin anew, as I imagine you have done many times before."

"I am sure you searched our belongings and know what is in there. I appreciate that you have not annexed it for the church."

"No. I am not a thief. I believe there are those in the church who would steal from you, in fact, there are several around the table you just commanded who would, and they would do it not for the church but to enrich themselves."

To his assistants, he then said: "Now, take this baggage to the docks. The captain of the Sanctus awaits your arrival." He retrieved a sealed envelope from his desk and handed it to the most senior member of his staff. "You are to give this envelope to the captain. As you leave and secure my door, ensure the guards stand fast outside."

I sat with a heavy heart. Hosius correctly interpreted my body language and emotional countenance and held out both hands. It was a gesture designed to calm as well as persuade me to listen.

"I would imagine you have much to ask. Hold your peace and listen to what I have to say." While he said this to me, he removed a small dagger from his cloak and approached Elan and Sarah. Both flinched as he took their hands in his and severed the ropes that bound them.

"Sit, stay still. Make no sudden movements, make no sounds that would draw attention," he counseled.

Elan and Sarah rubbed their wrists and came to me. Both of them fell at my feet. Sarah sobbed.

"His men surprised us while we were napping, bound us, covered us with a dark sheet, and brought us here."

I looked up. "Was it necessary to cover and bind them? They are no threat. What is the meaning of this?"

Hosius shrugged and shook his head. "It was necessary to accomplish the task under the cover of darkness. I had my assistants use the sheet to ensure they could not be identified. I had them bound to prevent any attempt to escape, since I am sure you have contingency plans and meeting places already prepared should any of you ever be discovered."

He saw acknowledgment in my facial expression and knew what he'd said was true.

"Cassias is a great name to use. It fooled everyone who mattered. With your looks and build, you actually can pass for every ethnic group of people living within the territories made up of the old Roman Empire."

"Do what you will with me. But spare these two. They are innocent of any wrongdoing or deception you believe has occurred!"

With a slight smile, he spoke.

"Lazarus, who is truly innocent? You, of all people, understand that question. First, I wish I could say we will have many years together. I am jealous beyond my ability to express of what you three must have experienced. Of the life you have lived. Just think, you three are the people," he paused quickly and added, "You *are* people, right, not angels or something else?"

I nodded in affirmation. "Yes, bishop, we are, indeed, people. Human."

He continued. "Human? That is quite a humorous statement coming from Lazarus of Bethany. You three are hundreds of years old. I am not entirely sure that makes you human. However, I will accept your answer."

He paused for a moment, then continued. "I confess, on learning of you three, I had my doubts. It is very hard for me to even speak with you, the only people alive who actually *met* Jesus Christ, the Son of God. You touched him, heard his voice. Perhaps you watched his crucifixion. It is almost too much for me. Truthfully, even saying that is, almost incomprehensible to me."

He paused again and with both hands, rubbed his forehead, as if trying to stop his brain from what it was telling him.

"My friends, I cannot even begin to understand what it must have been like to sit and hear his voice, to hear his ministry. To witness the miracles."

He raised his voice just a bit. "Add to that the fact that you three have passed into the afterlife and come back."

The three of us had dealt with the drama he was rehashing so I interrupted with the only thing I cared about at the moment.

"How did you find us? Was it something I did?"

My question reoriented his mental gymnastics regarding our true identities. After a brief pause, he explained. "Oh, well, yes, of course, you'd be curious. There is one thing you failed to truly understand about the church my . . . old . . . friend."

He smirked saying that but continued.

"When someone such as yourself, someone very smart, resourceful, with seemingly endless monetary depth yet no desire to put their wealth on display, seemingly full of knowledge beyond their years, arrives and appears to have the means to live comfortably but there is no indication of how they achieved those means *and* within a short time is elevated to a position of power within the clergy or the church, someone, somewhere, takes notice. We do run a church, yes. But," and with this, he paused, which I believe was for dramatic effect. After all, as the most senior clergy in the region, I imagine dredging up emotions to salt into his words was an easy thing to do, "we also run a very sophisticated and large organization based on the gathering, analysis, and dissemination of intelligence. Sometimes we need to know what other countries are up to. Or what their leaders worry about. We even have spies in the emperor's court. Why, might you ask? Because it pays to know what the emperor thinks or believes. What do those who attend and worship at our churches truly think or believe? We wonder about a great many things."

I guess the blank looks of amazement on our faces were precisely what he had been hoping to see, so he continued.

"I know that you recall the actions Moses took after the Israelites had been released by the pharaoh to wander through the desert. Moses sent twelve spies over the mountain to determine if the Israelites could take possession of what God had promised them on reaching the promised land. Those twelve spies pale in comparison to the network the church has established. We use it for many things, such as the furtherance of the gospel, the well-being of God's people, and the spread of the holy word of God. Most of the time."

"Most?" I muttered.

Hosius laughed softly. "Yes, most." Turning his back to me, he brought out a glazed clay bottle and four cups. "I suppose the youngsters are old enough to join us?"

I honestly think he was making fun of us, but I sat silently. *What in the world is going on?*

"Yes, of course, they are of age enough to consume wine."

"Good. I seek not to loosen your collective tongues but to ease your apprehension regarding being discovered."

He poured and handed each of us our own cup of wine. "Bow your heads please."

I raised my eyebrows. Sarah and Elan, now seated on the floor at my feet, looked to me for guidance. I shrugged and did as he asked, though I did keep my eyes open, accessing our collective situations.

Making the sign of the cross over his forehead and chest, he began.

"God the Father, God the Son, and God the Holy Ghost. Keep us and protect us from evil, forgive our trespasses, and accept our souls into heaven when we pass from this life into the next. Open the hearts of your servants, Lazarus, Elan, and Sarah, so that they know no harm will come to them this day. Watch over them, as I know you have these hundreds of years since their deaths and resurrections at the hands of your Son, Jesus Christ. Strengthen in them the divine purpose for their continued existence. In your name, I ask all these things, Amen."

"Amen," the three of us said in unison.

"Now, drink while I speak."

I sipped and listened. Elan and Sarah waited. I think they were waiting to see if I'd been poisoned by the wine. Seeing no ill effects, they both sipped, though gingerly.

"So, I know of your story Lazarus, what of you my son?" he said, pointing towards Elan.

"I am Elan from the town of Nain."

Hosius looked quite happy as he nodded in understanding.

"Of course, you are. You are the widow's son, raised from the dead by Jesus just before you were to be buried!"

Hosius looked to Sarah next, and she answered without hesitation.

"I am Sarah, from Capernaum."

"Ah, the daughter of the temple leader."

I think I saw his face turn red as his voice accelerated a bit. "Your father sought out our Lord and brought him to your bedside though you were already dead. Is that correct? Are the scriptures we have in our possession correct on that matter?"

She nodded and looked at me. I believe there was relief in her eyes to meet someone who knew the truth and who wasn't trying to kill us.

He nodded in my direction and took a deep breath, "And, as I said earlier, you are Lazarus of Bethany."

I nodded in return. He looked so happy as he sat into an ornate chair, his posture was as if he was trying not to crack eggs as he settled in. He said nothing for several minutes. Finally, he seemed to have come to a decision, so he took a long sip from the cup of wine and began to speak.

"Then, may I call you by your given name and not Cassias, the false one you have used for such a very long time?"

I confess there was a tinge of relief in my heart to hear my given name from the lips of someone other than Elan and Sarah after living so long without it.

"Yes, please. I have only heard it from these two," I said, motioning towards Elan and Sarah. "Even though they have been trained to try and use the false names we've manufactured every new place we go, they slip up now and then."

"Yes, I would venture to say that your name seems to have gone out of style, I would say. Much like the name, Judas."

At the mention of the name Judas, Elan snorted loudly.

"Judas? What do *you* know of Judas?"

This took Hosius aback for a moment.

"What do you mean Elan?"

"It is a simple question for a learned man such as yourself. What do you know of Judas?"

I wanted to smack him for his insolence but resisted.

Hosius indulged Elan with an answer worthy of the gracious, intelligent man that he was.

"Well Elan, religious scholars, in their pursuit of details regarding the savior and his disciples, have uncovered numerous letters, scrolls, and writings, some of which we know were authored by the apostles before their deaths. I refer to one that was written by an apostle named Mark, one of the original men selected by Christ. It was written sometime before Mark's death."

That piece of information took me by surprise. Before I knew it, I had blurted out, "Mark? The cousin of Barnabas? He brought me water to drink after my resurrection. He had such a beautiful, peaceful manner. He wrote something of the Rabbi Master . . . how did I miss this fact? I must acquire it and include it in my papers!"

Hosius fell silent for a few seconds and the look on his face was one of utter disbelief and fear. I wondered why the emotion of fear, and was going to ask about it when Elan decided to barge past my verbal moment of introspection when he plowed ahead with, "and?"

Hosius visibly swallowed and cleared his throat. He sat back as if a great moment had arrived and whatever he needed to decide had been decided.

"Well, we have confirmed that Mark traveled with another apostle, Peter, some years after the crucifixion of Jesus. They traveled for a year preaching, healing the sick, and establishing churches. During their travels, apostle Mark took great care to memorialize their experiences. He paid great attention to his own interactions with Jesus, and in the scroll regarding the arrest, trial, and crucifixion of Jesus, he identifies a traitor within the apostles, a man named Judas, who sells information to the Sanhedrin. This act ultimately leads to the arrest of Jesus."

At this point, the writings he had been mentioning finally made sense, and once again, I broke into the conversation.

"Ah, you are referring to the writings, letters, and scrolls by the disciples . . . "

I never got to finish my question because Hosius interrupted me quickly.

"Yes, many of the men known as the disciples, or the apostles, authored material regarding Jesus and his life. Most are in the form of letters to the various congregations with whom they associated. In three of the four of these letters are clear descriptions of each of you and how it is you came into contact with our Lord."

The collective look of surprise on our faces must have taken him aback as he paused, took another sip of wine, nodded, and continued.

"You are surprised? Yes, there is substantial information regarding your deaths and resurrections, just, as I mentioned previously. However, the names of your two companions are not in the narratives, so it is a joyous occasion that I, of all the scholars in the world, get to meet and put names to the two other individuals our Lord raised from the dead."

I sat back, somewhat in amazement and slightly in shock. I'm sure Hosius would have been hurt to know that my surprise wasn't about his brilliance at finding us but at hearing that others from the Rabbi Master's flock had written down the details of his life, death, and resurrection.

Hosius continued. "But, back to Judas. What is it you wish to say Elan?"

Elan looked to me again, which snapped me out of the mindset regarding my collection of material from the so-called apostles. His expression contained two things: contrition and a request. I nodded slightly that he should continue, though I had no real idea about what he would say.

"I start this discussion with a question: What kind of man was Judas? I suppose we will get to the circumstances that brought me into contact with the Rabbi Master and his disciples. But for now, you mentioned Judas, so that is where I shall begin. Judas was born and raised in Kerioth (known in modern times as El Kureitein.) His position among the apostles was tenuous at best. Though it was not spoken of, he was seen as a thief, a liar, and one whom no one could trust."

Hosius stopped Elan. "Wait, he was known as a thief and a liar? We have seen something like that in writings by Matthew and Luke, but we never knew if those details were true or added later by someone else who perhaps had issues with Judas. How is it he continued by the side of Jesus for so long?"

"I cannot answer that question. However, I once heard the Rabbi Master rebuking his apostles for some minor infraction. He said something like: "Did I not choose you twelve, and one of you is a devil?""

"So, he knew a traitor was in his midst the whole time?"

"Yes, it was also clear he meant for the traitor to hear his words, as if there were still time to change his mind about whatever he was about to do that was wrong."

This made Hosius sit up straighter in the chair. Clearly, it excited him to hear the details regarding something so fascinating.

"But this raises so many theological questions. If Jesus had persuaded the 'devil' as he called the traitor, then our history might be vastly different than it is, given his sacrifice for all mankind."

I broke into the conversation at that point. "Yes, we three have tried to understand topics and scenarios such as these many times. What if this had happened, and what if that had happened? But we must live within the world of what actually happened. There is no question among the faithful; Judas actually did betray the Rabbi Master."

Hosius turned to Elan. "Did you spend much time with our Lord or his apostles?

"Some. After my resurrection, I convinced my mother to give up her tepid devotion to the pagan gods, and we followed him for a time, watching and listening, learning the ways of the one, true God and his Son."

Hosius sat back, the stunned look fading from his face as he considered what Elan had offered. He smiled for a moment, turned his attention to me, and asked a question.

"Did you have any interaction with the Lord? The disciples? Do you have an opinion regarding Judas? Was he the devil?"

I considered his line of inquiry regarding Judas for a moment and decided to be completely honest in my reply.

"I met and followed our Lord, thanks to my sister Martha. After my death and resurrection, there was no time to tarry, as the religious authorities had already grown quite tired of his miracles and his assertion that he was the Son of God. I saw Judas and the look of fear and anger in his eyes after I was brought back to life was easy to discern. I had heard the grumbles of the faithful regarding how Judas mismanaged their funds, so I already knew he was not trustworthy, and the look in his eyes when I came back was one of true fear. I have no idea if he was truly possessed by the devil. Not long after we three fled Judea for Cyprus, a story circulated among the early churches that the man who had befriended and then betrayed Jesus felt remorse for his actions and tried to return the money he had been paid. Of course, I eventually found out what happened to him. And if the description of his death is true, then Judas died a horrible and painful death. I shed no tears for him."

Hosius was nodding as I finished speaking. "Indeed. The three documents I am familiar with relate two different versions of what happened to him; he either hung himself and died, twisting in the wind as he frantically tried to undo the knot holding him or hung himself and the limb on which he'd tied the rope was too rotten to hold his weight. It broke, causing him to crash to the ground, where he hit a sharp rock protruding from the ground, which opened a large wound, spilling his innards out onto the ground. Either way, it is a horrible way to die, though fitting for the one who betrayed our Lord"

That earned an expression of displeasure and a gag from Sarah.

However, now I was intrigued. *So much detail! I must add these details to my own manuscripts!*

"But, Elan, you met the man who betrayed our Lord," Hosius said. "I cannot believe it was all just for the money, which I might add, he disavowed!"

Elan sat still. He had just displayed a depth of character I'd not seen. He wasn't finished surprising me.

"I believe Judas was ruled by jealousy and envy. After my mother and I became followers of the Rabbi Master, I recall the sick feeling I had in the pit of my stomach. Somehow, I knew a traitor was among his closest followers. It turned out that I was correct. So, in my opinion, the name Judas deserves to disappear from the earth forever."

Hosius sat quietly, contemplating the things Elan had just said.

"True, if I were comparing the lives of Judas and Lazarus, they were completely different. But I was not comparing them. After the death, resurrection, and eventual ascension of our Lord and savior, I was merely saying that those two names have been entirely lost to history. Matthew, Mark, Luke, John, James, Paul, all are well-known disciples of Jesus Christ. Joseph and Mary, who everyone knows as the human parents of Jesus; their names have been and are being used regularly by the rich, the poor, peasants, and royalty. But you Lazarus, somehow your name has been forgotten. I dare say, perhaps there has been some divine intervention on your behalf to encourage such far-reaching and permanent forgetfulness."

At the mention of Paul, Elan and Sarah had reacted with a start, which Hosius noticed.

"Why the reaction when I mentioned the apostle Paul?" He looked like he was trying to retrieve a lost bit of information from the back of his brain when it hit him. We had lived in Cyprus at the same period in time.

"When you were living on Cyprus, did you know or interact with Paul? It is an established fact that he traveled there, fathering churches," he said. "In fact, I have read that you played a significant part in Paul's ministry in Cyprus. But it is written that you died a natural death at an old age and are buried on in the cliffs there, overlooking the sea towards your homeland!"

I shrugged. We'd been caught, so I thought, *what harm could it cause now?*

"Of course, we all knew Paul. He was a constant friend until he left Cyprus for Rome," said Elan. "It still hurts that they eventually made a martyr of him."

"Yes, he was a gentle soul who loved the Rabbi Master more than you can even imagine. I know the Romans took his head, and I am sure those responsible will pay for that action in the afterlife," said Sarah.

Since neither of them thought to address the question regarding the other Lazarus on Cyprus, I did.

"And, yes, there was a man who called himself Lazarus in Cyprus who did great works for the faith, but it was not me. Paul brought him to Cyprus at the suggestion of the risen Lord to give me time to regain my humanity and prepare for the long journey ahead. Paul is the one who told us that our resurrections conveyed immortality until the return of the Lord at the end of days. He reinforced the charge given to us by the Rabbi Master, and I am quite thankful that he was sent to us. However, I am the one who buried the other Lazarus after his death."

Hosius appeared to be shocked even more so than when he had revealed the knowledge of our true identities. He stood and paced for a few moments, then he turned and began speaking again.

"The evidence regarding you three was conclusive, and I thought I was prepared to address all this with you. But now that the three of you are here, and listening to what you have said, I don't know. I may never be able to grasp exactly how important it has been meeting you. Perhaps I was guided to you by the Lord himself, to save you from those who still seek you out. Add the fact that you truly knew the Lord and his apostles? It is almost more than I can take. It is very difficult, even for a learned man such as me, to begin to understand what you must have seen and heard."

With that, he took a large gulp of the wine and quickly refreshed his glass. He offered us more, but Elan and Sarah followed my example and declined.

I decided to pick up where he had stopped.

"Regarding the disappearance of my birth name, it has not happened as a result of any prayers I have made to God for his assistance. Perhaps it just ran its course in history and never needed to be used again."

What I said seemed to bring him back to reality. "That may be so. However, the truth is that I have never met another Judas or Lazarus. Both names have disappeared from the earth."

Now I was curious since he seemed intent on reliving our previous couple of hundred years. "Hosius, if you don't mean to harm us, why, this?" I asked, holding up the cup of wine and pointing to the ropes that had held my Elan and Sarah.

"Your assistance with our new creed has been exactly as I had hoped. I requested your appointment to the council of elders because I already had in my possession the details of your true identity."

This caused me more than a bit of surprise, and I very nearly jumped out of the chair.

Hosius held out both arms again and asked that we remain calm. "Wait. You are safe. I have told no one. Over the last couple of years, I have had my network gathering bits and pieces of information about your lives. An astute scholar such as I was required to put the pieces of the puzzle together. But once I did put them together, I knew I had to meet you to understand just what you have been doing all these years. But I am sad to report that my search has alerted those who continue to seek the three of you. Surely, you must have realized that somewhere, someone was still searching and watching for three individuals who never aged properly, or who acquired wealth and then disappeared mysteriously."

"What do you mean, those who would seek the three of us?" asked Elan.

Hosius shook his head as he answered.

"My son, you must realize that soon after our Lord's crucifixion, an organization sprung up to preserve, let's say, a certain viewpoint on his life, death and teachings. If it were common knowledge that you three were still among the living, this news would run counter to their established opinion. In their dogma, three individuals such as yourselves cannot be allowed to continue their lives unabated. It is believed that the people might begin to focus attention on you and turn their eyes away from the Lord."

We sat silent for a moment.

"But we have not done miracles! We haven't gathered followers and threatened the status quo of the ruling religious class! We have only returned from the dead, and even that was by his hand!" Sarah said from the floor, where she still held a tight grasp on my left leg.

"While the facts as you state them are true dear Sarah, they regard your continued life as an abomination. Apparently, they believe that you were supposed to live a productive and normal life and then die at a normal age. And you either forgot to die, or just didn't want to. They discount that the Lord himself keeps you alive and prosperous for his own reasons."

"Does this organization have a name?" Elan interrupted.

"It does. They call themselves *'Custodes de Resurrecturis.'*"

"Guardians or Protectors of the Resurrection?" I muttered. This was news to me and not at all good news. How had their existence not been revealed to me?

"Both guardians and protectors. And they are quite serious about it. They shorten their name to simply 'the Protectors' when searching the records for the three of you."

"The Protectors? Are you sure of this information?"

"My intelligence is beyond question. If they ever find you, it is their intention to immediately return you, Elan, and Sarah back to the afterlife. I've heard they even have a plan to do it in such a way that even your immortal bodies wouldn't be able to survive. There have been rumors among the hierarchy of the church that you exist somewhere out there. I thought nothing of them until the details regarding you came to my attention. I am certain the Protectors have been alerted as well, which is why I took the precipitous action against Elan and Sarah and have brought you together here, under my personal protection."

This was too much for Elan. He turned to me and said, in a very forceful way, I might add, "See, I told you this would happen. I am beginning to wish I'd never been brought back to this life; all we ever do is look over our shoulders and prepare for the next time we must run away. No church we establish is worth all this aggravation! I am so tired of always wondering why I was brought back, and what am I to do with this gift." The way Elan pronounced the word "gift" it was clear he might not view his resurrection as a gift.

This was not the first time I had heard Elan complaining about his return from the dead.

"Quiet, Elan, let the bishop speak," I said. His look was one of distinct displeasure, and I could tell Elan wasn't interested in complying.

With some measure of agility, Hosius moved from his seat and knelt in front of Elan. Taking his chin into his hands, he said the most interesting thing.

"Young man, yes, it is a 'gift,' as you so derisively put it. One that is immeasurable in human terms. You have seen the other side. You, along with Sarah and Lazarus, can tell everyone there is an afterlife and describe it. People need to know that what they do in life, what they believe, and whom they worship has consequences. Consequences that are real and eternal. The nonsense with these men who seek you and their belief that your resurrection should be undone cannot cloud the reasons *for* your resurrection."

He stopped for a moment, considering. I could see what he was thinking and knew the next question would be the one he was most interested in asking.

"In fact, exactly what was your experience in the afterlife? Are you able to share it with me?"

Elan glanced my direction once again.

I nodded. Elan looked down, then up, and took a deep breath.

"It was negative beyond my human ability to describe. You cannot even begin to imagine the horror, the pain, the complete futility of eternal damnation without the hope of redemption. Add to that the knowledge that my circumstances would never change. Forever. And trust me when I say that the concept of forever isn't one you, a still-living human, can even begin to grasp. However, as a being who has passed from the living world to the dead one and returned, I know just how long forever is going to be. If you are there, you are there forever, and that is never going to change. It is permanent and unending. The sense of hopelessness permeated virtually every part of my soul. And what I just described wasn't even the most hurtful part—which was the knowledge of my eternal separation from everyone and everything. I was completely alone. I knew my dead family members were there because I could sense their pain. The heat was unbearable, and the stench of sulfur overwhelmed me immediately. I knew I could never move, could never change the fact that I was on the wrong side of eternity without relief. Forever. Oh, one last thing: I could see the 'other' side, the one where there was happiness, peace, and security. I don't know if others there could see it. I have often wondered, after the fact of course, if I was given a glimpse of it so that I would know it existed. I knew it was there, but it was forever out of reach. Across the great divide there was love, there was beauty. There was God. And I knew it would never, ever be mine."

Hosius was shocked into silence. He stood transfixed, clearly trying to mentally catalog and understand what he had just heard. With one quick motion, he jerked his hands away as if Elan's face had turned to liquid fire. He reached for his chair and sat heavily.

"And yet, dear boy, even though you have been saved from that eternal damnation, and separation, as you put it, you speak out against the Savior of mankind who brought you back to the land of the living? You entirely miss the point of your resurrection. Perhaps it is purposeful. Perhaps, even though you are more than 300 years old, you are still too young to comprehend the magnitude of your gift. You have the opportunity to make amends, to begin your life again, to tell the people of the world what awaits if they reject salvation. Your desire to have never returned makes no sense and insults the Son of God, whom, I might add, can immediately return you to that place of pain and horror. At any time."

With the very forceful rebuke from Hosius ringing in his ears, Elan shrank from him and grew quiet. I expected nothing less. I knew of the resentment that had been growing in him, yet I also knew of the horrors he described. I could see that the bishop was trying to curb his anger and, in the process, seemed perplexed and suddenly unwell. I believed he was still processing the truth about us. But what Elan had said unnerved him. His skill at compartmentalizing things he didn't like must have been activated since he quickly returned to his previous train of thought.

"I told you of the network of spies that the church maintains. I revealed this information to you so that you would know what I am about to say is true. The Protectors are closing in on you. It is time to go into hiding once again. Other than what Elan and Sarah had ready, I had some clothing and items you might require on your journey." He looked directly at me and continued: "Inside the lining of the bag, you will find the gold and silver coins you have sewn into the lining. I am sorry that my inquiries have brought yet another misfortune to your lives. I know you wanted to stay. But you cannot. It is time to leave. I have booked overland passage to the southern port city of Izmir (a modern city in Turkey on the Mediterranean coast.) From there, you shall board a ship to Morocco and then onto parts unknown to me. The latter is done by design so that I can never be tortured to reveal your new location."

Seeing the look on Sarah's face, Hosius tried to calm her. "Fear not, Sarah. The ship is owned by the church, and my crew is entirely trustworthy. They know they face excommunication and eternal, well, separation, as Elan described it, if they go against my orders. The ship is exclusively for your use and once underway it will only stop for provisions at ports of call that the church considers safe to use."

She sank into herself. "Another voyage. I hate the sea."

I tried to comfort her but knew there was no way to lessen the blow of uprooting our lives again so suddenly.

Hosius stood and motioned that we were to follow. "Come, the guards who brought your two companions will escort you to the port and make sure you arrive safely. Lazarus, thank you for your contribution to the creed and to our Christian world. You should be proud of what we have accomplished. Through your leadership, the Christian church now has one thing which is needed so desperately. I can never repay you, but in providing you an escape from the Protectors and their plans to murder you, I pray that I find favor in the eyes of God."

Clasping my shoulders, he spoke in a voice broken with emotion. "Lazarus of Bethany, blessed of God Almighty, who knew and was raised from the dead by the only Son of God, the time has come. You must go. Your secret shall never pass my lips. Though, in truth, I shall never forget you."

Hosius clapped his hands sharply. The door opened, and the guards entered the room once again, though this time no restraints were involved. As we were rushed out, I glanced back at Hosius one last time. He stood there, knuckles white as he grasped the cup of wine. Hosius had become a man who found three world-changing secrets and would never be able to speak of them. As the door closed behind me, I glanced his way one last time. Tears were already beginning to stream down his face.

The sun has one kind of splendor, the moon another and the stars another; and star differs from star in splendor.

1 CORINTHIANS 15:41

27

I stood taking in the fresh, salty air. Over the years, I had learned to like the feel of a ship such as the Sanctus beneath my feet. Her movement through the water and the wind in my face was strangely comforting. It was early, so Elan and Sarah were still sleeping below. According to the marks Elan had been making on his bunk, we had been on board without stopping for at least twenty-five days and my singular question remained unanswered. *Maybe it's a good time to ask again.* I approached the captain and steeled my nerves. Instead of hitting him immediately with my question, I thought a bit of light conversation might smooth the way.

"Good Morning, captain. My compliments sir. Your vessel is quite comfortable. A ship this size must be a jewel of the church!"

He looked at me and smiled. I guess my attempt at sneaking my inquiry in was kind of transparent.

"You, of course, know it once belonged to a wealthy Roman whose sins were great. He gave it to the church as a form of penance. I know you are only trying to prepare a new way to ask the question regarding our intended destination, so, please, let's begin our daily dance."

Well, at least he had a sense of humor. "Of course, captain. I wonder if I could ask you a question?"

"Is it the same question you have asked every day since arriving on my ship?"

"Yes."

I could see on his face that he'd grown tired of not answering. I started to get just a little excited about his potential reaction. *Today might be the day.* He inhaled and finally provided details about our journey.

"Sir, the bishop's instructions were to take you as far away from Rome and Roman influence as possible. Since you have displayed a keen skill for observation, I am sure you noticed when we sailed between the Pillars of Hercules and turned with the wind. If you know this, then you also must know that we left the Mediterranean Sea many days ago, and we sail south, down the coast of Afri-Terra, the southernmost continent, following old trade sea routes."

I pointed to the speck of land visible on the horizon. "You mean where the Afri people live?" I was thinking about all the stories I had also heard regarding the various tribes of people the Romans had encountered. "Are these trade routes entirely safe?"

He seemed impressed. "So, you've heard of it?"

"Of course. I recall when ships sailed from Cyprus towards Carthage, bringing barter items, copper and timber, and other items from the wilds of that land, I also know that they often returned with slaves and precious stones, enriched by what they had discovered. Though, I am sure people lived there for many years before the Romans claimed to have discovered them."

I paused, then went forward with something I'd once heard.

"I have been told of tribes that practice cannibalism on their conquests. They consume their enemies in an attempt to absorb the strength of those they have bested."

His face darkened. "Yes, sadly, what you have heard is true. Though I have obviously never experienced it, I have heard tales from sailors I trust of finding human bones and ceremonial fire pits. It is a vile practice, one that should earn those who participate a seat in Hades forever."

To his statement I had an affirmative answer. "Trust me, it does," which earned me a quizzical glance. Then, understanding swept over his face, transmitting his knowledge of exactly who I was. He shivered a bit and shook his head.

"Yes, I guess you, of all people, would know this information. Before you boarded, the bishop described you three in great detail, including why you were being sent away. He felt it important that I know and understand who you were. I would try to question you about your experiences, but I believe your answers would simply frighten me and perhaps even be too stunning to take in and understand fully."

We stood silent for several minutes. His countenance returned to normal when he recalled what started our discussion.

With that, he turned and faced due east. He pointed towards a speck of land.

"In the distance is solid ground. Your cannibals can be found there, I have no doubt. However, most of the land you see off in the distance will probably be uninhabited and wild. We should be fine. I have consulted the maps of the region, and there are no enemy towers on the coast high enough for our ship to be discovered and pursued and no true settlements whose navy could be worthy of engaging a ship such as ours."

I appreciated the knowledge of the bishop's man. He certainly knew the trade route, his ship, and what she was capable of accomplishing. "So then, my question remains: Where are we going?"

"We go south, then east, we have already passed through the sea of darkness."

That got my attention.

"Sea of darkness?"

"Yes. I did not mention it before because I thought you might over-react to the name. I admit many ships and sailors have been lost there. Some attribute the losses to sea monsters. It is also a place of turbulent weather. The key is to wait for calm seas and a following wind and not temp the passage when seas are rough, or the sky is dark."

He leaned over as if to impart a world-shaking secret to me. "You know, ancient mariners believed that the oceans covering the world were separate entities, like lakes or ponds, with no mingled water, only much larger. We know better. All the oceans are connected, and one can, in theory, depart from one port and sail around the world and return to that port. It may take months or even years, and while we have yet to undertake such a mission, we believe it possible."

He relaxed a bit and swayed in sync with the ship. He saw the disbelief in my eyes and laughed as I muttered, "We?"

"The guild to which I belong has mapped most of the known world. This knowledge is kept so close that it is one of the most-important secrets of the church. I know that one day some of us will use it to find and convert the entire world to Christianity. For now, though, only the guild members and the highest echelons of the church know the secret. And even then, many still do not believe it. Our ships have established contact with almost every continent and every people to begin to spread the word of the Savior."

His eyes gleamed for a moment.

"Of course, we also search for treasure."

"Treasure?"

"Yes. The guild undertook our earliest exploration using maps based on a book of geography by an esteemed mathematician and geographer named Ptolemy. Rome took a great interest in his work and made heavy use of it to expand the empire to the east and the west. Trade throughout the known oceans is extensive, and many Roman trading ports were established in places you have never heard of or even imagined existed."

The captain saw a look of fear cross my face. So, I guess he felt it necessary to tell me not to worry.

"But you shouldn't fear. We are so far away from what is left of the Roman Empire of the east that we might as well be on the moon we see in the starlit sky."

Sarah emerged from below and clearly had been listening. She looked my way as if to ask permission. I shrugged, wondering what she wanted.

"Sir, I heard you say that your fleet of secret ships have been everywhere and seen everyone. Everyone? Surely there must be some you've missed."

He looked pained at the fact that she had overheard his comment, but I could also see the reconciliation in his face that we would never be back to tell anyone.

"Perhaps, but if so, one day we shall reach them."

I could see that she needed to follow the logical trail of his comment.

"Let's say, for the sake of argument, that you have missed some nations and peoples. We know that the Savior has established a pathway towards salvation for all." She pointed towards the speck of land still visible on the horizon. "What of the people living and dying there? They may be in hard-to-reach locations, jungles, mountains, caves. They are young, old, healthy, ill. Living and dying, just like the rest of the world, but they lack access to a church or bishops with details regarding salvation. They may practice voodoo or magic. Perhaps they are cannibals, eating each other or their enemies with abandon. What happens to them when they die?"

"This one is the smart one, isn't she?" the Captain said, mainly to the wind. Gathering his willpower, he provided an answer of sorts.

"Young lady, the church believes that it is better to walk in the light than to stumble around in the dark. The church has been sending missionaries throughout the known world to spread the true word of God. Yes, there have been many killed. Perhaps even eaten by savages who do not know better because we may not know their culture or language.

Some missionaries survive the trip only to succumb to a disease or from an untended wound. The truth is that we've just begun to spread the word of God. It may take hundreds of years to reach every person in every part of the world."

"But what of those who never hear the truth?"

"We have no way to know. Perhaps one such as yourself, or Lazarus there, or Elan down below can tell us. You ask, so I wonder if I may inquire: What do you believe will happen to them?"

Sarah contemplated the question for just a moment.

"Well, to begin with, when I died, an angel stood beside my bed and held my hand. All around me flew hundreds of other angels. They surrounded me and comforted me until the Rabbi Master spoke the words that raised me from the dead."

I had heard this story before and wondered if there would be a reaction from the captain. I was not disappointed.

His voice cracked a bit. I could tell what she'd just said opened a new door for him, bringing a new emotion to his world.

"Angels? You truly saw actual, real angels? From heaven?"

"Yes. They were the most beautiful beings you can imagine. Shining with an inner light, wings draping over their shoulders. They flew around me in a circle, singing and praising God. I cannot begin to adequately describe the peace I felt as they spoke to me."

I saw the captain's jawline clenching. "I know we run from those who wish to do you harm, but I implore you, please find a way to tell your story. The truth of your death and resurrection is too much to keep to yourself. Many would believe in the Lord and his saving grace and power if you could just speak up."

"You said it yourself, though many would try to kill us too."

"Yes, this is true. But there must be some way to tell your story and yet live to tell it again." With that, he looked directly at me. "Mr. Lazarus, find a way."

I was silent for a moment, thinking, *perhaps it was no accident that we'd been discovered and forced to flee in the company of this fine man.*

"Thank you, captain. Even if it takes a long time, I shall find a way. I make that promise to you."

"Good. Now, young lady, what were you saying?"

Sarah smiled. I could tell she was happy that the captain was paying attention to her.

"I was saying that I believe our God is compassionate and understanding. I knew that when I lay dead, surrounded by angels. If the tribesmen and savages in the jungles and caves are good people, keep their laws, whatever laws they may have to lead a clean, sober life and have a genuine, good heart, perhaps if even if they have never heard of God or his Son, there may be room in paradise for them."

That impressed me. I remained quiet and let Sarah's words float in the air a bit. The captain was clearly thinking about her answer when he turned to me. "Lazarus? What is your opinion on the matter?"

"My answer will be one you might not want to hear. But once, after my resurrection when I was following the Rabbi Master closely, I heard him say something in a sermon that I did not understand. Yet today in this discussion it has returned to me. He was asked by someone in the crowd about being a shepherd and protecting his flock of sheep, a reference clearly that he was the shepherd, and we were his flock, and how could he hope to protect us all from those who planned to harm us. He said: 'I have other flocks that you know not of,' which stuck in the back of my mind for some reason. Perhaps he, or an angel of his, has been here, visited these people, told them the truth, exposed them to God, and given them a pathway to salvation. If so, then it is on them to teach what they've been told, to make sure the truth of salvation is preserved and passed on in their community somehow."

"Perhaps you are right. Who is to know?" the captain mused quietly.

Sarah looked my way with a different look in her eyes, but it was the captain who surprised me with his next question.

"Have you ever looked out on a moonless night and seen the stars?"

Sarah almost fell over.

"What did you just ask?" she said quietly.

"The stars. Have you ever looked up at the lights in the sky on a moonless night and wondered?"

I think I understood Sarah's interest.

"Sarah, I recall your escape from Judea was on a moonless night, right?"

She nodded. "Yes, Elan and I escaped and started our journey to the waterfront to meet you on such a night. Elan used a grouping of stars to find our directions in the dark. I had never seen such a thing. Why do you speak of moonless nights?"

"On nights without a moon, I would set my gaze towards the heavens. When I was younger and understood less of the world, I would wonder if maybe those lights were angels looking down at us. Innumerable and uninvolved in our world, just watching and waiting for the Savior's return."

Not being one to look closely at the sky, I was intrigued.

"Do you really believe that?"

The captain shrugged a bit. "Perhaps, once, I was rock-solid in my beliefs regarding life and death. Now, I stand on shaky ground after meeting three humans who have died and been resurrected. I know the lights in the sky can't be angels. They move the same way each and every season. Therefore, they must be places such as ours, moving in their own way through the heavens. My guild maps once told us that the earth is flat, that it is the center of the universe, and that all heavenly bodies revolve around it in perfect circles. However, many in the guild believed those ideas were wrong and set out to prove it. The earth is not flat, it is a globe that has been measured and charted, and it is merely one body among the millions in the heavens that have been created to reveal the creator's glory. Perhaps somewhere else in the heavens, to others such as us, we are simply another shining light in the darkness."

He paused, considering if he'd said too much. Taking a breath, he pointed upwards and said: "In the guild, we are all taught how to use those very same lights in the sky to navigate as we sail in the open ocean." He stopped and wagged his finger as if to stop us from hearing what we'd just heard him say. "That of course, is the deepest of secrets in the guild. So, you must forget I ever mentioned it, please!"

The captain was smiling when he said that, so perhaps he was happy to have told someone his big secret. Convinced we would never divulge his secret of the stars, he continued: "So, I believe the lights in the heavens are not angels, but they were put in the sky by the Father for another reason."

Sarah was interested once again.

"Another reason?"

"Lazarus spoke of what the Rabbi Master said regarding his 'other flocks,' and I instantly thought about the lights in the night sky. I was thinking, what if they are other places, other worlds such as ours? What if the flocks that he spoke of are up there? What if he has been to those places too and offered himself as a sacrifice for their salvation? No one has ever asked those questions, but I will tell you that the guild asks them. Very quietly, of course, as none of us want to be branded heretics and crucified or burned at the stake. But still, we talk of it amongst ourselves in the security of our chambers."

I was quietly shocked by how Sarah answered him.

"It is possible, I guess. I am sure that if there are other flocks up there in the sky as you described, the Rabbi Master has been there and has secured their salvation. I will never doubt it, and I suppose one day we may find a way, as they did in Babel, to reach the sky and find out for ourselves."

He nodded. "Yes, I have heard the story about Babel. If, in our far-flung future, we are ever able to reach the sky, I just hope the outcome of our efforts are not as unsuccessful as theirs."

Elan poked his head out of the forward hatch.

"I've been listening to this conversation, and, I admit, I am intrigued. Through these years, I to have looked heavenward and pondered the lights in the dark sky. I learned to use them at night long ago through the hand of my father."

"Oh yes, he was a shipbuilder, right?"

"Yes. Though not a member of the secret guild," he nodded and smiled at the captain, who chuckled. "However, he knew how to use the lights in the sky to find his way around the Sea of Galilee and made sure I knew how to use them as well."

Elan continued as he looked skyward.

"I would love to find a way, better than the Tower of Babel, to go there and ask the Lord why he thought it necessary to bring me back. One day, perhaps I will get the chance."

We were all quiet for a while, digesting the possibility of life among the lights in the sky. I made a mental note to speak with Elan later about his statement. However, I was very impressed by the intellect of our captain and hoped to spend many more days talking with him regarding this mysterious guild and his other interests. Eventually, he glanced in my direction with a questioning look. I correctly guessed what he wanted to ask but let him voice it.

"Lazarus, I have never heard you speak of your time with our Savior. Perhaps you should do it more often. I am fascinated by this fact and am eager to hear about him and your experiences."

Sarah decided to return to our previous conversation. Maybe she didn't want to get into a discussion about my life before or after my resurrection.

"I wish to finish my thoughts regarding the possible savages on land who have never heard the Rabbi Master's teachings or the news of salvation. I believe that deep down, we all learn laws similar to the Mosaic law and the Ten Commandments that God handed down to Moses on Mount Sinai. If you have never heard of God or his Son, yet you keep the laws of your people and lead a clean life of good standing, is there sin?"

Sarah continued to show her inner strength and knowledge when she closed our discussion with, "Once when Elan and I were listening to Paul speak in Cyprus, he said, 'Some say that where there is no law, people cannot be charged for breaking it.' He spoke regarding the reign of death over the earth. He was answering a Pharisee trying to disrupt Paul's message by mentioning the time between the creation of the first man and women, their original sin, and the law as given to Moses. The Pharisee said that with no law to break, the people of that time were sinless and have been in paradise since their deaths. Paul disagreed, saying that all people have sinned because of the fruit of the original sin, and sin brings death because you have broken God's law. The Pharisee countered with, 'if you'd never heard of the law, how then can you break it?' Someone else shouted that they did not understand how a compassionate and loving God could deny paradise when you die if you have never heard the law. Paul contended that original sin outweighs the lack of knowledge and must be addressed before entry into heaven can be granted. He also said very clearly that everyone within the sound of his voice has been told the truth and that there certainly was no excuse for them."

It was clear to me that this whole discussion was unnerving to the captain, and he was ready to end it.

"Perhaps you are right, Sarah. Those who have never heard the truth are still guilty of the original sin. This is a sobering thought, one I may need time to understand. Thank you for sharing."

"You are welcome, sir," she purred as she turned and went back below deck.

The captain looked in my direction once again and shook his head. "You three are very dangerous. I truly understand now why you are being sought. The way you speak the truth is so clear and easy to understand that the church and those who wish to control how the people worship and what they believe must keep you silent. Please, do not stay silent. Do something that puts the truth of our Lord and Savior into every hand on earth. Now, if you will, please go below. We are approaching a part of our journey where we must skirt around the tip of the continent. It will not be easy or smooth. Prepare for rough seas and pray we find fair weather and winds."

I did as he asked and went below to prepare Elan and Sarah for the potentially rough crossing.

I confess to being somewhat saddened to have been summarily exiled from the Mediterranean. It had been our home since escaping Judea. The ship Hosius gave us was large, and we grew accustomed to her noises and movements. Even Sarah came to appreciate the sturdy nature of the great ship. When we initially set sail, I had no idea though, that the feeling of solid ground underfoot wouldn't be ours for many more years.

Though we stopped many places, we kept moving. The captain was curious about everything and had a serious case of wanderlust, which was shared and encouraged by Elan, who also wished to see the world.

Just before the fourth century, I learned from a missionary on one of our stops for provisions of new religious councils, one in Hippo in 393 and one in Carthage in 397. Their purpose was to formally accept a twenty-seven book New Testament, which would be known as the earliest complete list of the New Testament books. They were found in a letter written by an obscure and unknown fourth-century bishop to someone in Alexandria, Egypt. As I listened to the missionary describing the events, I was pleased to hear that the religious authorities of the time paid attention to material of such great importance.

Long before we left Cyprus, I had begun collecting every scrap of information and letter written by those called apostles who had associated with the Rabbi Master or his ministry. I was driven by the need to archive everything I could while it was still fresh in the minds of those who had actually lived through the experiences. I did not include anything I had written because I felt it wasn't my place to write about him, since I'd only been associated with his ministry a shorter time than all of his other close followers.

For every letter or parchment I received, I made several copies, hiding them in various places along our journey. When Hosius packed for us, I was pleased that he included the documents I had made for my most-recent acquisitions. I spent years trying to arrange them in a fashion that made sense because I wanted a compilation book that told his story from beginning to end. Thus, when I heard that the material I'd buried in Carthage had been discovered and taken seriously. I was pleased. For once, I finally felt the great charge and challenge given to me by the Rabbi Master had been met. I recall thinking: *Finally, I guess I should be happy, but it is just the beginning. I pray the religious authorities accept my truths and don't try to change what they disagree with.*

I guess I should have known better. Okay, I should have known better.

28

We spent many years traveling and observing the cultures and religions of areas we'd never even heard of or imagined. Soon, Elan and Sarah had mastered navigation of the ship, which negated the need to replenish our crew once they became aged and feeble. I'll never forget the look in the eyes of our original captain once it became clear to him that though they had all grown old, we had not. Before they were all too old to handle the open ocean, we put into a port near the equator and purchased a new boat. This one was no match for the Sanctus, but it would do for the three of us. We told our original crew that they had faithfully discharged their purpose, and after refitting their ship, we sent them home to live the rest of their days with their families. I pray they made it and died in the arms of their loved ones. Once wholly in command of our own ship, it was interesting to watch Elan and Sarah work together. Two not-quite-adults caught between youth and maturity; each sharing the duties of captain and crew.

On our journeys, we continued to encounter people who had never heard of the Rabbi Master and his great sacrifice. Madagascar, India, the islands of the Indian Ocean; all were full of people eager to hear of the Savior. Some were anxious for us to leave because we upset the established order of things. Some listened with their hearts and were saved. There were times when we almost tested the notion that we were immortal since we barely escaped with our lives. We tried to bring the good news of his sacrifice and salvation to as many as possible, but it was clear some were not far removed from the savages we'd heard about and cared only about food, shelter, and reproduction. The closer we got to the so-called "spice and silk lands," we were surprised to see some measure of

Roman influence in culture and governance, as well as acceptance of the message the Master preached of repentance and forgiveness.

We stood off and watched as many countries invaded their neighbors, only to enslave large segments. The government in that part of the world was disjointed and warlike. What religion we did encounter was a mixture of everything except the truth and was very bizarre to the three of us.

When we hit the 500-year mark of our journey, we laid the keel for our fifth ship, and once it was finished, we decided to seek out a different climate and people. Sarah frequently spoke of her immense boredom with travel by ship. I lost count of the number of times she expressed her opinion that a land-based journey would be much more exciting. To the contrary, Elan's eyes glistened at nightfall on the ocean, especially as darkness would take hold and the lights in the sky would begin to sparkle. Regardless of what Sarah wished for, I thought it prudent that we escape the area where we'd spent a considerable number of years, so we set sail for the Orient. We'd been told of open lands and beautiful places among the people there, so with good wind and nothing but time on our hands, we eventually found ourselves in Hokkaido, a northern-most section on the island nation of Japan.

Unexpectedly, Elan seemed to come alive. He embraced their ancient culture and found comfort in the men who gathered together to practice a series of movements related to using military implements like swords and spears. I should have been concerned, but by that time, I had concluded that Elan and Sarah needed to live their own lives, as much as possible. So, I ignored his interests in Japanese warfare training. He spent hours listening and learning, which I thought odd given that he'd never expressed an interest in learning languages or about the cultures of the other people we'd encountered. Now, quite suddenly, he was very interested.

One man in particular paid close attention to Elan: Mr. Gao. I'd watch as they'd spar, both wielding swords, daggers, and wooden poles hardened over an open flame. The clanging of metal on metal or the occasional broken staff made it clear they were not pretending. Elan would return home the happiest I'd ever seen him. Intrigued, first I and then Sarah began to train with Mr. Gao, which seemed to make Elan even more happy. One day, I made my way over to Mr. Gao's, and the sound of a fierce battle resonated from his courtyard. I quickened my pace, worried that Elan, Sarah, and Mr. Gao were engaged with robbers or kidnappers.

Rushing through the doors, the sounds got more intense, then I slowed when I heard Mr. Gao intensely providing instruction to the fighters, which is when I realized the two fighters were Elan and Sarah.

"Sarah! You must always be moving, spinning. Be fluid as water falls over rocks. You fight for clearance and awareness of space."

I paused and watched as she drove Elan backward with frenetic energy.

Mr. Gao was quite pleased and immediately reacted.

"Yes, driving your opponent backward is an excellent tactic. It is when you can engage in a flurry attack and keep the blade of your enemy in sight, always preparing to evade that which is coming."

Without warning, Elan pulled a short dagger out of his tunic and counterattacked. I saw no surprise on Sarah's face. However, the contentment on Mr. Gao's face made it clear to me that he'd told Elan to use the second weapon. To my amazement, Sarah quickly parried and moved to sweep Elan off his feet. He landed hard on the ground, dust billowing for a moment from where he lay. With both hands, he rolled and avoided the strike Sarah directed at his midsection. This was almost too much for me. I believe she would have run him through if he'd not moved. I prepared to yell for their attention when he stopped for a moment. They both looked towards Mr. Gao.

"You two are exceptionally skilled. Very evenly matched. Elan, I have finally destroyed the poor instruction you once received as a Roman and turned you into a fine swordsman. Sarah, you are a formidable warrior in your own right! HAI! This is very good."

This statement shook me. *What did he just say? Does Mr. Gao actually know who we are?* He continued: "It is critical in a one-on-one battle to create distance. Shoving away your opponent is a valid tactic. Control of your opponent's weapon arm is a must. Restraining the hand that controls the weapon becomes more important than removing the weapons. This is especially true if the opponent is doing dual sword wielding, such as I had directed Elan to do. Your attack needs to be reserved yet planned. Intense yet practical. Sarah, you focused on the small blade. This was the correct course of action. However, never remove from your mind the other weapon."

Elan and Sarah both wiped their foreheads and saw me. Elan smiled and raised his sword in salute. Sarah did the same. Mr. Gao continued as if I was not present.

"Blades do break. Oxidation, poor construction, or lack of care are the enemies of your steel, so remember these facts. Most important for you to think about, even before you ever engage in battle, is to be prepared for that moment of conclusion. Never let your opponent manage your space. Never stand still. Always be moving. You are in a life and death battle. There must be no emotion associated with what you are doing. Be pure in all things."

Apparently, Mr. Gao thought that was enough for the day as he bowed, smiled at Elan and Sarah, and then disappeared. Elan and Sarah put away their weapons and came to my side.

"What'd you think?" Elan asked.

"I'm not sure why, but I guess the skills we've acquired here will be helpful one day. Come, let's make our way home."

As we walked, I made a mental note to ask what Mr. Gao knew about us one day.

All the lessons Mr. Gao had been sharing with Elan made sense many years after we'd put down roots in Hokkaido. One late-spring day, without even a proper greeting, Elan presented himself to me and announced that he had decided to leave. He wanted to join an army and fight. I was taken aback just a bit, given that we had never discussed a plan for our collective future that included him doing anything like that. I believe he started the conversation in a manner designed for the shock value, and it worked.

"What did you just say?" I asked, trying not to become angry, though it was clear to him that he had my immediate attention.

He smiled. "I know you heard me. Your hearing is as good today as it was 500 years ago."

I quickly muttered the prayer under my breath that I'd been saying for a very long time. *"Lord, for all the time Elan, Sarah and I have been together I have tried to be the father he never had. Yet how is it possible that my 500-year-old teenager still lacks the maturity to avoid risky behavior?"*

"Well? Do you have nothing to say? Old age got your tongue?"

"I am not much older than you are. Perhaps you'd like to stop trying to anger me and speak and act more like a man than a petulant child," I snapped back.

"I am speaking as a man," he replied too quickly. "This has been on my mind for many years now. I have learned that my skills are such that now I believe it is my duty, as a former member of the Roman Legion, to offer my services to a nation in defense of her borders."

I had to pause and take a breath for a moment and hope that I could re-orient Elan's point of view. I could see him seething beneath the surface and wanted to calm him. But I knew he wasn't going to like my next question.

"Remind me again, which battles did you fight as a member of the Roman Legion?"

He stood taller, squinted, and replied, "What are you trying to say? That I wasn't a true soldier? My training was brutal and deadly. That I did not fall on the field of battle means nothing. I was a Roman warrior."

I needed him to have a calm discussion, so I tried to argue my points.

"I will give you that point. However, you stated that you wish to fight for a nation. Which one? Japan? China? India to our west? Rome? Elan, Rome is no more. Even when we were young and on our first lives, Rome was an old, dying woman. When you enlisted and began training, Rome was on her death bed. She died a slow, painful death over hundreds of years at the hands of barbarians and corrupt politicians. I would add that Rome's lust for depravity, conflict, and the desire to conquer every neighboring nation added significantly to her demise. How is that even an honorable death?"

I was trying to get him to question his motives, but it seemed to be failing miserably.

"What is your point?"

"You need not go to war. There is no Rome. There is no Roman Legion. After Romulus Augustulus was deposed by Odoacer, there is literally no more Rome," I said.

"You are focused too much on Rome. Even if Rome, the Rome we knew, has ceased to exist, and is split into different empires, someone somewhere needs soldiers," said Elan. "Just look to the eastern Roman Empire. We've heard tales of their battles with the Persians. Those potential experiences call to me. Therefore, why wouldn't I return and volunteer? I must fulfill the duties I started so long ago. You need not fear. I shall not use my real name. I'll just do what we've been doing for 500 years and assume one. I have hundreds of years' worth of experience; I am a very good fighter. Mr. Gao says I am the best hakujin he has ever taught mastery of the staff and blade. Of course, I believe I am also the only one he has ever taught, other than you and Sarah. Not to mention I am an excellent horseman. I must use these skills for a country."

"Again, for whom will you fight? For which country will you fight?"

"Maybe the Visigoths, or the Franks. From rumors I have picked up at various ports we've visited, the Saxons are engaged in some fighting worthy of a former member of the Roman legion. Perhaps I will undertake a sea journey and join the fight!"

I had to stop him.

"Elan, the legion as you perhaps will recall, trained you to fight and kill and then tasked you with scraping out human waste and dead animals from inside the public latrines."

When I said that, he shrugged. My arguments were not deterring him.

"Then perhaps here in Japan. The Japanese require soldiers in their ongoing conflicts with their aggressive neighbors to the north. Mr. Gao believes I can contribute significantly given my current skill level and ability to learn. He has instilled in me a love for this land and her people."

"No. I know Mr. Gao is an excellent teacher, but you are not one of them. They will never accept you into their ranks. You know this."

"Perhaps," he mumbled. Thinking I was making headway with him, I foolishly tried to force the issue.

"It is madness, and I forbid it."

I've had lots of time to think about that phrase, and, looking back on it, forbidding him to leave clearly wasn't the right thing to say.

Elan's anger was immediate. I could see it rising in him even as I finished speaking.

"You forbid it? Just who do you think you are?"

I had to stop and suppress my own growing anger. Elan had always been headstrong, and I did not want him to leave us. Once again, I tried to calm the conversation with a logical argument.

"Elan, what will you do? Arrive at a recruiting facility and announce that you once were a Roman legionnaire? The only action you'll see after saying something like that will get you is up close and personal time in a tower or a hole in the ground dedicated to those who are beset by *lunaticus* and suffer from extreme bouts of madness."

"You don't know what you are talking about. I believe you just want me to stay here, hiding from the world. Well, I can no longer be that person. I need to get out, to see the world, to test this immortality of ours. We've never been ill; we've never suffered seasonal maladies. Even cuts seem to heal so quickly there isn't time to apply poultices or leaches. That alone spurs me to act, to take steps to position myself where I can contribute to the strength of a nation."

Anger and persuasion were not effective. Maybe if I asked nicely. I tried to think of something different to try when a soft voice interjected itself into our discussion.

"Elan, please, no."

Ugh. That was Sarah who had just spoken, and I was unhappy she had heard our argument. Neither of us had seen Sarah spying from just outside the room.

Elan turned to face Sarah as she entered and sat, her face clouded by pain and anger.

She cleared her throat and asked, "Why must you go now?" She said so softly that we had to lean towards her to hear.

"Sarah, I must. I need to go spread my wings, to get out and experience life. Honestly, you should too. I would take you with me, but where I am going a woman cannot go."

Sarah pierced the air between them with a look I'd never seen.

"One day, a woman shall lead a great army. And when that happens, I will be expecting a sincere apology and your recognition that a woman's ability to lead warriors into battle and kill her enemies is equal to or superior to that of men."

I was not happy. *Where did that come from? Why the sudden desire in both of them to speak of waging war?*

Then it hit me, and I looked at her with new recognition.

"You knew, didn't you?"

She glanced down, then at Elan, who shrugged. "Yes, but I never believed Elan would actually leave. I know he has been training for years, but I always thought he would grow out of it. I also know he's had a local swordsmith make a *gladius* and *pugio*."

That was more surprising news.

"You had a *gladius* made?"

Elan smiled and pointed towards a long leather bag. "It's beautiful. The metal is folded more than a thousand times. The edge cuts right through bone and muscle. We've tested it on cattle. The swordsmith loved the style since everything they use here has a thin, curved blade. He says he may add it to the armaments he makes for the warrior class."

Now it began to dawn on me the long-term thinking that had gone into Elan's plan. Sarah decided to speak up before I was able to do so.

"Being so far from Rome, especially once news reached us that Rome had split and different factions started warring with each other, I grew concerned that he would leave and return there to fight. My concern grew more pronounced when I heard of the *gladius* and *pugio*. I don't know what he expects, but if he is injured and heals, who knows what they might do to him. They may think he is a wizard or a demon, or at least in league with Satan. How can he be truthful with them if they see him healing from a wound that would surely kill other men?"

Elan jumped back into the conversation. "Yes, she knew. I have discussed this with Sarah many times. I feel trapped, unable to move, sometimes unable to breathe. I believe I was resurrected for a reason that does not include hiding under a rock and running every time someone figures out just exactly who we are. It is time, and I am leaving. If I were actually eighteen years old, I would still wish to make my own way and leave the family. Like you and Sarah, though, I remain at the age I was when I was resurrected. I am literally more than eighteen years old, and it is time for me to go, and you cannot stop me."

Sarah shook her head for a minute. Then, her face hardened, and her jaw clenched like I'd never seen. "Like I said, I don't know what could happen if you are injured or killed. I believe you waste the gift given by the Rabbi Master." She turned to look at me as she finished her thought: "Just as your friend Hosius chastised him for doing 200 years ago, I believe his desires have outweighed his ability to reason. If Elan insists on leaving, then I hope he goes so far away that he can never return."

With that, it was clear that she considered the matter closed.

Elan stood, reached for a pack of clothing, and paused.

"Goodbye, Lazarus. Thank you for being my protector all these years. You became like a father to me. But like every other man my age, it is time for me to leave the nest and find my destiny."

I chuckled inwardly at his comment but fought to hide it, not wishing to anger him further. There are no other "men his age" except for me, and I am certainly not about to charge off to fight someone else's war.

Elan looked to Sarah, who to my amazement, was still not crying. In fact, she wasn't shedding a tear at all.

"Sarah, take care of Lazarus. Take care of yourself. I love you."

Without looking up, she replied: "If you really loved me, you wouldn't leave. But you have your destiny to find, so good luck. Now, you should just go."

He stood, silent for a heartbeat. Without saying another word, he nodded my direction, turned, and left.

Looking at Sarah, I stood.

"Don't go after him, let him leave."

"I will let him leave," I said. "But first, I must speak to him one more time."

Leaving the house, I saw Elan picking up a long sack that clearly had metal of some kind inside by the sounds it made. Catching up with him, I implored him to stay for just a moment. He was adamant in his determination to go.

"You can't stop me. I have made my choice. Please, just let me go."

"I did not come to stop you, but what you said has made me think about what we have been doing these 500 years. I only ask that you consider this; recall when we fled Cyprus and stopped to resupply before calling Gaul home for a while. Don't go to war immediately, or if you do, when you have satisfied the lust for war that is inside you, return to the places where we buried some of the wealth we'd acquired. I know you remember the locations. One is just outside Carthage, there is one up in the kingdoms of Gaul, and another far inland on Cyprus. Go there. Find what we buried and use it to begin establishing yourself. Though you may believe you appear young, you are not. You are mature beyond any other man you will encounter. Take the time to do whatever you must to feel complete. Then, take some of the silver and gold we buried and do whatever you wish with it."

"Really? Why?"

It was time for honesty.

"I can see that, soon, Sarah will also grow tired of the lifestyle here. When that happens, I will speak to her and determine where her heart is regarding our situation. If you take my advice and go back to Gaul and then Cyprus, wait there. I believe we may follow in your footsteps, but it might take years. Just wait. Use the skills you have learned to thrive there. Perhaps someone needs what you have learned. You are smart. You speak virtually every language there is, your training with Mr. Gao has made you a formidable warrior so it should be easy for you to do whatever you please."

I could see that Elan had not expected such encouragement from me. He stood still, considering what I'd said. There was war in his emotions, and I had used the one tactic I hoped would turn the tide of battle in my direction.

Nodding, he finally answered. "This is acceptable. I have made my plans. I will take my journey to the sea, retracing our travels around the African continent. I will go to do as you ask and eventually return to Cyprus. I yearn to see the Mediterranean once again and walk the lands of my birth. But I will wait for you while I unearth the riches we buried and establish myself as the scion of a wealthy family. I'll work with the local population and kingdoms as little as possible. However, I will be using what I've learned here. I give you my word that I will wait. But I will not wait forever. I know Sarah is angry with me. I pray she understands someday why I had to go."

With that, we clasped arms more like brothers than father and son. I felt a corner had been turned concerning his emotional maturity.

"There is one more thing, Lazarus, I am happy the Protectors never found us here. For some reason, I think of this place as where we had time to grow and prepare."

I interrupted. "The possibility of the Protectors pursuing us is one of the reasons I kept the ship and her crew away from home for so long. When we finally released the crew and built the new ship, there was no way for them to be tortured to reveal our location."

"I understand, and I completely agree with your tactic. However, I am certain the Protectors still exist, and I have considered finding one or two and asking a few polite questions."

I smiled at the word "polite" given that I'd never associated it with Elan.

"Polite questions? Before you cut off their heads?"

"Perhaps. Regardless, I shall be careful, thoughtful, and I will do as you have asked regarding the wealth we have buried."

I nodded my acceptance and understanding and squeezed his arms. "May God guide your footsteps Elan."

"May the Lord God guide yours and Sarah's."

With that, he smiled, turned, and left.

I returned to the room where Sarah waited. The look on her face told me not to speak, so I left and went back to my workbench to finish the piece I had started.

Sarah stayed to herself for a while. I could tell inside of her swirled emotions that were not ready to be expressed.

Bear with one another and, if one has a complaint against another, forgive each other; as the Lord has forgiven you, so you also must forgive.

COLOSSIANS 3:13

29

When we first moved to Japan, I was intrigued by the workmanship in Japanese woodcarvings, which completely rekindled my interest in woodworking. I soon found work as a lowly apprentice to a local artist, and spent years trying to master the art of *mokuga*, an indigenous art form for making a picture out of wood by painstakingly carving one piece of wood to create the effect of overlaid pieces of wood. Today we would call the look "three dimensional." No one knew of three dimensions back then. Instead, it was just a beautiful way to exploit the natural beauty the artist discovered inside the wood. On this particular day, I was outside bent over a piece of wood about the size of a fist, intent on the tiny movements necessary to make it come alive when Sarah appeared at my side.

"Lazarus, may I interrupt you for a minute?"

I stopped working the wood and put down my tools. "Not at all. What do you need?"

She paused for a second, then proceeded with the one question I had been waiting to hear.

"Do you miss Elan?"

It was as simple as that. I had hoped she would ask it much earlier, but at least she finally came around. Elan had been gone for years, and even though I had told Elan we would someday reunite with him, I had yet to broach the subject of abandoning what had become, for the most part, a comfortable existence in Japan. We had lived in the northern mountains of Japan for more than 50 years, and I wondered if Sarah was growing weary of the tribal warfare that had started around us. I looked up and over her head, noticing that the mountains in the distance were capped with newly fallen snow.

"Am I to surmise that you are growing restless here?" I pointed towards the mountains. "Do you wish to leave before another season in which the entire landscape is covered in snow?"

She ignored my remark and repeated her question. "You never answered me. Do you miss Elan?"

"Do I miss Elan?" To be truthful, I was trying to gain perspective and time to form a decent answer.

She laughed. "Don't turn my question around with another question! You've tried that technique with me too many times. You will not succeed because I know how tricky you have become with language!"

I also laughed and finally stopped what I was doing. What she'd said was true. She was quite familiar with all the tricks I might use to avoid a topic I had no desire to engage. It seemed inevitable that this conversation was finally going to happen.

"Yes. Of course, I miss Elan. Even though he was occasionally troublesome, he had some endearing qualities, which I came to appreciate."

"He is our brother! His endearing qualities as you put it, should not figure into this discussion. Do you think he is still alive?"

"I believe so."

"Why?"

I hesitated for a moment. Though Sarah retained the appearance of a young woman, her demeanor and intelligence had matured significantly. Mentally she was the equal of any adult I had ever met. In my heart, I knew also she was a warrior with a profound intellect. I decided to respond in my own way.

"Though it was a very long time ago, you know that the Rabbi Master told me I would meet two others."

She interrupted. "I hope this is you trying to answer my question and not some strategy to avoid answering my question."

I decided to change my response and be as direct as possible.

"Yes. I miss Elan. To be honest, he has been on my mind for a long time, and it is my mistake not to have broached this topic with you before now."

She considered this for a moment.

"And?"

"And, when the Rabbi Master told me that I was going to meet you two and that you would be my traveling companions, and together the three of us would become keepers of the faith, responsible for spreading the word of God to the world, I had no idea what my life would be like.

How could I have known that more than five hundred years later I would live in a land as foreign as this one. I had no way to know that we'd have been chased by people who wanted to kill us. I don't know if we will live another one hundred, or even one thousand years. I wish I could know; it might help. But even my prayers for guidance seemingly go unanswered."

"Maybe they are not unanswered. Maybe you just don't like the answer."

Have I mentioned that Sarah was annoyingly smart? I shook my head at the fact she had become so skillful in her ability to get to the center of an issue.

"Perhaps that is true. I know we have been here in the winter mountains for many years, and that Elan is gone from us. But, in my heart, I know we will see him again, and when we all are together, perhaps the life we have lived, both together and apart, will make us more prepared to undertake the Son of God's mission."

Sarah thought about this and then said, "Thank you."

I let her words sit between us for a few heartbeats.

"Thank you? Why do you thank me?"

"You were straightforward and answered my question without pretense, without trying to hide your true feelings or meaning. I feel it in my heart that we will see Elan again, and when we do, he and I will be better friends and better companions for you. So, thank you, Lazarus."

I nodded. *Indeed, she is a formidable warrior.*

I did not tell her that when Elan left to pursue his desire to wage war, I tried not to remain angry. His departure was a bitter pill for me, and I knew he would fight for a cause or a government he did not even believe in. I had expended a small measure of our treasure to find the men with whom he had been training. I learned that he had told them his plan to purchase or fight his way back to Rome and join an army either for or against the barbarian invaders, who were quickly annexing parts of old Rome. I was happy that at least he hadn't told them he was immortal. After I learned the details of his plans, I was gratified that I had taken the time to speak to him before he left for good and found the wealth we'd hidden, and my hope to eventually follow him.

Sarah had been sitting, watching me think. Finally, she stood, approached, and waited for me to be ready to hear what she had to say. The expression on my face apparently kept her silent for a while longer, then, feeling comfortable, she spoke.

"Lazarus, in all our years together, I have never said this before, but, in my heart and soul, I believe it is time for us to leave here. It is time for us to begin a journey that will return us to the land of our births. Our destiny is not here in this land. Elan is our family. Perhaps he waits in Cyprus for us. Wherever he is, we should be there. I have a feeling that you may even know how to find him. How long it takes us to get back isn't important. We need to go. This new pagan religion brought by the invaders from across the sea of Japan is growing. It is easily overtaking every other belief, and eventually, it will be problematic for us. The fighting between the factions vying for power is growing, so I believe we will be in serious danger if we continue here. It is time for us to leave."

There was no reason to argue. It was time to go. I nodded my acceptance.

"Then, it is decided. I will go pack. Why don't you also gather your things."

Putting my tools in their case, I noticed that she pointed towards a valise sitting on the floor. Somehow, I had missed the fact that it had been there, just waiting.

"I am ready whenever you are ready."

I should have anticipated that.

"I understand. However, I will need a few days. I guess it's good that after Elan left, I purchased a large, two-masted vessel from a local purveyor."

She smiled and replied, "I know. I can go anytime. And for your information, I have already packed as if I shall never return."

I should have known better than to try to keep any secrets from her.

30

Using our newly purchased vessel of Japanese design, Sarah and I made our way past India, around the continent of Africa, up the coastline, and eventually into the Mediterranean Sea. I was grateful we had chosen to bury what we did so far away from civilization. Every place we stopped for provisions or to purchase supplies, it was clear that humanity had grown exponentially and now covered far more land than even I had thought possible. Luckily, the markers that pointed to where we'd buried things of value were chiefly geographic, which meant we had no trouble finding and retrieving our buried gold and silver to continue our journey. Often, we discovered letters written by Elan which provided details about his adventures and directed us onward.

One letter was particularly troubling, yet Sarah demanded that I read it aloud. I kept it all these years and now I know why. What follows is a complete transcription of his letter.

Through the grace of our Lord and Savior, I have made it this far without serious challenge or incident. I hope your journey from the east hasn't been too demanding. I bet Lazarus even had a ship built just for the voyage, right? If Sarah is shaking her head in agreement, it means that even in our separation, I know and understand you both better than you imagine. If you are reading this, then you must have uncovered the silver and gold we buried just outside of old Unica Colonia, now called Oran and under the control of the Moors. I'm not sure of the exact route you took to arrive here, so you might not have noticed that there have been many political changes since we left. However, as I understand it, something of the old Roman Empire still exists. So, my intention remains to find a suitable way to contribute to their war effort. Lazarus, please tell Sarah not to worry. I have been and will continue to be very careful. I mingled in disguise amongst the native population and learned that the formerly Roman northeastern provinces have come to be called Europe. It is primarily Christian, except for the people who've come from the area of the Nile valley and the Red Sea. Those are the people you may have heard about who have begun to follow a prophet whose name was Mohammed. He is neither gentile nor Hebrew. Instead, his religion, which he has called "Islam," is similar to both, yet different. His followers call themselves Muslims. Their governmental structure is called a caliphate or emirate. They are fierce warriors, and their religion teaches that they must fight every man who does not convert to their faith. Yet, they appear to value family and familial connections over everything else. It is a conundrum of some measure.

The current sovereign of the Roman Empire is a man named Charlemagne. Apparently, he is responsible for the broad cultural revival and renaissance taking place in the region. I hope to find a way to meet him and contribute to his war effort.

After a long and singular voyage, I successfully piloted my ship through the straits and into the Mediterranean. Not knowing what to expect from pirates loyal to the followers of the Emirate of Qurtubah or the Protectors, I made that entire journey prepared for battle. I prayed that my tiny, one-man ship would not present an attractive target of opportunity for treasures or slaves, and so far, I have been unmolested.

Before you left the Orient, did you hear rumors or see any evidence of the compound invented by alchemists associated with the Chinese Tang Dynasty? It is called "black powder," and is very flammable. Even small amounts of the substance are capable of amazing fire and destruction. I have seen it demonstrated here, and frankly, it will fundamentally transform the way war is waged. Though most warriors and armies still carry and use bladed weapons, I believe that eventually this powder will come to be used by every army. Even here, there are some who experiment with it to kill their enemies. It is an impersonal weapon used to kill or maim large numbers of warriors without the need to face them in battle. I am very curious about it and plan to make inquiries about acquiring some and becoming proficient in its use.

I have also heard that Norsemen, the north's warrior brutes, invaded and occupied much of northern Gaul. I encountered a ship of slavers here telling me that the Norsemen tried to take the islands of Britain from the Christians but were beaten back. They then turned their attention towards the Gaelic lands and were more successful. After the battle, one powerful monarch unified his entire country and stands with a firm grip on the population. I am interested in traveling there someday, so mention it to me when we are together again and allow me to persuade you both to accompany me.

Now, to my main reason for writing this letter. While uncovering the cache of gold and silver, I encountered three of the warriors from the group Hosius, our benefactor of long ago, warned us about. Do you recall that conversation? He called them the "Protectors." We've not spoken of this group for a very long time. Three men ambushed me here, and it was clear that they had established a residence nearby and had set a watch over the cache, patiently waiting for one or more of us to return. If you'd like to see how they lived, take a bearing away from the sun at daybreak, walk about one thousand paces, and you will find a cleverly hidden domicile. They were not what I would call brave. Indeed, they were duplicitous and cowardly fighters, stooping below the belt in both their fighting technique and its execution. During our battle, two were mortally wounded and chose to end their own lives. This tactic is similar to what we saw in Japan. Wounded warriors on the losing side were required to disembowel themselves, either to avoid capture or to atone for their lack of success. The third warrior was prepared to follow his comrades, but I intervened and was able to knock him unconscious.

When he awoke and realized his arms and legs had been bound, he began to thrash around quite violently. Once he discovered his bindings could not be shaken loose, he calmed down. At that point, I followed a tactic I learned from Mr. Gao, and I offered him some food and new wine. He believed that I would kill him outright, which I confess, I had thought about doing. However, once he'd consumed sufficient quantities of the wine, he had a much calmer demeanor. Thusly medicated, he was receptive to my questions.

"Why are you here?"

"To kill you, Lazarus, and Sarah."

"Why is that so important?"

"We believe you were never meant to be immortal. Immortality is only for God and his Son, Jesus the Christ. God is incorruptible. Man is not. Surely, you have been corrupted by your extended lifespan. Sarah and Lazarus as well. We must see that only God remains immortal. Your continued existence is an affront to his holy word."

I was pleased. He had exposed the flaw in their reasoning without me even asking about it.

"If that is so, why hasn't he taken the immortality away from us? Has the Lord been too busy to remember he left the three of us alive and immortal here on earth?" I asked. Before he could answer, I followed up with another question. "I also know some of the holy writings . . . the apostle Timothy once wrote in a letter that the "Savior abolished death and brought life and immortality"" Who are you to say that we are not the embodiment of what Timothy wrote? Are you saying that he wasn't writing the word of God?"

He sneered and answered. "You twist the words of the apostle to suit your own needs. This is to be expected from one such as you. The devil has turned your soul."

I shook my head and wondered at the programming he'd endured. He really was convinced of our demonic origins. I countered with: "What of the words, attributed to the Savior, by his close disciple John, who wrote that anyone who keeps the word of God will never see death."

"Once again, you twist the meaning to satisfy your own corrupted and human needs. You haven't been keeping the word of God. You've not even been here, fighting for the Lord. You ran as soon as we closed in on you long ago. A simple farmer found your buried treasure, and once we heard of it, we came, compensated him for his effort, and waited."

I snorted and interrupted, "You mean you killed him, his family, and anyone who asked after them, don't you?"

He sneered once again as he answered, "We are the hand of God, as he stays his almighty anger, we do not."

I shook my head. "And you see nothing wrong with your convoluted logic?" Seeing no reaction, I motioned for him to continue, which he did.

"We knew you'd return one day, and here you are." He stopped speaking, looked over my shoulder at the waning light. In his hesitation, I decided to ask a question.

"You profess to be a follower of the Savior?"

"Of course."

"And a central tenant of your organization is that our resurrections, and continued existence, is somehow an abomination and must be reversed?"

"Yes."

"All because we are still alive?"

"Yes."

"So, let me ask you, are you truly schooled in the writings of the apostles?"

He nodded slowly. "Of course. Before we can be allowed to pursue our holy missions, we are instructed in the holy words written by the apostles of Christ. Why?"

"What about the words of the prophets from the time of Adam?"

"I do not see how that question is relevant. Why do you ask?"

"Surely you have heard the names of Enoch and Elijah?" I watched as he thought for a few heartbeats about my question. He shifted in his seat and said nothing. "Well?" I persisted.

"Why do you ask? Enoch and Elijah are not you, or Lazarus, or Sarah. They do not roam the earth. They were caught up into the heavens by the Lord Almighty and sit with him, awaiting their appointment as witnesses to his glory during the end of days."

"You sound pretty sure of yourself. Let me speak from your perspective for a moment . . . if what you say is true, Enoch and Elijah were caught up into the heavens, and did not die, then the same power that took them to heaven is the same power that resurrected us from the grave. Their future witness, as you describe it, is in the future. Our witness is like the Holy Trinity, past, present, and future. Surely you know that Lazarus has been writing about his experiences with our Lord and has been collecting and hiding letters written by the apostles and others. He hopes to create a book of the Savior's words one day, from the time of creation at the hands of the Lord to the prophecies of the apostles regarding our combined future. Think about this. Isn't it possible that what Lazarus, Sarah, and I are doing is setting the groundwork, the foundation if you will, for the Enoch and Elijah you described to appear at the end of days?"

The look on his face was one of confusion. After a few quick exhalations, he began to speak again.

"I do not know if what you three do harms or helps bring about the end of days, or the great celebration when all sin is vanquished, and God reigns over the people of the earth."

I sat back, sheathed my blade. The movement did not go unnoticed by my captive. He appeared to relax even more, given the evidence that I had decided not to kill him. Instead, I decided to give him some insight into our resurrected existence.

"Yes, we were raised from the dead. Perhaps if you'd taken the time to speak with us once you found us, you might have heard of our experiences in the afterlife. Of the three of us, only Sarah had what I would call a positive experience. Personally, I was eternally separated from God, which was so horrible that I can hardly even describe it to you. I won't speak for

Lazarus, but before you try to kill us, which I'm not even sure you can do, you should have opened a dialogue with us first. Hiding in the shadows, ready to pounce and kill without question, isn't a way to live. I feel sorry for you, my friend."

He looked uncertain as he asked the only question that mattered. "What are you going to do with me?"

I stood and walked behind him. He tensed as if he expected a blade to be drawn across his neck. Instead, I cut away the ropes that bound him and spoke softly.

"Relax. I am letting you go. I would have saved your colleagues too if they'd given me a chance to speak before they attacked. Go home. Or go back to your organization and tell them what I just said. It makes no sense for you to continue our pursuit, and it isn't in line with what the Son of God did by resurrecting us. If you've been taught, as you said, the words of the apostles and the Son of God are true, then surely my words will ring true with you and with your superiors."

He stood, rubbed his wrists, and made no move to leave. Instead, he spoke in a clear and concise voice.

"I was unsure what to expect. It has been said that you three were seduced by Satan after your resurrections. However, speaking with you, I am convinced that what we have been told is not the truth. We have been fed a diet of lies. Perhaps jealousy is to blame, perhaps nothing other than simple human hatred. I will do as you ask and return with the words that you have said. They may not be received well, though, so I ask that you not hold me accountable if the next members of my society you meet still try to kill you. However, I shall not be one of those. Thank you for sparing my life. I shall recount your kindness, as well as your ferocious abilities as a warrior to my superiors. I hope they hear me."

"I do, too," I said. "Now, go with God. I pray they heed your words."

He bowed, turned, and left. I hoped that he would be successful once he returned home, but, knowing human nature, I wondered if the issue could be closed so easily. We all know how hard it is to convince humanity not to kill.

I hope you've not met any of the Protectors, but if you have, know that I tried to dissuade them from searching for us and undertaking any further attacks.

Anyway, since you are reading this, I assume you are here, safe and sound, and hopefully on your way back to me. This brings me great happiness, regardless of what year it is or how long it's been. Do what you must to come home. I have missed you both and have prepared a new home where we can live for some time. My love to you and heartfelt wishes to see your faces again very soon.

Elan

I finished reading that last sentence and, without speaking, folded the message and put it into my pack. I looked at Sarah just as a tear of what I figured to be both joy and apprehension ran down her face.

"We must hurry. Elan needs us."

I nodded in agreement and grunted as I lugged a small container of silver towards our ship. "Let's go. I'm sure Elan has been causing trouble."

"You know he has," she said with a slight giggle.

31

It was a joyful day when we brought our weary boat into the shipyard in Larnaca Bay, a place we both knew well (and still exists to this day.) As we searched for a spot to dock, we drew quite a bit of attention, given many there had never seen a ship of Japanese design. Finally tied up to the dock, several captains and shipbuilders asked for permission to come aboard, marveling at how wide our craft was, at the squared-off bow and stern, at how the sails had vertical and horizontal spines and how only a crew of two could manage the open ocean. One captain summoned a shipbuilder who was still onboard, taking note of the improvements that had been made by their Japanese counterparts, when we left for town.

Though happy to have arrived, Sarah and I were a bit out of sorts, given the number of years we had been gone. As we looked around, it was clear that virtually everything in town had changed. There were so many new buildings and people, many dressed in fashions we did not recognize, that we stopped frequently in amazement. We were happy to discover that the streets were mostly unchanged, though. The center of town was still the center of town. Approaching it, we were surprised to see a huge church on one corner.

We stopped and a sign told us we were in front of the Orthodox Basilica Church. To be completely honest, it made my head swim just a bit. The large structure had three imposing domes and a tall bell tower. It was quite ornate, with a portico whose steps led down into what must have been a sanctuary that could easily hold several hundred people. The church's stonework was sturdy and built of square limestone blocks that appeared thick enough to stand undisturbed for thousands of years.

"When did this get built? It is huge!" I muttered to myself.

"It's beautiful, isn't it?" came a voice from behind me. "Always amazes me that they could build a bell tower that high."

I turned to see who had spoken and found a woman carrying two children. A flask of water was also slung across her shoulders. Sarah put down her small satchel, smiled, and motioned to her. The woman understood and handed the smallest child over to Sarah, who cradled the baby and began cooing and dancing around with it.

I was surprised at Sarah's actions and tried to hide it. "Yes. It is, striking. When was this built?"

"The Greek Orthodox began to build it, oh, perhaps 300 years ago." She paused and leaned towards me as if to impart some secret knowledge about the building. "You know, some of his bones are enshrined inside."

This took me by surprise. "What did you say? Some of whose bones are inside?"

"Lazarus. The one raised from the dead by Jesus Christ."

She stopped again. I believe it was to judge our reaction to such an outrageous statement, and to give us time to process what she'd just said.

"His bones? From Lazarus? There are bones from Lazarus inside this church?" Sarah asked, making a comical facial expression.

"Oh, yes. When the Arabs overran Cyprus, they discovered his tomb and were in the process of looting it, when a great earthquake occurred. The Arabs, being very superstitious, believed that God was telling them to leave it unmolested. So, they let it be. I guess they just forgot about it, or perhaps the one true God removed the knowledge of it from them. Then, just 100 years or so ago, some children rediscovered the tomb. An inscription was still visible on the stone arch over the tomb! It read: "Lazarus, friend of Christ."

When I heard that, I was thrilled. *Just as I had hoped. That stone cutter was quite the craftsman.* "The tomb of the actual Lazarus. What happened after it had been rediscovered?"

"Soon thereafter, a great battle occurred during which the Arabs were defeated by men at arms employed by the emperor. The army was led by a fearless warrior. He fought with such fierceness that even his own men were somewhat afraid of him. He carried weapons that were foreign-looking and deadly. Legend has it that he was never injured. Arrows and swords seemed to bounce off him! Can you imagine? Many thought he was an angel sent by God to protect Lazarus and his remains. When the battle was won and the fearless soldier was made aware of the tomb, he took a few of the remains back to Constantinople, handing them over to the emperor. It is said that the emperor then sought to have them consecrated by the papal leadership."

"Fearless, you say? And he couldn't be injured?" Sarah asked. The look on her face was almost too much for me to take. I could tell we were thinking of the same warrior. "That sounds like a fable. It can't possibly be true!"

"But it is true! 'The mad warrior,' the Arabs called him. He was always yelling about how Jesus Christ himself had instructed him to fight the ungodly. It made his enemies fearful and angry. In their confusion they fought so poorly that he drove them from Cyprus with very little trouble. I've heard that he even resides here, though I am sure it is just rumor." She looked as if she doubted her own statement, shrugged, and concluded with, "Perhaps out in the mountains? Who really knows."

Sarah interrupted, "But why did he take the bones they thought belonged to Lazarus?"

The mother of two smiled. "Perhaps the emperor wanted them because he believed the bones held special powers, given that Lazarus had been raised from the dead by Christ. The habits of the highborn were, and still are, very foreign to us. Perhaps they ground them into dust and drank them with their wine or sprinkled them into their food. Power makes people do foolish things, so nothing would surprise me."

"So, you say that some of the bones said to belong to the remains of Lazarus are inside? Maybe they didn't drink all of his bone dust? Maybe they left some, perhaps for use in some other mysterious way?"

When Sarah asked that question, she slyly looked my way. Her sense of humor had not diminished in all these years.

The woman snorted a bit in reaction to Sarah's question and inference.

"No child. We heard that eventually the Pope repented taking such holy relics looted from the tomb of one who knew Christ. He saw to it that what remained of the bones were returned to Cyprus and placed within the tomb. The papal leaders who returned them kept a few bones out and directed that they be enshrined here, inside the church."

She stopped speaking. I guess the whole idea of the thing was too much for her to contemplate. She motioned to Sarah, who returned the young child to her mother's arms.

"Thank you for educating us regarding this beautiful church and the legend of Lazarus."

She frowned slightly. "Oh, it is not a legend. Lazarus was truly here in Cyprus. He was raised from the dead by the Savior and was sent here to minister to those in need of salvation. It is a fact that he lived here and eventually died here after a long and quite impactful life."

With that, she shrugged, gathered her things, and started walking again. Once she had disappeared, a lone voice called out from behind one of the stone portico columns. "So, I hear you are interested in Lazarus?"

"Elan!" Sarah yelled, racing towards the voice.

Stepping from the shadow cast by one of the columns, Elan was immediately engulfed by Sarah and almost fell to the ground.

I waited until their reunion was calmer before I approached. He, Sarah, and I shared a hug that seemed to go on for days.

I pulled back and couldn't resist poking a little fun at his adopted name.

"The mad warrior? Really? Was that your idea?"

He laughed heartily as he cast a furtive glance around.

"Be careful, someone might hear you call me by that name."

"Okay. I will never mention it again."

"That suits me." With just a slight pause, he continued, "And by the way, no, it was not my idea. I just embraced it. Anyway, welcome back to Cyprus. Come, let's go home."

I looked startled, which is why he quickly replied, "To clarify, to my home. Not the one we shared hundreds of years ago. That block of homes no longer stands. I understand our tunnels were discovered, and they razed the buildings searching for us or for the buried treasure they believed existed there."

I was relieved, but very interested in what Elan had been doing. "I have so many questions, but I will hold most of them until we are no longer in the public square. How did you know we would be here?"

He raised his right hand and tapped three fingers on his forehead.

"Something told me that I should visit the church today. So, since I had business to conduct nearby, I traveled here and waited to see what our Rabbi Master had in store for me. I was elated when I saw you both! But before I could rush forward, the woman with the young child approached. I remained in the shadows and listened with interest as she regaled you with tales of my exploits until it was safe to reveal myself."

"You just came here today because you had a feeling we might be arriving? Well, I am glad you followed your intuition."

He smiled. "I always do now. I hung back in the shadow of the church and kept quiet until the woman disappeared because there are always inquiring eyes, especially given what I have been doing here and who everyone thinks I am."

That made me curious, but I held my tongue and motioned for him to continue.

"For now, just know that I retrieved the things we discussed when I left the Orient and made my way here. I stopped in Gaul and Carthage along the way."

"We know! We found your letters!" Sarah said quickly. "Thank you for thinking to leave them. It let us know that you were safe and had been there."

Elan nodded. "You are welcome. It just made sense to let you know I was okay and where I was going next." He paused for a moment and then continued. "As you heard, I was able to satisfy my desire to be a holy warrior. When I felt I had done what I set out to do, I settled down here near the island's interior. I think you'll recognize it, though it is quite different from when we first arrived."

"Wait, you don't mean?"

He nodded.

"Yes. The farm Marcus gifted us with funds provided to him by the Rabbi Master nearly 850 years ago? Those 7,000 trees are now more than 20,000. The originals are still producing!"

Elan led us down the street in the afternoon light to a place where we found four horses tied to a pole. Elan fondly rubbed the nose of the largest one.

"These are mine," he said.

Sarah reacted with glee and cupped her hands around the largest horse's nose and face. The animal clearly was appreciative, as it gave a quiet snort, stomped once, and pursed its lips, letting out a soft, friendly sound.

Elan laughed. "That means he is very happy."

Sarah buried her face in the long mane, and the horse let out another series of snorts.

"He likes you."

"I've always wanted a horse," she said. That took me by surprise since it was the first time I'd ever heard her mention wanting a horse, although I knew her training with Mr. Gao had included mounted warfare. I had even tried it a few times, though I never got as comfort in the saddle as she was.

"Come, let us begin the journey as the ride will take half a day. Though the island has changed, the distances we must cover on horseback have not," Elan said. He helped Sarah up onto the saddle and directed that I put our belongings into the baskets slung over the backs of the other horses. Mounting, we turned and made our way out of town.

"Are we really returning to the olive tree farm?" Sarah asked excitedly.

"Of course. If you recall, it's in the flatlands between the Kyrenia and Troodos mountain ranges," Elan said. "Since you saw it last, the Arabs have cut down many trees to use building their fortresses. Thank God they needed the olive trees for other uses, so they spared every one of those! What was once woods is now pastureland. And as I recall, you always enjoyed the small herds of goats and sheep that we had on the olive farm. Well, I have many more, and I hope you will love it. No more talk, let's get there."

Sitting in the saddle, I was impressed with this Elan. He had matured into a man, and I was interested to hear just how that had happened.

If my people, who are called by my name, will humble themselves and pray and seek my face and turn from their wicked ways, then I will hear from heaven, and I will forgive their sin and will heal their land.

2 CHRONICLES 7:14

3 2

"I call this council to order!" barked Gourmand, the Patriarch of Jerusalem as he banged the thick, well-hewn gavel in his gnarled right hand. "The question has been put to the table: Do we, the followers of Christ, continue to turn the other cheek? Or in the name of the Lord God Almighty, do we take decisive military action against these murderers?"

His question started the entire room, the men sitting around the huge, square table, and the backbenchers standing or sitting in the room, arguing loudly.

Elan and I were seated in a back row, with interested members of the community who'd been invited because of our perceived wealth and station in life. *If only they knew just how familiar we are with this entire area.* We'd both commented about this fact when we received the invitation.

One very imposing man, the constable of Jerusalem, stood and began speaking in a soft voice, so soft that all the men around the table became silent in order to hear him.

"Brothers. None other than the apostle Paul used the language of warfare to describe the battle for the soul of mankind. He told us to take on the "armor of God" and to stand against the devil's schemes. I cannot recite the verse word for word. I am sure I could call on some of the more learned men or clergy around this table for a perfect translation. But in essence, Paul wrote that we struggle not against flesh and blood, but against rulers, against the authorities, against the powers of this dark world, and against spiritual forces of evil in heavenly realms."

From the other side of the room, a brave soul interrupted the constable.

"Yes, but our current struggle is against flesh and blood, not a spiritual power we cannot see. These devils bleed and die just as do you and I."

The table erupted like boisterous children.

I looked over at Elan and motioned, curious if he knew who had interrupted the constable.

Elan leaned over and whispered, "That is a Frenchman, Hugh of Payens. Hugh believes the previous battles fought against the caliphate armies were not forceful enough and he wishes to make holy war on the armies that continue to attack Christian pilgrims. He has formed some sort of a military organization and wants official recognition for it."

"You mean, like the Knights Hospitallers?"

A sly look crossed Elan's face.

"Or you could also call them by their other name, the Military and Hospitaller Order of Saint Lazarus of Jerusalem. They're a different organization than the other Knights Hospitallers but share a common name."

At this point in history, I'd been alive for more than 1,000 years. I thought I couldn't be shocked by anything. I was wrong. I recall no hesitation in my reply.

"What did you just say?" which elicited a sustained, but subdued laugh from Elan.

"Apparently, you've never heard of them. They're a new order, approved and authorized by none other than King Fulk of Jerusalem. They are not fully warriors, but they will fight for what they see as their "Christian rights." Their main focus is, as you described, with the Knights Hospitallers to give care to the sick and wounded.

Well, now I understood, sort of. The Hospitallers were initially chartered to provide medical care for pilgrims. A couple of years ago, news had spread that they were transitioning from a medical operation to one that took up arms and fought. I believe they did it for two reasons: First, in reaction to the things they saw the Frenchman Hugh doing, and second, because no one can tolerate being attacked every day without seeking some measure of revenge.

"Do they really call themselves the Order of Saint Lazarus of Jerusalem?"

"Yes. Yes, they do," said Elan, smiling. "I'm still waiting for the Order of Saint Elan, but I guess my resurrection wasn't as memorable to people as yours."

I worried someone might hear his joke, so I looked around with a furtive glance. No one was paying any attention to us, so I relaxed a bit as he quickly retorted: "I'm just kidding about being jealous. Yes, they do call themselves the Order of Saint Lazarus of Jerusalem, among other things. It's good that someone remembers you. Think of it that way."

I shook my head, curious about what they believed, but aware that I could never approach them. It would just be too weird. I had too many questions about an order using my name so instead, I returned to our previous conversation regarding Hugh of Payens.

"What do you think Hugh has in mind?"

Elan didn't hesitate. "In my opinion, all Hugh wants is to kill people and not go to hell for doing it."

I laughed. "Well, have you heard his reasoning? Is it sound?"

Elan nodded perceptibly. "While he is prone to hyperbole, I do believe his reasoning is mostly sound. His argument is wrapped around mysticism and the cross. The caliphate armies usually take no prisoners unless they have some significant value. They love capturing a knight or a high-ranking person, and he argues very forcefully for permission to kill anyone associated with the caliphate."

Elan stopped for a moment to let a couple of people pass by. With them out of hearing range, he resumed.

"And I will admit, someone, needs to protect the Christians who come here." Leaning back towards my ear, he whispered, "You may notice the look on the king's face. I understand he holds the Frenchman Hugh in high regard and is inclined to work this council in such a way as to give him an army to command."

I sat back and listened while, as Elan had suggested, Hugh followed his initial outburst with a decent argument.

"We must make real warfare on those who would kill Christians. There can be no middle ground on the matter! I have begun to raise an army of godly men to bring the fight to the land of our Lord. I seek an agreement on a set of rules which would define our engagement with the enemies of Christ." Hugh, feeling empowered, pointed directly in the direction of the King. "Sire, we beseech you to grant our petition and support our effort to remove the ungodly invaders from the Holy Lands of our Lord and Savior, Jesus Christ."

There was considerable murmuring around the room. Elan, still leaning in my direction, gave a low chuckle.

"Well, nothing like forcing the King into a corner. If Hugh doesn't get what he wants, I believe his next move will be easy; just tell everyone and anyone who will listen that the King hates God."

The King, an unhappy look on his face, motioned for silence.

Hugh sat quickly and appeared content to wait for the King to respond. He didn't have to wait long as the King sat upright and cleared his throat. Taking a sip of wine, he pointed directly at Hugh and motioned for him to stand. Hugh did, and the King began his response.

"I understand the honored gentleman from France seeks rules from this body which would establish the legal framework for godly men, such as himself, to take up arms against the heathens and unbelievers who are killing our Christian pilgrims in the name of their false god."

Hugh looked like he wanted to speak again, but he temporarily held his tongue in deference to the King.

The King understood and nodded, motioning with one hand for Hugh to speak if he was so inclined, which he was.

"Yes, my Lord. The caliphate and its soldiers seek nothing less than control of the entire world. If we allow them control over the holy places, what is to stop them from eventually taking Rome? Paris? I have access to the spaces adjacent to the temple of the Lord in the king's palace where we may berth a number of like-minded Christian knights whose fealty and faith will be to the Lord and his temple."

He added, as if sorry to have missed the connection, "and of course, to yourself, my Lordship.

The King ignored the minor slight. "This company of knights you envision would kill the enemies of the cross?"

"Yes, sire. Ours will be an order of men dedicated to penance and removing the murderous caliphate from the Holy Land of our Savior's birth. But we would seek to do so without committing the sin of Cain, the son of Adam. One of our Lord's commandment's specifically states, 'Thou shalt not kill.' Since we will be acting under orders promulgated by you and this council, which takes its love of our Savior to heart, we would seek to be held harmless in the eyes of God."

Hugh paused for a moment and prepared his big pitch.

"Your Lordship knows we are under attack by an evil force sent from the depths of hell, and all I ask is that you provide the framework for the pursuit of action against our common enemy. History will remember that with your help, we won God's war."

"He is very well spoken and persuasive," I muttered to Elan. "But 'God's war?' Perhaps he exaggerates for a reason?"

"It is his way. He hopes to flatter and cajole the King in to action, even if it is unofficial, which, I believe it will be."

"Unofficial?"

"I just don't see a rule for killing coming from this body. He may get what he wants, but I bet it will not be written down, just in case it does not go well. Let's excuse ourselves and go out to the courtyard."

We left and found seats outside. I needed to understand just what was going on in Elan's mind, so I started with the obvious.

"So, are you interested in joining Hugh's band of holy warriors? I would have thought you'd had enough fighting over the last 200 years. Especially when you were fighting for Charles, King of the Franks. You have told us that his campaigns took you all over the known world."

Elan laughed. "Charlemagne? It has been a very long time since I thought of him. He really preferred the title 'Holy Roman Emperor' over any other, especially Charles the Great or any of the other names people called him."

"But you did fight for him."

"Of course, I did. I fought the Franks, the Saxon's, the Lombards, the Moors, the Slavs . . . "

I interrupted him. "It would seem your Holy Roman Emperor had a disagreement with virtually every other kingdom on earth. I would think you'd have had your fill of battle."

"At first, I believed his intentions were entirely Christian in nature. Then, as his power grew, it became clear that he was just another tyrant bent on world domination. And besides, he wanted to change the creed that you shepherded through the First Emperor's Council, back in Nicaea! When I heard that, I was already on my way out. That helped push me to leave because I knew if you ever found out I was involved in something like that, you would be very disappointed, if not angry that I'd had a hand in it."

That took me back for a moment. Elan had truly matured.

"Was he successful in changing it?"

"No. He wanted to substantially change the original creed. His idea was to add statements of fact about Pilate's involvement and create other new basic tenets of the faith. Oh, the church leaders of the time also wanted to add that the Holy Spirit proceeds from the Father and the Son. I heard he wasn't happy when he was told that Pope Leo III opposed the changes. However, the Pope did agree with the emperor's ideas in principle and directed the additions to be made when instructing new Christians about the Trinity. I think he did that to avoid being permanently retired by the King."

"Well, at least the creed is safe, for now. With regard to joining this fight against the Caliphate, though, I am not sure."

Elan chuckled. "It has been a very long time since I had a good fight. One thing I came to appreciate during my time with Charlemagne's armies was that I could fight without regard for my personal well-being."

"Do you believe being immortal makes you a better fighter?"

He looked around with some measure of angst. "I can't believe you would say that out here in the open!"

"No one is listening. Besides, I'm sure you've thought about it."

"I'd have to say, yes. That knowledge gave me more time for studying battle tactics and preparation and less time worrying about losing my life."

"So, yes or no? Aren't you tempted to be one of this Frenchman's knights?"

"No, but I might hang around and fight. You should, too."

That surprised me.

"I know you have the training," Elan said. "Sarah says that after I left you both in Japan you remained engaged with Mr. Gao and then his successor when he passed away. She says you still possess several weapons from our time there."

I'll have to speak with Sarah about this later.

"Perhaps that it true. What do you hear regarding Hugh's request?"

"Like all kings, this king has sinned."

"Uh, what does that have to do with anything. All kings sin, as do all men."

"Yes, but this king, the one who can sway the council to approve what Hugh has requested, has committed the almost unpardonable sin of not paying tithes to the church on time. This, of course, is a sin that can be moved into the pardonable category by making up for it and overpaying more tithes to the church. Thus, I expect the religious leaders will ask him to make some form of penance, comprising money or treasure, which will then be used to fund a holy war against those who attack the pilgrims. Like most politicians, they attack the result, not the cause."

"What do you mean by that?"

"The root of the issue is the continuous flow of pilgrims. Something should be done in all the countries, all the places where they originate to discourage them from undertaking such a difficult journey."

"Interesting. Please, finish what you were saying about the sins of the King."

"Many believe that the sins of the King and the people have brought on the caliphate's attacks, as well as the frequent earthquakes, swarms of locusts eating crops, and legions of mice that are spreading disease. It is spoken loudly in the churches, markets, and public places that these sins must be addressed before Jerusalem can prosper. An added benefit to whatever penance the church extracts from the King for his alleged sins will be that Christians on pilgrimage to the tomb of Christ and other holy sites may be safe in their travels."

"So, some actually believe that to bring an end to this string of man-made and natural calamities, the King just needs to say that it's alright for Hugh to form his army and attack the caliphate? That seems pretty simple."

"No, there is more to be considered when they finally make a decision. There has been an excessive-to-abundant supply of adultery, both in the populace and in the clergy. I'm sure that will be dealt with swiftly and permanently. I expect there will be lots of severing of body parts as well as people getting burned at the stake."

"And?"

"I suppose, if Hugh gets his way, the clergy will also be excused from the prohibition regarding taking up arms. I expect many, especially those in the clergy with grievous personal sins hanging over their eternal heads, will seek penance through service in a war many will consider holy."

"Clergy taking up arms. How has it really come to that?"

"The caliphate attacks have been brutal, especially on those who have been identified as clergy. Their wounds are the most vicious and permanent because they do not defend themselves. Many clergy wish to fight but are unable to, given the current rules. Suppose Hugh is successful in persuading the council to alter the rules of engagement for the clergy? In that case, I am sure there will also be many edicts about dress, interaction with men and women who are members of the caliphate, and what to do if one is attacked without provocation."

"It seems that you have spent considerable time thinking about what Hugh is requesting. And yet, you profess no desire to join his group."

Elan smiled and stood. "No. It holds no interest for me, and I have no need to support a king or a specific kingdom in this endeavor. However, that doesn't mean we can't just go off and do something similar on our own! Come, let's return to the deliberations. I don't know how long the council will meet, but by the time they come to a decision, I expect Hugh will have gotten almost everything he wants and more."

"And just how does that affect us?" I wondered aloud.

Elan smiled a devilish smile. "I was wondering when you'd get around to that question," he said as he stood and motioned me to follow him. This gave me no confidence for the future or for plans I was not involved in creating.

As we made our way back inside, I was not surprised that Elan had found a way to fight once again. I should have known he'd want to go off on some crazy new adventure.

33

Just as Elan predicted, the King gave approval to Hugh, and he formed a new army. They called themselves the Poor Fellow Soldiers of Christ and of the Temple of Solomon. Everyone just called them "the Templars." I knew that the King's approval might prove interesting, so Sarah, Elan, and I took up residence not far from the seashore, just to the south of the seaport and immense fortifications in the seaside town of Acre, located on the Mediterranean Sea. (It is still known today as Acre and is one of the oldest inhabited cities in the world! I could give them a list of other cities, but no one has ever asked). We could see the port from the beach in front of our home, so we knew when ships arrived without going to the port master and asking. Every ship was full of pilgrims, and even though we did not join one of the groups protecting them, we did figure out a way to participate from time to time.

While we were happy to be living together once again in Judea, we all still dreamed of revisiting the lands of our births, deaths, and resurrections. Though I knew that my sisters, Mary, and Martha, had been dead for centuries, I did wonder if anything was left of our town. Sarah had heard that her father's temple still stood. Would it be possible that the foundations of my workshop might still exist? On slow days, we would contemplate a journey to find out, however most of the country was under serious oppression by a powerful leader named Saladin. So, we resolved to wait until the hostilities had ended. Of course, we also knew we could just wait until everyone involved grew old and died. Given that fact, we were left with nothing to do except escort the occasional group of pilgrims from Acre to the king's stronghold in Jerusalem.

The three of us were seen as an oddity, two men and a woman not afraid to fight, but unwilling or uninterested in joining one of the officially blessed warrior groups. Tongues wagged, as they are apt to do, until one day we were enjoying the salty air and a bit of wine when three Templars decided to test us at a local outdoor market. They chose Elan first, and apparently his attackers had never heard of, nor encountered, a man skilled in the Japanese martial arts. When the largest man attacked Elan without provocation, he easily blocked the strike. He stepped closer to his attacker, grabbed him by the collar, and with one movement flipped him over his back and onto the floor. The man's head made a thick sounding 'thud' as it struck the floor. Elan placed one foot on his stunned attacker's chest and proclaimed in a loud voice, "Stay down!"

Another moved quickly and grabbed Elan from behind. As if slathered in oil, Elan turned inside the grasp, which put him face-to-face with the other man. He shrugged, raising his arms up as if he were trying to emulate a bird taking flight, and pushed upwards. He dipped slightly and bent at the knees, which freed his arms entirely. He bent again, to the left, and wrapped his arms around the man, one below his waist, and one above. In one movement, Elan flipped the man and dropped him hard to the floor where he joined his comrade. Both men yelled loudly for assistance and another man tried to join the fight, but he wasn't quick enough to avoid Sarah or her unsheathed tanto knife. With a kick to his shin, the man fell to his knees, and Sarah was behind him in a heartbeat, her blade hovering over the man's exposed neck. Sarah smiled and simply said, "Life? Or death? Choose one."

Seeing all this take place, their commander stepped forward and bellowed, "HOLD!" A collective sigh went through the crowd. Clearly we were not dilettantes pretending to be fighters. The commander had seen enough. "No more! They are to be left alone. This is my order! Obey it!"

With a smile, Elan bent over and helped the two men to their feet. Sarah patted the head of her attacker, sheathed her knife, and returned to the table. This earned us significant credit with the Templars, and from that moment on no one else challenged us. They also grudgingly announced their acceptance of us as freelancers.

With the issue of our worthiness to participate finally settled, we started escorting small groups or individuals from the waterfront to holy sites and then on to the king's compound in Jerusalem. It was easier than we expected. When pilgrims would off-load from their ships, Templar or Hospitaller guides usually waited, ready to immediately set off with them into the hostile countryside. The pilgrims who had not made previous arrangements for supervision were occasionally sent to us. We did not share the desire to immediately set off for the Holy Lands. Instead, we took a more relaxed approach.

Acre was a beautiful place, and though most making the pilgrimage were from countries with access to the ocean, people of that time never relaxed. We thought it important to encourage the pilgrims who purchased our services to take a day or two and enjoy life, especially given that the road ahead would be filled with danger. The Templars had recently announced their intention to build a huge tunnel from their castle on the western edge of Acre to a location near the seaport. When asked, they would respond that if the city were ever overrun by the caliphate, it could be used to secretly transport men and equipment to the safety of waiting ships. Everyone actually believed they were either using it to store their holy relics, or that it would be used to protect their treasury from the invaders. If they ever finished the tunnel it would be an impressive feat of engineering. So as they excavated, we would often stop to watch the men bringing out the dirt and rocks, dressed in all their soldiers armor, which must have been uncomfortable to say the least. Just imagine chafing in the twelfth century.

One day sticks in my mind because of Elan. After being engaged by a group of pilgrims to escort them to the king's palace in Jerusalem, we spent some time gathering provisions, wandering around the city, and watching the tunnel workers. The next day we set out to the sites currently open to crusading pilgrims. Elan, Sarah, and I were on horseback. We had three other horses pulling carts loaded with provisions. The pilgrims, Christians from Italy, were making quite a bit of noise. We exhorted them to remain quiet and vigilant. I expected to be waylaid by caliphate warriors as soon as we left the protected confines of the city.

It was not an unusual trip for us to take, as we had become well known for providing safe escorts on the road to Jerusalem. Our reputation had spread, and our services were frequently sought out by smaller groups.

We were making our way on a well-beaten path, lovely fields of wheat on both sides, when I noticed a beautiful grove of olive trees. Of course, seeing them brought back wonderful memories of the farm we once owned in Cyprus. My reminiscing was interrupted when Elan's horse bucked a bit, and without warning, he found himself flat on the ground.

One second later, I discovered what had spooked his horse when caliphate warriors charged our direction. We'd had no warning of their stealthy attack.

Elan, still on his back in the dust, pulled his sword as one of the riders dismounted, and ran full speed his direction. Not one to respond to a fight at a disadvantage, Elan quickly jumped to his feet and engaged the warrior. The soldier who attacked him was larger and slower than Elan, and with a few well-placed swipes from his sword, Elan stood victorious over his body. I even heard Elan giving the dead man a lecture.

"My friend, the ambush was a great idea. However, I cannot forgive your poor foresight and battle tactics."

I shook my head and yelled, "Fight more. Talk less!"

The one Elan killed had been holding a deadly pole spear as he fell to the ground. Elan plunged his sword into the dead man's body, stooped and picked up the pole spear just as the dead man's partner stepped forward and swung a large ax. It was a beautiful swing, the arc was one that, if it had struck flesh, Elan would have been cut into two pieces. Elan deflected the second blow from the ax and parried with the pole spear in both hands, turning swiftly so that when the warrior tried to spin on his feet and swing his heavy ax, it was too late. With a deft movement born in the tactics of the nascent shogun, Elan shoved the spear through the neck of the warrior, placing the blow precisely at the joint between his back armor and his helmet. The warrior dropped his sword and grasped at the tip of the spear. It was clear his attacker was trying to breathe and the spear sticking out of his neck made it quite difficult. The warrior's colleague kept trying to get at Elan, but he used the pole spear like a puppet master would a puppet, constantly moving the dying man's body to ward off further attack from the other. Tiring of this action, Elan twisted the blade side-to-side, and the soldier toppled over, face down in the dirt. Elan placed one foot against the quivering body and withdrew the pole spear. He raised one leg with a deft movement, snapped the spear into two pieces, and tossed them into the wheat. With a grunt, Elan withdrew his sword, faced the next attacker, and stood perfectly still. He smiled and motioned for the man to approach. This tactic seemed to anger the man, who yelled in Arabic something about Sarah, which was kind of a mistake. While I dealt with my attacker, I heard Elan yell, "Kee-Yah!" when his sword struck bone. Just like that, three of our attackers were mortally wounded. Two of them were twitching on the ground, wailing in Arabic.

The men who attacked us, most likely Syrians in Saladin's army by their dress and weaponry, thought we were going to die quickly and easily. We'd faced warriors such as these before and they all believed their skills with swords and pole spears were unmatched. This always seemed to hurt Elan and Sarah's feelings and, without my blessing they had picked up the habit of lecturing the dead or dying on their poor tactics.

Behind me, I heard metal on metal and risked a quick glance at the pack of pilgrims. Sarah had just relieved one warrior of his head, and another was about to lose some body parts. I heard the warriors who were still alive comment to each other that with the others dead, the riches they were going to share after killing us would be easier and more profitable to split.

Sarah held out one hand and yelled, "Hold!" in their language. That they stopped their approach was actually kind of amazing. At the time I believed that perhaps they thought we were about to yield and seek quarter. They all held their fighting stance but waited. It was then that Sarah spoke in a clear and strong voice.

"First, do you think you'll be richer because the price on our heads would be split between a smaller number of men? You must know, we can defeat you as easily as we have your brothers whose bodies now lay at our feet. Second, we know you have been told of the reward for killing us." It was evident that they were surprised to be addressed in such a fashion by a woman in their own language. "Weeks ago, one of your soldiers, a survivor we kept alive long enough to interrogate, told us that Saladin's anger with the three mysterious fighters is great."

Hearing this, the men did not move, but grunt in recognition.

Sarah continued. "We were also told Saladin was most angry because the warriors who face us never return. Is it true that there is a special prize offered to anyone who can deliver our heads to Saladin?"

Still confused, they all nodded. Sarah smiled. Sweeping off the scarf she'd been wearing that covered her head, her dark hair fell below her shoulders. She smiled again and what she said next actually surprised me.

"And, for a beautiful, 1,000-year-old Hebrew woman's head, is there a special bonus of some kind?"

This took them by surprise, I can assure you. But she wasn't done yet.

"And am I to believe that you pathetic excuses for warriors think you will be the lucky ones to take our heads? To take this beautiful head?"

This was too much for one of one of them and he kicked sand towards Sarah and yelled: "How is it that this infidel speaks our tongue? Is this real?"

The man next to him didn't even hesitate "They are demons! Kill them!" He stepped forward quickly and swung for me. I believe they must have practiced this move and used it before to catch opponents off guard. It was unsuccessful as my blade diverted his with ease. Of course, I diverted his sword directly into his colleague's face. I believe in terms of warfare today, they would call the grievous wound "friendly fire."

I believe this was the reaction Sarah wanted, since she responded with a yell: "So be it! Then let there be no quarter given!"

"None asked," the one in front of me yelled in return as he removed his sword from his friend's throat. Blood gushed onto the dirt as the wounded man fell to the ground.

"Then, you shall die," she muttered as she feigned to the left, and sprinted forward in a move I recognized as one Mr. Gao taught her. It took her attacker by surprise. He grunted and with one movement raised his sword and brought it down point first, but it imbedded itself into the dirt, as Sarah was already behind him. She twisted her sword and sliced at his leg just below his crotch, behind the armor that protected his upper thigh. She braced herself as she thrust her blade back into the same cut. As she twisted, blood spurted out of the wound as the warrior fell to the ground on one knee. He shifted his head backward to yell and met her blade directly, the tip protruding through his skull with enough force to dislodge the armor designed to protect his head.

It was clear to me that he had misjudged his female adversary.

As I watched Sarah, still a bit awed by her abilities, she yelled my name and pointed with urgency over my shoulder. Perhaps I shouldn't have allowed myself to be distracted since I was almost run through by yet another warrior wielding pole. Unprepared, the square tip of the wood caught me in the chest, and I went down hard.

He dropped the pole, unsheathed his sword, and repositioned himself over me for a kill strike. As he thrust it down, I used the handle of my Odachi to divert his blade away from me and into the looped iron rings that covered his left foot. Apparently, his sword found a void in his own armor, and he leaped, screaming as the blade cut clean through his foot, which gave me time to stand.

As his foot leaked blood, he staggered, trying to regroup mentally. He lunged at me, and I parried the strike intended to end my life.

Instinctively, I transitioned from a low-level stance designed to accept an enemy attack, leaving them off-balance due to their inability to conserve the full energy of a strike designed to kill, to an aggressive posture that allowed fast draw and two-handed cuts. My attacker was large, but size usually is truly no match for skill. And he overestimated his. As he fell, his life spewing from the wound on his neck, I wiped the blood from my blade with my cloak. We quickly checked on the pilgrims. All ten were shaken but safe.

"I am curious about this ambush party," Sarah said as we prepared to resume our journey. "I believe they were expecting us, given what at least the two I overheard were yelling before they fell. I would have liked to save one, like we did last time, to confirm my suspicions."

"Are you thinking that a spy in Acre told them we'd be here?"

Sarah nodded while Elan continued: "And, you could have 'saved' yours. I would have, but I was too busy trying not to get killed. Plus, I was a bit busy defending our guests."

She looked at him in mock disgust. "We were all busy," which elicited a shrug from him. "And, besides, mine needed to die after what he said about my mother."

Elan considered what she'd just said for a moment, as did I. This warrior Sarah was vastly different from farm-girl Sarah we'd first encountered so long ago.

"What did he say about your mother?"

"It isn't important. Just know that I can never give quarter to anyone who curses my family. A true warrior never does such a thing." She moved on to another topic quickly. "By the way, they knew I was the female warrior they'd been told to expect even though my hair was hidden. One of them said something like 'these are the three warriors who don't wear suits of armor' and something about we were all going to die, and they were all going to be rich once Saladin gifted them the bounties on our heads."

Sheathing his blade, Elan looked at the bodies arrayed around us. "And that did not happen," he said.

She ignored Elan's quip, "If I were a betting woman, I would say we'll face more, very soon."

Elan chewed on his lip for a second.

"You may be right. On the previous two trips, we have faced more opposition than usual. The price on our heads must have grown and attracted a lot of attention."

We took a quick look around to make sure we had everything and everyone. Sarah went to comfort one pilgrim in particular dismay, so I took advantage of her being a bit out of earshot to chat with Elan.

"Elan, I see what attracted you to studying and perfecting the skill of bladed, man-to-man combat! Every time we encounter raiders like these it is always the same; to the death with no quarter asked or given, even when it's a knife fight They are great fighters, without equal in some respects, and are totally devoted to their cause. One day, the world may face something similar, and if that day comes, I wonder if we, or they, will prevail."

Elan nodded. The look on his face was grave.

"They demonstrate a singular purpose, killing the enemy. I would agree with you since it seems that Saladin's fighters obey his commands without question. If their army continues with this discipline throughout the ages, then indeed, the world could be conquered."

He bent over and looked at the field kit of the nearest dead soldier. Removing a cloth from it, he ran it over his hands. I noticed that he raised his eyebrows in admiration.

"This is softer than anything I have," Elan muttered. Looking down at the fallen man, he said, "Thank you, sir. I honor your commitment to war, though I disagree with your reason and tactics, which were poorly thought out and executed, I should add. I take this cloth as my prize. Now, every time I clean my weapon, I shall think of you."

He then sat on an overturned and rusty hand cart on the side of the road, no doubt debris from another, more successful raid by these same warriors, and used the cloth to clean his blade. Shaking it to remove debris and sand, he folded it into a catch pocket.

"Nice. Remind me, what was it you were saying just before these men interrupted us?"

"That I think it was smart of us to be clear with the authorities that we are not aligned with either the Templars or the Hospitallers. There is far too much loose talk amongst the people regarding their bizarre initiation rites and practices."

Looking back at the pilgrims, I saw that Sarah had instructed them to sit patiently and share a bladder of wine. Satisfied they were obeying her direction, I put my gear down and took off my tunic. It had a diagonal cut across the chest which would be challenging to mend, so I put it away and donned a new one. As I did this, I wanted to hear more of what Elan had to say.

"Initiation rites?"

"It's ugly. Lots of kissing one another, other, exceptionally bizarre requirements. I also hear that a new recruit must deny Christ and spit on the cross. Things like that."

I wasn't surprised, given the few I'd met who professed to belong to either group. But it seemed foolish to have such ridiculous practices.

"Why would they have requirements like that? It seems so stupid. And why demand these rituals be done among their group, and not in secret, to signify membership? That is an endeavor destined for failure. The discovery of secrets such as these could easily lead to imprisonment or death. Careless tongues loosed by drink or lascivious behavior could undo every good deed they have accomplished and destroy their entire order. You know, it wouldn't take much for the Pope or the King to use information such as this against them, especially if they become too powerful to control."

"You are correct. So much for their 'secret society of warriors.' I expect they will run afoul of the church eventually, and I have no desire to find out if we can survive being burned at the stake or beheaded."

The brush to my left rustled with a metallic human sound, and I yelled, "Neither do I!" More caliphate fighters appeared, running at full speed directly towards us from behind a stand of trees near the edge of the wheat field. As they ran, their armor sounded like a cart full of kitchen metal headed my direction.

Elan grunted and dodged a spear thrown from within the group of men.

The attackers split into three groups. Several came at Elan, four sprinted at me, and two others ran towards Sarah and the cowering pilgrims. The men approached Elan at a run. The looks on their faces said they attacked, believing him to be nothing but a young man of no skill, weak and vulnerable. This was not the best decision they'd ever made. I heard him yell as he struck first. That man fell with a heavy sound, screaming in pain, his armor rattling as he rolled away from the melee. One arm flopped on the ground beside him, sword still clutched by the hand attached to the severed limb. He left a bloody, macabre trail in the dust as he crawled away from the battle to die. The other warriors attacked, their lances flying as if threshing wheat. The combination of metal hitting metal, our screams, and those of the pilgrims created a chaotic symphony.

Recalling Mr. Gao's constant admonition, "There must be violence of action to be victorious in battle, power perceived is power achieved," I gritted my teeth and sank my Odachi into the neck of the closest fighter whose force of attack carried him beyond me. His action carelessly opened his back. I quickly twisted my wrists using a two-handed grip and pulled the blade sideways, separating his head from his body. I stepped sideways to avoid his partner, who had moved close enough to swing his sword. It glanced harmlessly off my forearm. With one hand on my Odachi, I forced his attention on my long blade, giving me the opening I anticipated. With a quick flash, my twelve-inch dagger was out, and through his chin, poking out of the tip of his skull, his weight now supported by its hilt and my arm. Pulling it out, he collapsed at my feet. Sarah had been holding her own against the other two who, seeing the battle turning bad for their brothers in arms, attacked with even greater anger. It did them no good.

I looked over at Elan, who had just killed his twelfth man since morning. He had everything under control.

Glancing back at Sarah, I could see she was standing between the two soldiers who had gone past Elan and me directly at her and the pilgrims. One looked in my direction and promptly lost a leg. As he fell, the other looked as if to redouble his attack on Sarah. I tightened my grip on the Odachi, smiled, and yelled at him. This stopped him for a moment. He stood, sword up at the ready and took in the blood and gore that was all that was left of his colleagues. I could see the uncertainty in his eyes, so I addressed it directly.

"Yes, you heard me correctly. I said your friends died just as quickly as you shall. Today, you return to the dust from whence you came." I pointed the tip of my blade in Sarah's direction and finished with, "and it shall be at the hands of a woman."

He turned towards Sarah just in time to see her blade slicing him into two warrior halves.

A hammer blow struck the back of my head and I stumbled. Turning quickly, I was preparing to strike back when Elan's sword appeared suddenly, its tip breaching the outerwear of my attacker. Elan twisted the sword and removed it, leaving a gaping, bloody slice where my attacker's heart should be. The warrior was dead on the ground before his brain knew he was dead.

I caught up with the one I had injured and would have killed him outright, but it was clear his fighting days were at an end. My blade had

struck an artery in his right leg. I saw with interest that he had tried to attach a rudimentary cloth and stick tourniquet to stem the river of blood,
but he bled out as I watched. His curses becoming softer and softer until
he was almost silent.

Sarah couldn't help replying while he was still alive.

"No, my friend, we are not spawn of the devil. On the contrary, we
are sent by the One, True God. Not your false God, but the actual, real
one. And your remark about my mother? Well, for your information, she
lived not too far from here, though it was more than 1,100 years ago.
This has always been the land of my people. It is my land, too, and I shall
defend it. Now I hope you enjoy your very painful afterlife."

The man gurgled, his eyes wide open as he made the transition into
eternity.

I wiped the blood of my enemies from my face.

"It's going to be a long day," I said. "We should probably not tarry
too long. I am sure the next wave of fighters could appear at any time."

"I agree," Elan said, putting his back against the nearest tree. He
pulled a water bladder from his pack and took a long drink. I did the
same as Sarah checked with the pilgrims, making sure none had been injured in the battle. She soon called out from the group of pilgrims, asking
the question we wrestled with on occasion, especially after battles such as
we'd just been through.

"Do you think this is anything like what the Rabbi Master had in
mind when he said we were to become the 'keepers of the faith?'"

The three of us had argued about this question every day since arriving in Judea and undertaking our escort duty. So, her question was not
one I was unprepared to consider.

"We fight in his name. I don't need the church to grant me absolution for defending God. By undertaking this fight I believe we fulfill, at
least in part, his great charge to us. And perhaps in doing so, we help
bring about his kingdom."

She arched her eyebrows and shrugged.

"Then, your answer is yes?" Elan asked.

"Yes. Of course, it is yes. It is the answer I give you every time one of
you asks this question."

Elan chuckled.

"Just making sure."

And with that, he took another long drink, swished it around in his
mouth, and spit it out.

The pilgrims, eyes wide in terror, looked at the three of us as if we were something other than human.

Their leader, a pious-looking reverend, approached slowly and posed a question he'd suddenly thought of asking.

"How is it you are uninjured and able to undertake such a calm conversation between yourselves? We have quietly marveled that you don't wear a suit of armor such as most wear. Instead, you all wear some kind of leather tunic, and your tactics are, to be blunt, foreign, and swift. We have never seen weapons such as you wield either. What kind of knights are you?"

"My friend, whoever back on your ship, or in Acre, told you we were knights was mistaken to do so. We are not knights," Elan said with a smile. "At least not in the traditional sense of the word." This statement spawned a few more looks of discomfort from the members of the group. He laughed at their dubious expressions. "You have no reason to be concerned about us. You are in the best of hands." He waved his dagger at them as he spoke. "The one who saved all your lives today is Sarah, the daughter of Jarius. He was the leader of the temple at Capernaum. I am Elan, son of the widow from Nain."

He pointed my way, and though I was shaking my head in an attempt to dissuade him from continuing, he said: "And this is Lazarus of Bethany, friend of Christ! We are fine without armor because we three were made immortal at the hands of the Savior when he resurrected us from the dead. This land once was our home, so spilling the blood of these Godless invaders means more to me than you can understand."

Sheathing the dagger, he looked pretty happy with himself.

"Now, pick up your things. There is still quite a bit of road to travel, and I expect we'll meet more of Saladin's warriors on the way."

Some of the pilgrims smiled, thinking he was joking. Most stood mute, surrounded by the detritus that is a bloody battlefield after the fighting is over. They were not quite sure what to say or do next.

"The man said, 'come on, let's go,'" Sarah said with some force. "The longer we stay outside the walls of the king's fortress, the longer we are all at risk."

The tone of her voice made them refocus their energy into leaving, and they gathered up the items they'd discarded as the battle was unfolding and regrouped.

I called my horse over and adjusted the saddle and stirrups. Reaching into my food bag, I retrieved an apple and cut it into two sections. I took a bite and then fed it to my stallion. I decided not to ride and instead started to walk, keeping an eye out for additional attackers.

As we walked, I thought that one of these pilgrims might say something about what Elan had said. But I was distracted when Elan, also on foot, stooped down to retrieve the last of the swords our attackers had wielded. He examined it closely and then shoved it into his gear with the other weapons he'd taken. It was not the first time I'd seen him do this. I knew he'd presented a few of them to the King, like some domesticated animal bringing a nuisance rodent to their owner as proof of their prowess, so I saw no reason to question him about it. He, on the other hand, felt it necessary to talk about the sword.

"That sword is very similar to the others I have collected, but there is a difference to it as well that makes me wonder about the blacksmiths in Saladin's court."

"How so?" Sarah asked from ten paces behind.

"Well, the three of us carry long swords we acquired during our time in the Orient. Lazarus has the Odachi, as do you. It is a great sword, but too long for me. I preferred to learn and use the Nodachi, which is typically used in field of battle for close quarter attacks. However, though they are different, they were made by the same swordsmith, from Japanese steel, which is vastly different from every other sword I've encountered. Ours is a light, very sharp blade, one that holds its sharpness even under the most extreme circumstances."

"In other words, ours are fighting swords, not to be used for meaningless ceremonies?" Sarah chimed in. "Oh, they can also be wielded in deadly fashion by men and women."

One of the pilgrims asked Elan a good question.

"What is the difference between a swordsmith and a blacksmith? I heard you use that term and I've never heard it before."

Elan was happy to have a receptive audience. He stopped his forward movement and we all ground to a halt. I could feel him getting ready for a small lecture on steel and sword construction. It was a favorite topic of his and I wasn't disappointed.

"It is a simple difference really. A swordsmith makes only swords. A blacksmith forges iron into tools to be used, sometimes they may make swords, other times hammers or axes. All the weapons I've collected recently were made using what the blacksmiths who also make swords call the 'Damascus' method." He turned very quickly and pulled one of the swords to use as an example. "See, the steel has a very distinct pattern to it, where ours is highly polished. I suspect the steel in our swords is equal in all ways to theirs, however, the workmanship of the oriental smiths was such that they felt the blade was not complete until it was finely ground and polished. The blacksmiths in Saladin's court are highly capable of folding the steel, but I believe they purposely do not polish the blades, leaving them with this beautiful pattern. Notice the banding and mottling It reminds me of flowing water. As we've seen, their blades are tough, resistant to shattering, and capable of being honed to a sharp, resilient edge. I have even heard the rumor that Saladin's blade, the one he keeps at his side, is the sharpest blade in the world."

"Is that possible? That it be the sharpest in the world?" a different pilgrim asked.

Elan replied with a bit of sarcasm in his voice: "So now you hear me, but not when we're yelling at you to defend yourself?"

I looked over at Elan with a less-than-pleased look on my face, and he then spoke loudly enough to be heard, "Well, I'm not sure how we'd test that unless you're volunteering."

Once again, I shook my head at his comment. I shrugged and sent my best 'what is your problem' glance his way. He smiled and returned my shrug with a mischievous smile. He could feel my displeasure, so to escape any more looks from me, he announced: "I'll ride ahead, see if there are any more surprises planned."

"Be careful, Elan," Sarah said. "Don't ride all the way to the court of Saladin just because you are interested in his blade."

I hadn't thought of that, so I immediately felt it necessary to reinforce what Sarah had just said.

"Elan now is not the time to test your immortality by riding up to Saladin and telling him our swords are better than his. Remember, there is still a price on our heads, and I've grown fond of seeing yours attached to your body."

"Why thank you, my friend," he said with a smile as he dipped his head, and with a gentle push from his stirrups, his mount broke into a trot. Soon, Elan and his horse were dusty specters.

And ye shall know the truth, and the truth shall make you free.

JOHN 8:32

34

With our pilgrims safely delivered, we started for home. But half-way there we were waylaid by an early season snow. Since we were in territory considered somewhat safe, we found shelter in a large cavern to ride out the storm. Sarah and I cut and used long evergreen branches to soften the jagged and dirty floor of the cave while Elan started a fire and cooked two rabbits he'd taken during the day. While I organized and cleaned my gear, Sarah went outside and cut more evergreens. I watched, curious as she placed them upright across the mouth of the cave. The way she wove them together was so effective that they blocked the snow from drifting in and kept the heat generated by the fire from escaping. We were warm, and soon our bellies were full. It snowed for a while, and finally the weather seemed to be passing as the wind picked up and the flakes stopped. Sarah stood, made her way forward, and removed a few of the larger boughs that had protected the entrance to our cave. What she said next surprised me.

"You know, this peaceful end to a very dangerous and physical day is nice. I'd prefer it if we ended every pilgrimage protection journey in a cave, cooking over an open fire as the snow flies outside. It reminds me of a simpler, less-complex time."

"Yes, it was much simpler when we didn't have to defend ourselves to the point of killing our adversaries, wasn't it?" Elan muttered as he stirred a pot full of melting snow for water.

"You know what I meant," she replied. Looking out, she studied the landscape for a moment and then remarked: "The clouds have started to clear. Look, I can even see the stars. Elan, I've noticed that those two lights to the east have been getting closer and closer. Is it possible that we approach the time of the birth of the savior? That bright light in the sky, might it be similar to the light that the wise men of old followed?"

Elan leaned back, his mood, uncharacteristically quiet. I recognized his quietness as deep contemplation of her question. He was quiet for a few minutes as he stirred the pot full of melting snow. After he'd formulated an answer, he replied.

"Yes, it is possible, I suppose. Though, I don't believe it is a star at all. It's more likely that the lights we see in the sky are actually other bodies in the sky or far away bodies in the heavens. You know, the scientific study of the sky has been around since the time of the first man, Adam."

"Really?" Sarah said quickly.

"Yes. His son Seth, and Seth's son, Enoch, all studied the sky. It is written that they were very interested in the firmaments above their heads. According to oral histories, Adam, given his personal interaction with the creator, was always looking up at the sky. I suppose he was curious about where his creator came from since it was clear to him that the creator must have come from the sky." Elan raised an arm and pointed: "The most logical guess would have been the creator came to earth from up there."

I felt that I should interrupt Elan.

"I don't know why you persist in having this discussion about the night sky. I seem to recall a conversation like this with our sea captain long ago."

Elan nodded.

"Right. If I recall, his thought was that the lights in the sky might be other places like our world. To be honest, I have no way to know if there is another place like ours out there. One day, perhaps, we will know. Personally, I would like to know. I might also like to go there."

Without turning Sarah added a new layer to the discussion.

"Elan, I recall your parchment paper demonstration of long ago. Now you say there's another piece of parchment paper involved?"

He shrugged. "Perhaps. But for now, until it is either proven or disproven, my opinion is that many of the lights in the sky move just as the earth moves, and what Sarah sees right now, two very bright lights getting closer together, are not magical or mystical. It is simply the way the creation of God works."

I knew this wouldn't dissuade Sarah.

"Then, it is possible that those bright lights could have been what led the magi to the manger where the Son of God was born? In the time of Herod?"

I noticed his smirk by the firelight.

"What I hear you asking leads me to believe you do not subscribe to the popular belief in religious circles. None other than a Pope of the Holy Catholic Church almost 1,000 years ago said that the Rabbi Master was born during the festival of Saturnalia. Which, if I know my sky well enough, could not possibly have happened during the festival. The sky would be different at that time. So, the Pope was wrong? Is that what you think?"

I could tell he wanted to talk about it, and tonight, so did she.

"Elan, we all know that the actual date of his birth is lost to history. Therefore, the date doesn't matter to me. I know he was born, as do you. I know he lived, as do you. He raised me from the dead, as were you and Lazarus. Since then, we three have been wanderers. With time on our hands, some nights I look up into the same night sky, just as you do. It is the same sky every other man, woman, and child sees. All of us observe the lights in the sky, the, 'stars' as you have been calling them. Anyone with half a brain can calculate that they move as the earth does. My point was that when the Master was born, we know that three magi followed a light that led them to his birthplace. If I understand you correctly, you believe that two or three of the lights in the sky might become aligned and produce a brightness many would associate with a guiding light. Did I correctly describe your thoughts on the matter?"

Elan indicated his agreement with a nod.

"Then, why does it matter what a long-dead pope had to say about when the Son of God was born. It is done, and there is nothing we can do about it. We could, of course, use our knowledge of the Master to change the practice, but still, we do not know his exact date of birth. I would note, that would require revealing ourselves, and I don't think we are ready for that. I know I'm not. I don't think the world is ready either."

"I agree. In fact, I don't foresee any time when we will tell the rest of the world, not just a few scared pilgrims, our true identities. Who we really are. Isn't that right, Lazarus," he asked as he turned towards me.

That took me by surprise, and I had to gather my thoughts for a moment or two before responding.

"Perhaps, sometime in the future we will be able to reveal ourselves. However, that day is not upon us. The world is full of fear and anger, much like in the time of Noah when the great flood rid the earth of sinful man. If those lights in the sky are what led the wise men to the manger, then it is the will of God. If they are just lights in the sky, getting closer together, then, once again, it is the will of God. I see no reason to debate the existence of the lights. They are right there," I said as I pointed towards the roof of the cave. "Though I cannot see them through this rock, I know they are there. I have faith they are there, and I will see them when I step outside. We live today because of the will of God. What we do, we do for his glory and not for our own. Now Sarah, put the cover back across the entrance, the cold has begun to seep in, and I would like to get some rest."

Sarah had been strangely quiet for a while, just standing there, looking out at the landscape. Finally, she pulled the large evergreen boughs back in place, Elan stoked the fire and added more dry wood. He dropped dried berries and leaves to the pot of melted snow and stirred them in, making one of his favorite teas. As the flames rose and the heat increased, I pulled my blanket in place, laid back, and started a quick prayer under my breath. Then Sarah decided it was time to speak what she'd clearly been contemplating.

"Lazarus."

"Yes Sarah?"

"In the morning, we should go to Acre, gather what we need and go back to sea. There is nothing here for us except more violence, ungrateful pilgrims and uncertainty."

"I agree," Elan said without hesitation from across the fire. "We should hire a crew and build a new ship or purchase one and rejoin our previous sea journey. It is clear the battle cannot be won against this enemy, and all the kingly forces brought here will ultimately prove no match for them, even with our assistance."

I was silent. I'd never heard them both agree so quickly on something. Especially something as momentous as going back to sea. I felt no need to resist. What they had said was clearly true.

"Yes, there is wisdom in what you both say. And I agree with you. We return to Acre, purchase a boat, donate the rest of our goods and supplies in an appropriate manner, and leave."

Resting my head once again against my saddle, I pulled the field blanket over my shoulders and said a quick prayer.

"Lord, thank you for today. Continue to guide our footsteps, and if the day comes when Elan is actually able to reach the sky and ask the questions he has, give him the strength to accept your answers."

35

I finished packing the fired clay jars I was using to store my most up-to-date written histories. Not wanting to keep them on board in case of bad weather, I spent time scouring the shoreline of an island we'd chanced by for a place to hide them. The rocky cliffs in the distance seemed to hold potential, so we dropped anchor in the shallow water offshore of an island known by the locals as Suquṭrā (a large island in the Indian Ocean, claimed today by Yemen.) The following day, just as the sun was beginning its journey across the sky, I set off on my mission.

"Careful, those are important," I said as the jars were handed over the side to me. I cradled each and placed them securely under lashings before leaving the ship and making my way shoreward. The small, three-person craft Elan had constructed three months prior was easy to pilot, and I yelled over my shoulder that I'd be back before sunset. Sarah waved her understanding and resumed fishing.

Paddling along the coast, I found a spot that suited my needs and quickly made my way towards a large, rocky promenade jutting up from a sandy beach. Beaching the rowboat, I made torches from driftwood for light and investigated the cave. It was deep, with a sloping floor that told me it would remain dry. *The perfect place to store my treasure.* As I started carrying each jar inside the cave, I noticed signs of previous habitation. Someone had written on the walls just inside the cave, and there was clear evidence of fires that had been used to cook a meal or two. One item that caught my eye was a relic left by the lone survivor of a shipwreck, a carved wooden tablet that told the story of his life and how he came to be alone on the island. I didn't see any bones, but incense pots and broken pottery were nearby. I like to think he survived and was rescued.

Before I started digging, I made sure the spots I selected were above the highest waterline I could find. Using a sharp trenching tool that I had constructed years earlier when I tried my hand at blacksmithing, I created several holes in the soft stone deep enough to accept my jars. Satisfied, I sat and took a drink from the bladder of wine, contemplating my past and my future.

Elan, Sarah, and I have built churches. We have changed lives through the power of the Son's message of hope and salvation. I believe we have given the world a Christian community and fought the enemies of Christ. Lord, I pray that you continue to find favor with us.

It had been a little less than a year since we'd left the Holy Land after the complete failure of the Crusades wars. We'd taken once again to the sea just before the arrests of the Templar leadership for various actual and made-up crimes. Turns out Elan was right; spies told the religious authorities about the atrocious initiation rites practiced by the various crusade armies, and for the most part, it cost everyone involved their lives.

I could see the tide turning in countries whose religious leaders supported the creation of tribunals for upholding their own versions of dogma. While they claimed their purpose was to purge heretics and non-believers, I knew that once the power to elicit confessions through torturous means was given, it would be misused. This was the sole reason we'd sailed as far away as possible from the growing instability of the known church and tyrannical religious control over it. I found my voice echoing off the walls, my mutterings coming back to me.

"They are too quick to convict those with whom they disagree. This is not God's plan. It is a plan wrought by man." I stopped talking for a moment and turned. Looking at the entrance, I contemplated the first time that I had emerged from a similar cavern. *That was so long-ago Lord. I know you must have a plan for us, for me. But, if you were to call me home today, this moment, could I justify my actions on the balance sheet of my life, given the great gift you have given to me?*

That thought was a sobering one, so I bowed my head and asked once again for his divine guidance. I did the only thing I knew to do. I knelt and prayed.

"Lord, I have done the best I could with the life you gave back to me. Please find it acceptable in your eyes and give me the strength to carry on until your Son returns to establish his everlasting kingdom. I feel in my heart that you are not done with me, with us, yet. If that is your will, then your will be done."

Feeling his approval in my spirit, I placed the clay pots into the holes I'd carved in the cave walls. Sealing them with wet mud and sea grass, I used a stick dipped in charcoal and lamb's blood to write a message on the ceiling directing whoever might find it towards the sealed clay pots hidden there. I knew that one day they'd be discovered, and I prayed they would be well received.

My task complete, I moved to the beach and spent the next few moments watching the sun hanging low on the horizon. When the trees started to cast their shadows, I knew it was time to leave. *I best get back; Sarah will not be happy if I'm out after sundown.*

I put my back into rowing against the incoming tide, and halfway around the point, I turned to make sure I was going in the right direction. In the distance, I could see Elan and Sarah, backlit by the setting sun. I assumed they were playing with the brass telescope Elan had acquired before we left the Mediterranean. It was going to be a moonless night and I was sure that after our evening meal, Elan would take the rowboat I was using, bring some provisions and his telescope, and spend all night examining the heavens, dreaming of how to get up there to interrogate his creator.

While I paddled towards our ship, the words on that first parchment, sealed inside the smallest clay jar, ran through my mind. I knew that someday someone would find what I had buried. I wondered what would happen once the scrolls were discovered. When I buried them, I had placed that parchment, a very important one, so that it would be the first one found.

"What I have buried in this cave, secured in clay jars, and marked in Palmyrene Aramaic and Latin are for all humanity. They contain the story of my life thus far. On them you will find my recollections of the life, death, and resurrection of Jesus, the Son of God, and the truth of salvation he offers to mankind. Of all these things, I am sure. I should know, I was raised from the dead by the Son of God more than 1,200 years ago in Bethany, Judea and have been doing his will ever since."

I signed it simply, *"I am Lazarus."*

How long, Lord? Will you forget me forever? How long will you hide your face from me?

PSALMS 13:1

Acknowledgments

If you made it this far, thank you for reading "I am Lazarus." It's a book that I had percolating in the back of my brain for a very long time. The story of Lazarus has intrigued me since I first heard it as a young teen. In our modern times there are those who insist that they "died" and "went to hell or heaven" for 33 minutes and returned to tell us about it in books, movies, or on talk shows. I've always been interested in their stories. According to the biblical account on which I base this novel, Lazarus was dead for a full four days, and then he returned to life at the spoken command of Jesus to "come forth." The part of the story I that created, namely that anyone raised from the dead by the Son of God is immortal, gave me the idea to bring Lazarus and the other two people whom Jesus raised from the dead through history together and into modern times. He is accompanied by Sarah and Elan, names I selected because they are not named in the Bible accounts of their resurrections. This group of three made crafting a narrative of their experiences and lives more interesting to me, and I hope more interesting for you too.

I was very sick as a young child and spent a lot of time in various hospitals in Louisiana and Texas. The experience I have attributed to Sarah at her death actually happened to me. I died in one of those hospitals from my illness and was immediately surrounded by angels and light. It was amazing, and though the angel who was holding my hand never spoke, I knew it wasn't my time and that I had to go back. I know, I said above that I was skeptical about people who claim great heavenly journeys, like meeting Jesus or Moses, but mine was different. I floated, held hands with a smiling, wonderous angel, and then I was back in my body.

The sheer number of biblical reference books, scripture-interpretation Internet sites and historical data such as maps, logbooks, PhD thesis papers on weapons, warfare, and naval history of all kinds, made this a learning experience as well as an exciting project for me. In a way, preparing for and writing this book also reconnected me with a faith I had all but abandoned many decades ago. Maybe I was supposed to write this book now. I kind of like that idea, so I'm sticking with it.

For me, the Japanese material was the easiest to understand and use, given my interest in all things Japan, and the huge volume of material I have available from my previous book, "*Trinity* 3.11."

I have tried to be thorough and careful in my research, especially because no historical record of Sarah or Elan exists after their return from the afterlife. But we do know the stories of their resurrections from the Bible as told in Mark 5:21-43, Matthew 9:18-26, Luke 8:40-56 (related to the raising of the daughter of Jarius) and Luke 7:11-17 (raising of the son of the widow from Nain.) Lazarus on the other hand, was a busy boy when he returned from the dead. According to every resource I located, sometime after the resurrection of Jesus Christ Lazarus really did flee Judea and settle in Cyprus and lived for another thirty years. Eastern Orthodox and Roman Catholic traditions offer varying accounts of the later events of his life, but all agree he became the first bishop of Kition (Larnaka), and Provence, where he is said to have been the first bishop of Marseille.

Thank you to publisher Wipf and Stock for its immediate interest in this book.

And the Walters Art Museum in Baltimore, Maryland, never hesitated when I asked if the circa 1426 Giovanni di Paolo masterpiece, "The Resurrection of Lazarus," was available to use as the cover of my book. Their response was immediate and positive.

My advance readers: Catharine Gibson, Rick Ware, Tom Corridon, L.Y. Marlow, Lynne Perler, Scot M. Faulkner, and Terri Hasdorff were instrumental in helping with questions, insights, or suggestions.

If you are an author and are looking for a new copy editor, let me humbly suggest mine. Mindy Fetterman, formerly of USA Today. Mindy was thoroughly fabulous. Her copy edits, suggestions, additions, questions, deletions, and nudges actually pushed my narrative forward in ways that amazed me. I highly recommend her.

My writing mentor, L.Y. Marlow, has been the greatest coach and fan of my writing that I could have wanted. L.Y. is the talented author of three very influential books. If you've never read "Color Me Butterfly," "A Life Apart" or "Don't Look at the Monster," you should.

The encouragement, attention to detail, love, and support from my wife, Ann, as I sat at the dining room table hunched over the glowing screen of my MacBook Pro or thumbing through reference books was unending and unwavering. Thank you, Ann.

Glossary

Acta diurna: (Also called *Acta populi*, or *Acta publica*) Said to date from before 59 BCE, recorded official business and matters of public interest. Under the empire (after 27 BCE), the *Acta diurna* constituted a type of daily gazette, and thus it was, in a sense, the prototype of the modern newspaper.

Apostle Paul: The Apostle Paul, who started as one of Christianity's most zealous enemies, was hand-picked by Jesus Christ to become the gospel's most ardent messenger. Paul traveled tirelessly through the ancient world, taking the message of salvation to the Gentiles. Paul is considered one of the greatest Apostles of Christ.

Apostle John: One of the Twelve Apostles of Jesus and traditionally believed to be the author of the three Letters of John, the Fourth Gospel, and the Revelation to John in the New Testament.

Barnabas: Born Joseph, was according to tradition an early Christian, one of the prominent Christian disciples in Jerusalem. According to Acts 4:36, Barnabas was a Cypriot Jew. Named an apostle in Acts 14:14, he and Paul the Apostle undertook missionary journeys together and defended Gentile converts.

Church of St. Lazarus: A late-9th century church in Larnaca, Cyprus. It belongs to the Church of Cyprus, an autocephalous Greek Orthodox Church. The Church of Saint Lazarus is named for New Testament figure Lazarus of Bethany, the subject of a miracle recounted in the Gospel of John, in which Jesus raises him from the dead. According to Orthodox tradition, sometime after the Resurrection of Christ, Lazarus was forced to flee Judea because of rumored plots on his life and came to Cyprus. There he was appointed by Paul and Barnabas as the first bishop of Kition (present-day Larnaca). He is said to have lived for thirty more years and on his death was buried there for the second and last time.

Council of Nablus: A council of ecclesiastic and secular lords in the crusader Kingdom of Jerusalem in the year 1120.

Council of Nicaea: The First Council of Nicaea was a Council of Christian bishops convened in the Bithynian city of Nicaea (now İznik, Turkey) by the Roman Emperor Constantine I in AD 325. This ecumenical Council was the first effort to attain consensus in the church through an assembly representing all of Christendom.

Crusades: A series of religious wars initiated, supported, and sometimes directed by the Latin Church in the medieval period. The term refers especially to the Eastern Mediterranean campaigns in the period between 1096 and 1271 that had the objective of recovering the Holy Land from Islamic rule.

Daughter of Jarius: The record of the daughter of Jairus is found in the first three books of the New Testament. The story immediately follows the exorcism at Gerasa. Jairus, a patron or ruler of a Galilee temple, had asked Jesus to heal his daughter, who in Mark's and Luke's accounts was dying, and in Matthew's simplified account, had already died.

Emperor Constantine: Constantine I, or Constantine the Great, was a Roman Emperor who ruled early in the 4th century. He was the first Christian Emperor and saw the empire begin to become a Christian state.

Gunpowder/Black Powder: Invented in China by the 900s and brought to Europe in the 1200s, soon became the key ingredient in a revolution in ballistic (projectile-firing) weapons.

Hosius of Corduba: (c. 256–359) Also known as Osius or Ossius, was a bishop of Corduba (now Córdoba, Spain) and an important and prominent advocate for Homoousion Christianity in the Arian controversy that divided early Christianity. He likely presided at the First Council of Nicaea and also presided at the Council of Serdica. After Lactantius, he was the closest Christian advisor to Emperor Constantine the Great and guided the content of public utterances, such as Constantine's *Oration to the Saints*, addressed to the assembled bishops.

Hospitaller: The Knights Hospitaller were also known by such names as Knights of Rhodes, Knights of Malta, Cavaliers of Malta, and Order of

St John of Jerusalem. The Hospitallers grew out of a brotherhood for the care of sick pilgrims in a hospital at Jerusalem following the First Crusade in 1100 AD.

Hugh de Payens: Payens was the founder and First Grand Master of the Order of Knights Templar from 1118 to 1136. He did not have a personal coat of arms, because heraldry only came into being in the 12th Century. He was born in Troyes, Aube, Champagne-Ardenne, France and died in Palestine in 1131 at the age of 61.

Jesus: Also referred to as Jesus of Nazareth, Jesus Christ, Rabbi, Teacher, etc. Jesus is the central figure of Christianity, the world's largest religion. Christians believe he is the son of God and the awaited messiah prophesied in the Old Testament.

Kition: Now mostly buried under modern Larnaca, was an important ancient city. Originally settled by the Mycenaeans and the Phoenicians 3,000 years ago, it was the birthplace of Zeno the philosopher and, according to tradition, its first Christian bishop was Lazarus of Bethany after he fled Judea.

Lazarus: Lazarus of Bethany, also known as Saint Lazarus or Lazarus of the Four Days, venerated in the Eastern Orthodox Church as (Righteous) Lazarus the Four Days Dead after he rose again, is the subject of a prominent miracle of Jesus in the Gospel of John, in which Jesus restores him to life four days after his death.

Odachi: An Odachi (large/great sword) or Nodachi (field sword) was a type of traditionally made Japanese sword used by the samurai class of feudal Japan. The western battlefield equivalent (though less similar) is the longsword or claymore.

Pharisees: Considered a social movement and a school of thought in the Holy Land during the time of Second Temple Judaism. After the destruction of the Second Temple in 70 CE, their beliefs became the foundational, liturgical, and ritualistic basis for Rabbinic Judaism.

Sadducees: A sect or group of Jews who were active in Judea during the Second Temple period, starting from the second century CE through the destruction of the Temple in 70 CE. The Sadducees are often compared to other contemporaneous sects, including the Pharisees and the Essenes.

Saladin: Caliphate leader and Sultan of Egypt and Syria who captured Jerusalem in 1187 and defended it during the Third Crusade (approximately 1189-1192).

Son of the widow from Nain: The raising of the son of the widow of Nain (or Naim) is an account of a miracle by Jesus, recorded in the Gospel of Luke. Jesus arrived at the village of Nain during the burial ceremony for the son of a widow and raised the young man from the dead. (Luke 7:11–17) The location is the village of Nain, two miles south of Mount Tabor. This is the first of three miracles of Jesus in the canonical gospels in which he raises the dead, the other two being the raising of the daughter of Jarius, and of course, Lazarus.

Templar: A Templar knight of a religious military order established in the early 12th century in Jerusalem for the protection of pilgrims and the Holy Sepulcher.